CHRISTOPH
THE PLUMLEY II

CHRISTOPHER BUSH was born Charlie Christmas Bush in Norfolk in 1885. His father was a farm labourer and his mother a milliner. In the early years of his childhood he lived with his aunt and uncle in London before returning to Norfolk aged seven, later winning a scholarship to Thetford Grammar School.

As an adult, Bush worked as a schoolmaster for 27 years, pausing only to fight in World War One, until retiring aged 46 in 1931 to be a full-time novelist. His first novel featuring the eccentric Ludovic Travers was published in 1926, and was followed by 62 additional Travers mysteries. These are all to be republished by Dean Street Press.

Christopher Bush fought again in World War Two, and was elected a member of the prestigious Detection Club. He died in 1973.

By Christopher Bush

CHRISTOPHER BUSH

THE PLUMLEY INHERITANCE

With an introduction
by Curtis Evans

DEAN STREET PRESS

Published by Dean Street Press 2017

Introduction copyright © 2017 Curtis Evans

All Rights Reserved

The right of Christopher Bush to be identified as the
Author of the Work has been asserted by his estate in
accordance with the Copyright, Designs and Patents
Act 1988.

First published in 1926 by Jarrolds

Cover by DSP

ISBN 978 1 911579 85 4

www.deanstreetpress.co.uk

INTRODUCTION

THAT ONCE vast and mighty legion of bright young (and youngish) British crime writers who began publishing their ingenious tales of mystery and imagination during what is known as the Golden Age of detective fiction (traditionally dated from 1920 to 1939) had greatly diminished by the iconoclastic decade of the Sixties, many of these writers having become casualties of time. Of the 38 authors who during the Golden Age had belonged to the Detection Club, a London-based group which included within its ranks many of the finest writers of detective fiction then plying the craft in the United Kingdom, just over a third remained among the living by the second half of the 1960s, while merely seven—Agatha Christie, Anthony Gilbert, Gladys Mitchell, Margery Allingham, John Dickson Carr, Nicholas Blake and Christopher Bush—were still penning crime fiction.

In 1966--a year that saw the sad demise, at the too young age of 62, of Margery Allingham--an executive with the English book publishing firm Macdonald reflected on the continued popularity of the author who today is the least well known among this tiny but accomplished crime writing cohort: Christopher Bush (1885-1973), whose first of his three score and three series detective novels, *The Plumley Inheritance*, had appeared fully four decades earlier, in 1926. "He has a considerable public, a 'steady Bush public,' a public that has endured through many years," the executive boasted of Bush. "He never presents any problem to his publisher, who knows exactly how many copies of a title may be safely printed for the loyal Bush fans; the number is a healthy one too." Yet in 1968, just a couple of years after the Macdonald editor's affirmation of Bush's notable popular duration as a crime writer, the author, now in his 83rd year, bade farewell to mystery fiction with a final detective novel, *The Case of the Prodigal Daughter*, in which, like in Agatha Christie's *Third Girl* (1966), copious references are made, none too favorably, to youthful sex, drugs and rock and roll. Afterwards, outside of the reprinting in the UK in the early 1970s of a scattering of classic Bush titles from the Golden Age, Bush's books, in contrast with those of Christie, Carr, Allingham and Blake, disappeared from mass circulation in both the UK and the US, becoming fervently sought (and ever more unobtainable) treasures by collectors and connoisseurs of classic crime fiction. Now, in one of the signal developments in vintage mystery publishing, Dean Street Press is reprinting all 63 Christopher Bush detective novels. These will be published over a period of months, beginning with the release of books 1 to 10 in the series.

Few Golden Age British mystery writers had backgrounds as humble yet simultaneously mysterious, dotted with omissions and evasions, as Christopher Bush, who was born Charlie Christmas Bush on the day of the Nativity in 1885 in the Norfolk village of Great Hockham, to Charles Walter Bush and his second wife, Eva Margaret Long. While the father of Christopher Bush's Detection Club colleague and near exact contemporary Henry Wade (the pseudonym of Henry Lancelot Aubrey-Fletcher) was a baronet who lived in an elegant Georgian mansion and claimed extensive ownership of fertile English fields, Christopher's father resided in a cramped cottage and toiled in fields as a farm laborer, a term that in the late Victorian and Edwardian era, his son lamented many years afterward, "had in it something of contempt....There was something almost of serfdom about it."

Charles Walter Bush was a canny though mercurial individual, his only learning, his son recalled, having been "acquired at the Sunday school." A man of parts, Charles was a tenant farmer of three acres, a thatcher, bricklayer and carpenter (fittingly for the father of a detective novelist, coffins were his specialty), a village radical and a most adept poacher. After a flight from Great Hockham, possibly on account of his poaching activities, Charles, a widower with a baby son whom he had left in the care of his mother, resided in London, where he worked for a firm of spice importers. At a dance in the city, Charles met Christopher's mother, Eva Long, a lovely and sweet-natured young milliner and bonnet maker, sweeping her off her feet with a combination of "good looks and a certain plausibility." After their marriage the couple left London to live in a tiny rented cottage in Great Hockham, where Eva over the next eighteen years gave birth to three sons and five daughters and perforce learned the challenging ways of rural domestic economy.

Decades later an octogenarian Christopher Bush, in his memoir *Winter Harvest: A Norfolk Boyhood* (1967), characterized Great Hockham as a rustic rural redoubt where many of the words that fell from the tongues of the native inhabitants "were those of Shakespeare, Milton and the Authorised Version....Still in general use were words that were standard in Chaucer's time, but had since lost a certain respectability." Christopher amusingly recalled as a young boy telling his mother that a respectable neighbor woman had used profanity, explaining that in his hearing she had told her husband, "George, wipe you that shit off that pig's arse, do you'll datty your trousers," to which his mother had responded that although that particular usage of a four-letter word had not really been *swearing*, he was not to give vent to such language himself.

Great Hockham, which in Christopher Bush's youth had a population of about four hundred souls, was composed of a score or so of cottages, three public houses, a post-office, five shops, a couple of forges and a pair of churches, All Saint's and the Primitive Methodist Chapel, where the Bush family rather vocally worshipped. "The village lived by farming, and most of its men were labourers," Christopher recollected. "Most of the children left school as soon as the law permitted: boys to be absorbed somehow into the land and the girls to go into domestic service." There were three large farms and four smaller ones, and, in something of an anomaly, not one but two squires--the original squire, dubbed "Finch" by Christopher, having let the shooting rights at Little Hockham Hall to one "Green," a wealthy international banker, making the latter man a squire by courtesy. Finch owned most of the local houses and farms, in traditional form receiving rents for them personally on Michaelmas; and when Christopher's father fell out with Green, "a red-faced, pompous, blustering man," over a political election, he lost all of the banker's business, much to his mother's distress. Yet against all odds and adversities, Christopher's life greatly diverged from settled norms in Great Hockham, incidentally producing one of the most distinguished detective novelists from the Golden Age of detective fiction.

Although Christopher Bush was born in Great Hockham, he spent his earliest years in London living with his mother's much older sister, Elizabeth, and her husband, a fur dealer by the name of James Streeter, the couple having no children of their own. Almost certainly of illegitimate birth, Eva had been raised by the Long family from her infancy. She once told her youngest daughter how she recalled the Longs being visited, when she was a child, by a "fine lady in a carriage," whom she believed was her birth mother. Or is it possible that the "fine lady in a carriage" was simply an imaginary figment, like the aristocratic fantasies of Philippa Palfrey in P.D. James's *Innocent Blood* (1980), and that Eva's "sister" Elizabeth was in fact her mother?

The Streeters were a comfortably circumstanced couple at the time they took custody of Christopher. Their household included two maids and a governess for the young boy, whose doting but dutiful "Aunt Lizzie" devoted much of her time to the performance of "good works among the East End poor." When Christopher was seven years old, however, drastically straightened financial circumstances compelled the Streeters to return the boy to his birth parents in Great Hockham.

Fortunately the cause of the education of Christopher, who was not only a capable village cricketer but a precocious reader and scholar, was taken up both by his determined and devoted mother and an idealistic local elementary school headmaster. In his teens Christopher secured a scholarship to Norfolk's Thetford Grammar School, one of England's oldest educational institutions, where Thomas Paine had studied a century-and-a-half earlier. He left Thetford in 1904 to take a position as a junior schoolmaster, missing a chance to go to Cambridge University on yet another scholarship. (Later he proclaimed himself thankful for this turn of events, sardonically speculating that had he received a Cambridge degree he "might have become an exceedingly minor don or something as staid and static and respectable as a publisher.") Christopher would teach English in schools for the next twenty-seven years, retiring at the age of 46 in 1931, after he had established a successful career as a detective novelist.

Christopher's romantic relationships proved far rockier than his career path, not to mention every bit as murky as his mother's familial antecedents. In 1911, when Christopher was teaching in Wood Green School, a co-educational institution in Oxfordshire, he wed county council schoolteacher Ella Maria Pinner, a daughter of a baker neighbor of the Bushes in Great Hockham. The two appear never actually to have lived together, however, and in 1914, when Christopher at the age of 29 headed to war in the 16th (Public Schools) Battalion of the Middlesex Regiment, he falsely claimed in his attestation papers, under penalty of two years' imprisonment with hard labor, to be unmarried.

After four years of service in the Great War, including a year-long stint in Egypt, Christopher returned in 1919 to his position at Wood Green School, where he became involved in another romantic relationship, from which he soon desired to extricate himself. (A photo of the future author, taken at this time in Egypt, shows a rather dashing, thin-mustached man in uniform and is signed "Chris," suggesting that he had dispensed with "Charlie" and taken in its place a diminutive drawn from his middle name.) The next year Winifred Chart, a mathematics teacher at Wood Green, gave birth to a son, whom she named Geoffrey Bush. Christopher was the father of Geoffrey, who later in life became a noted English composer, though for reasons best known to himself Christopher never acknowledged his son. (A letter Geoffrey once sent him was returned unopened.) Winifred claimed that she and Christopher had married but separated, but she refused to speak of her purported spouse forever after and she destroyed all of his letters and other mementos, with the exception of a book of poetry that he had written for her during what she termed their engagement.

Christopher's true mate in life, though with her he had no children, was Florence Marjorie Barclay, the daughter of a draper from Ballymena, Northern Ireland, and, like Ella Pinner and Winifred Chart, a schoolteacher. Christopher and Marjorie likely had become romantically involved by 1929, when Christopher dedicated to her his second detective novel, *The Perfect Murder Case*; and they lived together as man and wife from the 1930s until her death in 1968 (after which, probably not coincidentally, Christopher stopped publishing novels). Christopher returned with Marjorie to the vicinity of Great Hockham when his writing career took flight, purchasing two adjoining cottages and commissioning his father and a stepbrother to build an extension consisting of a kitchen, two bedrooms and a new staircase. (The now sprawling structure, which Christopher called "Home Cottage," is now a bed and breakfast grandiloquently dubbed "Home Hall.") After a falling-out with his father, presumably over the conduct of Christopher's personal life, he and Marjorie in 1932 moved to Beckley, Sussex, where they purchased Horsepen, a lovely Tudor plaster and timber-framed house. In 1953 the couple settled at their final home, The Great House, a centuries-old structure (now a boutique hotel) in Lavenham, Suffolk.

From these three houses Christopher maintained a lucrative and critically esteemed career as a novelist, publishing both detective novels as Christopher Bush and, commencing in 1933 with the acclaimed book *Return* (in the UK, *God and the Rabbit*, 1934), regional novels purposefully drawing on his own life experience, under the pen name Michael Home. (During the 1940s he also published espionage novels under the Michael Home pseudonym.) Although his first detective novel, *The Plumley Inheritance*, made a limited impact, with his second, *The Perfect Murder Case*, Christopher struck gold. The latter novel, a big seller in both the UK and the US, was published in the former country by the prestigious Heinemann, soon to become the publisher of the detective novels of Margery Allingham and Carter Dickson (John Dickson Carr), and in the latter country by the Crime Club imprint of Doubleday, Doran, one of the most important publishers of mystery fiction in the United States.

Over the decade of the 1930s Christopher Bush published, in both the UK and the US as well as other countries around the world, some of the finest detective fiction of the Golden Age, prompting the brilliant Thirties crime fiction reviewer, author and Oxford University Press editor Charles Williams to avow: "Mr. Bush writes of as thoroughly enjoyable murders as any I know." (More recently, mystery genre authority B.A. Pike dubbed these novels by Bush, whom he praised as "one of the most reliable and resourceful of true detective writers", "Golden Age baroque, rendered remarkable by some extraordinary flights of fancy.") In 1937 Christopher Bush became, along with Nicholas Blake, E.C.R. Lorac and Newton Gayle (the writing team of Muna Lee and Maurice West Guinness), one of the final authors initiated into the Detection Club before the outbreak of the Second World War and with it the demise of the Golden Age. Afterward he continued publishing a detective novel or more a year, with his final book in 1968 reaching a total of 63, all of them detailing the investigative adventures of lanky and bespectacled gentleman amateur detective Ludovic Travers. Concurring as I do with the encomia of Charles Williams and B.A. Pike, I will end this introduction by thanking Avril MacArthur for providing invaluable biographical information on her great uncle, and simply wishing fans of classic crime fiction good times as they discover (or rediscover), with this latest splendid series of Dean Street Press classic crime fiction reissues, Christopher Bush's Ludovic Travers detective novels. May a new "Bush public" yet arise!

Curtis Evans

THE PLUMLEY INHERITANCE (1926)

INSTRUCTIONS FOR MARCH 18th

(a) Prepare a monograph of about 50 ll. on southern English conifers with specimens of needles and cones.

(b) Obtain descriptions, and a 7 lb. tin, of the best water-proof cement.

(c) Obtain three dozen of the best tennis balls.

(d) Precis to an easily followed essay, the best method of rendering transparent glass absolutely opaque.

(e) Obtain the gardening catalogues of the three leading English firms, with special reference to hardy perennials.

(f) Obtain 30 ft. rolls of copper, and aluminum wire, of the handiness of ordinary twine.

(g) Obtain specimens of bitumen damp-coursing and discuss the advantages of this over ordinary slate.

(h) Obtain three second-hand suit-cases in perfect repair with good locks.

(Complete within seven days, please.)

OUT-OF-PRINT for over nine decades and one of the rarest classic crime novels from the Golden Age of detective fiction, Christopher Bush's first of 63 Ludovic Travers mystery novels, *The Plumley Inheritance*, happily has been rediscovered at last and made available in a 2017 edition by Dean Street Press. The book before you is the first new edition of *The Plumley Inheritance* that has appeared since 1926, the year *Plumley* was originally published in the United Kingdom by Jarrolds. Presumably *The Plumley Inheritance* was part of Jarrolds' Monthly Mystery Novels series, which the publishing company had launched in 1924 with *The Murder Club*, a short story collection by Howel Evans, a Welsh actor and author credited by some authorities with having helped inspire, with his Jules Poiret stories serialized earlier in the century, the creation of the great Belgian detective Hercule Poirot by Christopher Bush's future Detection club colleague, Agatha Christie. Aside from *The Murder Club*, *The Plumley Inheritance* is the most notable entry in the Jarrolds series of which I am aware; and the reprinting of *Plumley*, 91 years after its original publication, is an exciting event indeed for fans of classic crime fiction.

Precisely set in July 1919, eight months after the signing of the Armistice ending hostilities in the Great War of 1914-18 (and recalling Agatha Christie's *The Secret Adversary*, 1922), *The Plumley Inheritance* tells the intriguing tale of the teasing treasure hunt (with murder as well, for fanciers of the fine art) that is pursued by Geoffrey Wrentham and his old childhood friend Ludovic "Ludo" Travers, the latter of whom would appear in all of the Christopher Bush detective novels, finally making his exit in 1968 from the mystery stage on which he performed for more than four decades, with *The Case of the Prodigal Daughter*. In *Plumley*, the lead character, Geoffrey Wrentham, is not exactly a prodigal son, but he has been an absent one, having spent the previous three years fighting in the British army in Palestine and Egypt (regions where the author himself had served in the late war)—a span of time and place, notes *Plumley*'s omniscient narrator poetically, "not likely to make a man wholly unresponsive to those intangible stirrings of shadowed grass, the fragrance of old flowers, and all the pageantry of the English year."

Back in England's green and pleasant land, Geoffrey is staying briefly in London prior to returning to Hainton, the lovely Breckland village where his father has long been installed as vicar. About in the City he unexpectedly encounters old Colonel Travers, pater to his old pal Ludovic. (This is the Colonel's only appearance in the series, as far as I am aware.) Both as youngsters and as young men, Geoffrey and Ludo, though dissimilar in many ways (Geoffrey was more of a doer and sportsman, Ludo more of a thinker and scholar), "had been almost like brothers"--though since their years at Halstead and Cambridge, their ways had largely parted, particularly during the war, from which Geoffrey "had escaped with a couple of flesh wounds" while Ludo "was left with impaired sight" on account of prolonged exposure to poison gas. (This misfortune left Ludo wearing hefty horn-rimmed glasses, which he routinely removes and polishes—this a nervous habit that he retains throughout the long series.)

From the loquacious Colonel Travers, Geoffrey learns that Ludo, having been invalided home, found a job with the Publicity Department of the War Office, then under direction of the colorful (some say cracked) magnate Henry Plumley--head of City Corporations, Ltd., a mammoth investment firm in which Geoffrey himself has inherited shares, and owner of Hainton Hall, a fine country estate in Geoffrey's home village--and that for the last eight months his old friend has been employed as Plumley's private secretary, in which position he has become increasingly troubled by the financier's eccentric and erratic behavior. Before leaving London, an intrigued Geoffrey takes time to attend a speech at the People's Hall that Plumley is making on behalf of the Social League, an organization formed to ameliorate postwar social dislocation. ("As you'll soon discover for yourself, my boy, there's a great deal of unrest about which started after the Armistice," explains the Colonel.) During the speech Plumley shockingly collapses and dies, vexedly to Geoffrey throwing the affairs of City Corporations into rather a confused state.

In discussion with Ludo, who passingly declares--somewhat surprisingly for a crime novel from this era—his great admiration for the late Henry Plumley ("I can see little in him that was not natural-born courtesy and kindliness of heart. He was a bit flamboyant, I admit, and even occasionally hectic, especially in public, but I'd rather have that than some of those damnable old fools you and I ran up against in the army."), Geoffrey learns that Ludo had received from Plumley in March a bizarre list of tasks to perform within a single week (see the top of this introduction). Other weird jobs followed for Plumley's perplexed private secretary. Geoffrey concludes that the answer to the "comic conundrum" of Henry Plumley's exceedingly odd behavior is that the magnate himself had hidden caches of notes for a sufficiently perspicacious investigator to discover. Why not himself, Wrentham wonders:

If City Corporations had gone west; if he, Wrentham, had by Plumley's incapacity, mismanagement, or roguery, been done out of a very large sum of money, was he not justified in helping himself if chance and sound scheming should give him the opportunity? He knew the position in law—findings are not keepings. He supposed the correct thing to do would be to hand them over to the creditors. That, he cynically calculated, might work out at twopence more apiece.

With this persuasive germ of thought planted in Geoffrey's martial brain, there commences a great adventure for both himself and Ludo, with not only mystery and mischief in the offing but murder too. Reminiscent of such lighter-hearted Twenties British mystery romps as Agatha Christie's *The Secret of Chimneys* (1925), J.J. Connington's *The Dangerfield Talisman* (1926) and Freeman Wills Crofts' *Inspector French and the Cheyne Mystery* (1926), *The Plumley Inheritance* made a charming opening act to what was destined to become one of the most durable, prolific and pleasing writing performances by an author from the Golden Age of detective fiction. It remains so today, nearly a century later.

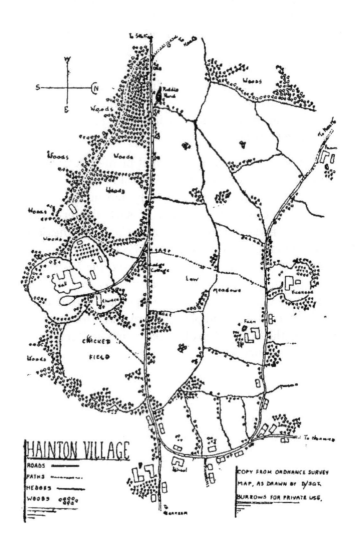

HAINTON VILLAGE

ROADS ▬▬▬
PATHS ▬▬▬
HEDGES ▬▬▬
WOODS ○○○○

COPY FROM ORDNANCE SURVEY
MAP, AS DRAWN BY B/SGT.
BURROWS FOR PRIVATE USE.

CHAPTER I
THE CURTAIN RISES

Geoffrey Wrentham yawned sleepily and stretched his long legs, then, eyes opening to the sun of a July evening, started up quickly. Twenty past six the clock said. He checked it by his watch; twenty past six it was. That left exactly a quarter of an hour to get to Liverpool Street. He scanned himself hastily in the glass, put on his cap and buckled on his belt. Fortunately the rest of his things were lying ready in the hotel lobby.

In three minutes he was in a taxi and on his way. The driver, having been told that haste was urgent, was already taking risks. Like a cyclist at a gymkhana he twisted here and there; purred impatiently behind a slowly moving vehicle as if in ambush and then darted again through the narrowest gaps. Then came a stop, half-way through the Strand—the cross traffic of Kingsway and Waterloo. He realised that impatience would do no good; but why on earth had he gone to sleep? It couldn't have been much after four when that cup of tea came up and he must have dozed off at once in the lounge chair in his room. A devilish expensive doze that! They were off again. He swayed to the forward lurch of the car. They might do it with any luck even now.

At thirty the blood is hardly to be stirred by thoughts of home. Most of the emotion that was in him had gone to the pleasant fields of Kent on yesterday's journey from Dover. Then there had been the taking of his draft for demobilisation far out of London, and the march through English lanes and by cottage gardens. Not that it was other than good to be home again. Three years in Palestine and Egypt are not likely to make a man wholly unresponsive to those intangible stirrings of shadowed grass, the fragrance of old flowers, and all the pageantry of the English year. It was only that in the hours he had already spent in England the first fine flush of the return had partially spent itself, and in departing had left the deep longing for one small village rather than the feeling that all was wonderful and desirous. So it was that the thought of his home and his father was different. He must buy that billiard-table and get it sent down. The village experts would probably play the deuce with it and Emma would have to be conciliated with regard to keeping it in order. Still, why worry? Who would meet him at the station? Wallace was back at the vicarage, so the last letter had said, and he could almost see the gardener and the old green-lined wagonette. His father would be sure to meet him too. And how green the paddock would be! And the bees would be busy in the lime trees.

Another stop! This time the Bank traffic. Only four minutes to go. They must have come in on the tail of the halt, for again the taxi moved on; crawling, darting, and then again crawling. Before them was a monstrous dray. "They oughtn't to allow those chaps on the road at this time of day," thought Wrentham angrily. Then at last the turn, down the slope, and number ten platform, and as he got out of the door a whistle blew shrill and urgent and the long train moved out.

And here, by rights, I should pause and, as the controller of dramatic irony, tell you of what tremendous trifles dire ills are born. I should wag at you a portentous forefinger and say with hushed impressiveness, "Why should a dray have been at that special spot at that particular time?" And the answer would be that but for that fortunate chance we should never have heard of the artist who painted the invisible, of the policeman who ran, of the divers uses of cement, and of the vicar who preached a pertinent sermon. That I do not wag at you this finger is because I have already done so.

There was no extraordinary perturbation visible on his face as he returned to the taxi. They drove round to the entrance of the Liverpool Street hotel where a room was soon found. That would be handier, thought Wrentham, than going all the way back to the Strand. As he paid off the driver a voice hailed him and he turned to confront Colonel Travers. The voices came together. "Hallo, Colonel!" "Hallo, Geoffrey!"

"What are you doing here?" The Colonel now got in ahead on the conversational mix-up. Wrentham related his misadventures. Jolly lucky running into the Colonel like that. He might get some news about Ludo. Why not ask him to eat a mouthful and then do a show? The Colonel had, however, to refuse.

"Not for me, young feller! Very good of you, but I absolutely promised to be in to-night. Why not come out with me to Highbury?"

"That's very nice of you, Colonel," said Wrentham, "but the fact is I had a dreadfully late night and must turn in early. Got to catch the seven-thirty in the morning. How's Ludo coming along these days?"

"Capital! Capital!" replied the other. "You in a hurry, my boy?"

Wrentham was not, and they moved along together towards the Moorgate Street Tube, talking of this and that, of meetings and familiar faces. Then, as they turned in by London Wall, a well-dressed man offered them a small printed bill. Travers waved his aside. Wrentham, less adroit, received his and was about to crumple it up to throw away, when his eye caught a name—HENRY PLUMLEY. He glanced rapidly through the notice.

"Rather an extraordinary coincidence that, Colonel," he remarked. "The first day I am in London after three years a stranger hands me a chit on which is the name of my neighbour."

The Colonel adjusted an eyeglass and scanned the bill.

"I expect you haven't heard anything of this movement," he said, "unless you read about it out there."

"What movement is that, sir?" asked Wrentham.

The Colonel pointed out the heading. "These people are connected with a society calling itself the Social League. I don't know exactly who they are, but there seem some very decent people among them. As you'll soon discover for yourself, my boy, there's a great deal of unrest about which started after the Armistice; demobilisation, inability to revert to male labour, and all that; so these fellers—I believe some are actually members of the Government—are going on the stump generally and holding meetings in big industrial centres. Let me see. Where's Plumley speaking?" The Colonel screwed in his glass and again consulted the bill. "Oh! the People's Hall, Aldgate."

"Do you know Plumley at all well, sir?" asked Wrentham.

"As well as most, between you and me," was the reply, a trifle angrily the other thought. "As a matter of fact, as you doubtless know, Ludo has been for the last eight months one of his secretaries."

Wrentham was certainly interested, for Ludo and he had been almost like brothers. True, their ways, since Halstead and Cambridge, had lain apart, and the war was a strange divider of interests. At the same time he was very surprised. The Colonel, however, went on.

"Yes, after he was invalided home the War Office found him a job at the Publicity Department. You knew Plumley had been in charge of a branch of that during the war?"

"I think I did hear something about it."

"Ludo knew there was not much point in hanging on, and so, when Plumley made him an offer—a dashed good offer too. He took it. Now he wishes to God he hadn't."

Wrentham hardly knew what to say. He was intrigued; more so than he cared to show. The other went on, this time his voice more lowered and confidential. "If one believes all that darn fool Ludo hints at, the fellow is going mad. All I can say is, 'Thank God I've no interest in City Corporations, Ltd.'"

While Wrentham was grasping this, the Colonel was making his excuses, and for a rapidly crowding lift at the same time. "Well, good-bye Geoffrey. Don't forget to come and see us when you return to Town. Remember me to the vicar," and hardly heeding the other's farewells he was gone.

It was inwardly, if not outwardly, a vastly different Wrentham who called, some ten minutes later, for a long whisky-and-soda in the lounge of the Great Eastern Hotel. Boys have a natural genius for the bestowal of nicknames, and those who gave him his title of "Rouster" were not the most incompetent at the job. It was the peculiarity of the man never to appear about to do anything; never to be concerned about preliminaries, but to face the event and leap into it. You may remember that 'Varsity match of his—he missed his Blue in his first year and a shoulder, crocked at soccer, kept him out of the next. Cambridge wanted eighty-three to win, with two bowlers, one of them Wrentham, to bat. His first ball he lammed for four; the next mid-off partially stopped, but they managed to get three for it. His second ball from Stonner—the great P.A.—scattered the ring at square-leg. When he was out, stumped some five feet from his crease, Cambridge had lost by four, and his total was seventy-one. "Why didn't he sit tight for the other five?" you may say. I do not know. There are the facts; for you is the analysis. And so with this other picture, if you will abide the digression. Sergeant Miller of C Company used him at times to impress new-comers to the Alexandria mess; not, I think, to shine in reflected glory. It appears, at least according to the sergeant, that one night in 1917, one sergeant and one captain found themselves about three hundred yards from the line by the Wadi Ghuzzeh, "Crawlin' on our bellies like a couple of bleedin' scorpines." They lay under a bank in the scant shade of a mass of distorted cactus. Here, perhaps, it would be as well to let the sergeant continue; his style, though being highly picturesque, having at least the merit of being direct.

"So the Captain he whispers to me, 'We'll stop here a bit, sergeant,' he says, 'and see if anything rolls up.' We'd been layin' there about a quarter of a hour when he sits up and cocks his ear. I look round his back and see something on the move like a couple of pi-dogs or them goats. He presses his left hand into the small of my back and there he sits like a blinkin' idol. Whatever it was, they must have thought he was somethin'. They come straight over to us, and who do you think it was? A couple of Johnnies! I could see their old dirty jackets and the round caps, and all the time he kep' on pushin' into my ribs. You talk about havin' the perishin' wind up! There he sat, and them two Johnnies must have thought he was some kind of ruddy animal"—it seems that the sergeant had never heard of Caliban and his bedfellow—"and they come right up and that's all I see. He must have given one a swipe over the jaw and the other a lift on the snout, because, when I got up, there was them two layin' flat and him whisperin' to me to drag one along. Well, we lugged them two Johnnies by the collar on the sand for a couple of mile I should think, until we got to the bend of the Wadi, and then, wot in 'ell do you think he done? 'Miller,' he says, 'I'm damned if I'm goin' to lug these fat swine any further. Nip off back and fetch a couple of orderlies.' And if one of them Johnnies hadn't started tryin' to get up, I'm damned if he wouldn't have made me done it."

But as Wrentham sat over his long drink it appeared to him with no little emphasis that something had rolled up. What did the Colonel mean about City Corporations? And what was that about Ludo hinting that Plumley was going mad? He hadn't looked much like going mad when he saw him at Hainton; but there, that was three years ago. He had never liked the man. Just a bit too plausible. He had no use for those financier fellows, in any case. Still, why worry? A brain-wave struck him. Why not go round to Bloomsbury Square in the morning and try to get hold of godfather Hallett? That was it—he'd telegraph to Hainton to meet the afternoon instead of the lunch train.

Why not try to get hold of old Ludo in the morning too? No, dash it all! he couldn't do that. Getting a chap to tell tales out of the office or whatever they called it. After all, it was probably a mare's nest. And another thought set that off—the very definite fact that ten thousand pounds is a devil of a lot of money, especially when it happens to be all you have. But what a fool he'd look if there was nothing in it. Heaven knows the war had produced enough tall yarns and doubtless the peace would not be left far behind. Perhaps there was no need to see his godfather. And if he did see him, how could he approach the subject without betraying the source of his information?

But during dinner his uneasiness persisted. It was not as if he had remembered something which he would fain forget, but rather as if he had forgotten something which he could not remember, so present at the back of his mind was the cloud of the evening's happenings. And while he was waiting in the lounge for his coffee he faced the problem and determined to forget it. And then, again, as he groped in his pocket for his pipe he felt the rustle of paper and pulled out the handbill!

He read it again. SOCIAL LEAGUE—PEOPLE'S HALL—ALDGATE. In the chair LORD CHARLES NEVVIN. He remembered Nevvin. Oh, yes! at the last shoot in 1913. He had been one of the house-party at the Hall. Thundering good billiard player Nevvin! Speakers—HENRY PLUMLEY, ESQ., MONTAGUE HEARST, ESQ. Hearst? Hearst? He'd never heard of him. AT 8.30 P.M. Extraordinary time of the year—July—to hold meetings. His eye caught the clock—the old Parliament clock at the end of the lounge—eight-thirty. Why not go to the meeting? If Ludo was one of the secretaries perhaps he would be there too. He would have plenty of time for Plumley, even if he missed the chairman. And somebody or other had told him that old Plumley could never speak unless he had a good dinner inside him. Two minutes later he was in a taxi and the driver was wondering why the devil his fare hadn't walked it.

CHAPTER II
ANOTHER CURTAIN FALLS

HAD WRENTHAM SPENT his last three years in England instead of in the East many things concerning the position of Henry Plumley would have been more clear to him. Had even his demobilisation not been delayed until this July of 1919 he might have been in a position to make, however unconsciously, certain reasonably obvious deductions. "What great ones do, the less will prattle of," is more true of a modern financier than it was of that mediaeval count, especially when the financier has decided tendencies towards the spectacular and flamboyant.

There was about Plumley little of that unctuousness, of that desire to add the keys of heaven to the dividends, which characterised those financial geniuses who went wrong a generation or two ago. Rather was he, and ostentatiously, a man of the world; a lover of all the things that money can buy, and as complement, of those things which cause money to melt. His racing stable was small but quality all through, and his breeding establishment at Chalton contained, besides that great sire Martext, two winners of the Oaks, and Volterra, the second mare of the century to win the St. Leger. At Hainton he had leased from the owner the Hall and one of the most famous partridge shoots in England, as soon as it had become vacant by the death of Sir Francis Bereston; which tenant had spent no inconsiderable sum of money upon improvements. At Hindhead he owned a small, well-timbered property of some forty acres. There, handy as it was for Town, he often stayed for a week-end's golf, at which game few played worse and none more enthusiastically. His Town house in Bellingham Square was said to contain the finest collection of the Flemish School in England, including Van Eyck's "John Baptising in Jordan." He owned two theatres, the "Capitol" and the "Metropolis"; one paper, the "Financial Herald," and was said to have a finger in certain other journalistic pies.

In Kingsway, the offices of City Corporations were, when first erected, one of the sights of London. Nothing like them had been seen before. It seemed as if the idea of the architect had been to convey the suggestion of weight; of sheer, ponderous, immovable and solid weight. To regard them was security and under their shadow was protection.

As to his origins, none could say for certain. There were some who professed to have known him, in the dark backward and abysm of time, as a solicitor's clerk or a kind of glorified insurance agent; but it is to be doubted whether such knowledge was other than it usually is in these cases, the boasting of some cheap liar broadcast into rumour. Nevertheless, from whatever source he had acquired it, he had in his nature that adaptability which is the greatest asset of the public man. With the man in the street he was the fearless defender of our institutions and the unfeed champion of the under-dog. In sport he would finance any defence of British prestige, whether in boxing, golf, or Olympic games. After his speech at York, following on the great munitions' strike, he was invited, it is said, to join the Coalition Government. Although unable to accept this, it is significant that in 1917 he became virtual head of the Publicity Department.

As to his business activities I cannot speak with any authority, save that financially he feared publicity as much as he courted it otherwise. Often as his photo appeared in the illustrated papers it was never as a wizard of finance. Governments never approached him for financial accommodations and currencies rocketed unhelped and unhindered by him. City Corporations, ostensibly his main interest, had many and various activities. It included in its scope such diverse methods of attracting the guileless investor as boring for oil in Nova Zembla or the marketing of synthetic alcohol. Less generally known was his connexion with Blacktons, the great steel mills; and Fortice & Ward, that formidable shipbuilding amalgamation of the Tyne and Glasgow yards. His name appeared as director on neither board, yet both firms were deeply involved in the world-wide ramifications of Apex Motors, in which he had large financial interests and whose policy he did so much to control. Of his operations on the rubber market when his attempted corner in 1913 fluttered the dovecotes of Europe and Wall Street, or of his rumoured negotiations with the New Oil Group, I cannot speak with certainty, knowing less of the real truth of them than any clerk in Mincing Lane.

His general appearance you may remember. In fashioning Henry Plumley, nature seemed to have achieved a masterpiece of incongruity, for never did a man have more the air of a stage deacon. Weak-kneed he looked and timorous and mildly deprecatory. His slight paunch seemed as if it must be merely a cushion and his trailing side-whiskers as if they must drop off. On his head was hardly a vestige of hair, but in compensation he had the most minatory of eyebrows. Give him an umbrella and a top hat and you would have said, "I don't know who that fellow on the stage is supposed to be, but whoever he is, he has overdone his make-up."

Yet, I suppose, as a public speaker there have been few as capable of so winding and insinuating himself into the heart of an audience. Put him on his legs and he spoke with the voice of men and angels, whether his theme and discourse were high imperial aims or political claptrap or merely those meanderings which occur after banqueting.

As he entered the People's Hall, Wrentham felt very uncomfortable. Only once before did he remember attending a meeting of this nature, rallying round Stonner when he tried to get in for

Mid-Norfolk. Somehow it didn't seem quite the thing to do. He narrowly escaped a species of usher and sat down on a form right at the back. The building was nearly full; between him and the nearest backs were not more than three or four benches. Nobody appeared to have the least interest in his entrance. Everybody must have been smoking, for a thin haze hung in the air like a grey veil. Flags were everywhere, clamorous and discordant. On the platform were about a dozen people, backed by an enormous Union Jack. Coming from the clear light of a perfect July evening Wrentham thought it all unreal and garish; and, despite the glare of the lights, a trifle shabby. He recognised Nevvin, seated behind a table draped with a less obvious flag. A tall, plump man was Nevvin, rather pinky, and wearing a moustache that looked as untidy as his clothes. He was leaning back in his seat, hands together, thumbs beneath his chin, forefingers caressing his nose—his whole pose one of obvious indifference to time and circumstance. The man with the black, close-cropped beard would probably be Hearst, whoever Hearst was.

Plumley was speaking. I do not suppose these various thoughts took more than a few moments to flash through Wrentham's mind. He settled to listen, but the fact that he was plunging abruptly into the speech and must gather for himself the connecting threads made, for a few minutes, concentration most necessary. He had in his mind no other idea than to listen to Plumley, to form his own judgment of the man after a three years' absence, and in the light of Travers' remarks, gnomic though they had been. The speaker was evidently at the moment fortifying some argument and stating his willingness to submit definite figures in support of certain statements. Immediately behind him and to his right hand was seated a man of foreign appearance; some kind of Latin, thought Wrentham. From him, almost without turning round, Plumley received a paper of some kind, evidently the figures required. The fellow must be a sort of secretary. Plumley read his statement as to the number of unemployed in a certain industry. They were meaningless to Wrentham, yet apparently a shrewd hit, for the audience laughed spontaneously and cheered delightedly. The secretary received back the list.

There was a smile on Plumley's lips as he waited for the applause to cease. His continuation was in a more serious vein. He was apparently making a comparison between the England of the close of the Napoleonic wars and that of 1919. From time to time he would lean forward and peck, as it were, at his audience, punctuating his points with jabs of his pince-nez. The voice itself was remarkable, else had the man provoked laughter and not hushed attention. Not Cyrano looked less a spell-binder than the insignificant and yet wholly contained figure before them. Some had said he was lucky in his secretaries, a comment which, while not beyond one's expectation of the man, yet gave no credit where it was due. In a way, as well discredit Shakespeare because of Boccaccio, or Grock because he was not the father of all such as deal in clown-age.

During the middle of this comparative exposition, and while the speaker was lingering upon the word "Peterloo," a sound of quick steps was heard and a messenger boy entered the hall. Before Wrentham could notice definitely his appearance he had passed quickly down the centre gangway and was pausing at the foot of the platform and holding up a letter. The speaker stopped and regarded the boy through his glasses, but, in a flash, the man whom Wrentham had, apparently rightly, taken for a secretary, leaned forward and took the note. It was evidently addressed to Plumley, who motioned with his hand as if to wave it away and made as if to resume his speech. The secretary, however, pointed out something on the envelope. Plumley turned and made a remark, inaudible to Wrentham, first to the chairman and then to the audience; slit open the note, glanced at it, and clenched it tightly in his fist. He stood so while one could count slowly up to twenty. Then he spoke again.

"There is one thing I would say, however, to the men of England, and it is this. Don't be led astray by the specious, by promises whose sole merit is their glitter. There is rarely in this world wealth to be acquired suddenly; there is nothing without effort. If you get something for nothing in this life it is generally worth it." Here a slow-dawning laughter ran along the hall. "There are to-day men holding up banks and post offices, and even small shopkeepers. The papers will tell you that all this is the desire for sudden having, the craze to possess without effort. Work will be the salvation of this country. He who has work will have no devil at his ear and no twitch to his fingers. Let me tell you something that may interest you." The speaker paused. It might be said dramatically; it might be merely to sip from the glass before him, to collect and review his thoughts.

"People have come to me. They have heard other foolish people term me a wizard, a financial genius. They have asked my advice on making fortunes. Sometimes they have been in actual need of money, and they have come to me as a savage would to his god to achieve the miraculous, to show them the shortest cut to wealth. What a delusion! We read that the King of Syria sent his servant, Naaman, by error to the King of Israel instead of to his prophet, to be cured of his leprosy. The king rent his garments. 'See,' he cried, 'how this man seeketh a quarrel against me! Am I god, to kill and make alive?'

"And yet there are at this moment, if we only knew it, opportunities for all of us. At this very second I might take you to a certain spot and say to you—" and here came the dramatic—nay, melodramatic—moment so characteristic of the man and in a way of his audiences. He leaned forward and pointed his finger at the packed forms. Only once did he seem to linger and then at some indefinite point in the front of his audience. You would have thought that heads would be turned, but it was the man who fascinated, not those unknown whom the fluttering finger half carelessly designated—"and say to you, and you, and you, 'Here before your eyes is what you wish. Here is money. Money! Help yourself! Take what you wish!' Then you would probably say to me, 'Where is it? I can see nothing. Here are grass and earth and trees and stones, but where is the money?' And yet there to your hand and for your taking it shall be, that gold for which we would all sell ourselves."

Again the speaker paused; then the voice went on, calmer but all as impressive. "And now you are saying, 'What is this tale of buried treasure he is telling us?' and then I reply, 'Life is all buried treasure and even treasure must be digged for.' But I would not affront your credulity with tales of the 'Arabian Nights.' Even the trees, the earth, and the stones may become treasure. One man threw on his fire a stone and it burnt; another saw a forest and it became paper. Another saw a kettle and it became a steam engine. Yet another watched a bird and one day flew."

In spite of himself Wrentham was interested. There are things which, written baldly on paper, have no appeal. Your actor—your great actor—has that faculty of emphasis which can make of triteness itself an epigram and of a platitude a thing to startle. And surely Plumley was an actor. Gesture, cadence, the knowledge of his audience, all were his. "A showman!" you say. Well, I grant you, but what a showman!

The speech was going on. "Out of chaos must come order. Chaos is annihilation; it feeds upon itself. It is this restraint, this order that I see evolving and that must evolve from every one of you. There is none so humble that he may escape order. Adam, the first gardener, dared not neglect the order of the seasons or they would have refused to obey him. In the first garden was law and order; the herb after his kind, the flower after his, and the fruit-bearing tree. We may learn much from gardens."

Again he stopped, and as he did so a figure came through the door at the back of the platform and sank unobtrusively into a chair. He was, as far as Wrentham could judge, a military man, as one might say, tall and carrying himself well. And yet he would not have been noticed but for the pause of the speaker, who had half turned at the slight noise of entry and had quickly scanned the entrant. Plumley again sipped his glass and stood as if to resume his speech. Had the thread escaped him? He stood silent and motionless, his gaze fixed upon a spot to the right of his audience. So he remained for fully a minute while the crowd waited, half expectant, half ashamed at the long silence. Then he swayed and fell. The glass, struck by his arm, crashed to the floor. There was a rising, a swaying of the crowd. Men stood on chairs to get a view. Speedily there was a hubbub.

All one could see on the platform was a blurred group and people rushing here and there.

Without waiting, Wrentham walked quickly to the street. Lord, what a day! It was not yet half-past nine and he strolled slowly back to the hotel. What an amazing speech it had been! Why on earth had Plumley switched off to talk about treasure at all and woven all that fantasy into a sober reasoning on unemployment? Was that a police inspector who had come to arrest him? And why had he talked about gardens to *that* audience? He couldn't make head or tail of it all. Oh, what did it all matter, after all? The morning would clear it all up. He refused to think about it more. The devil was in the day's proceedings anyhow. He pushed the bell and called for a long drink. Then he picked up the evening paper and for some time turned over the pages aimlessly. Nothing there to interest him in any case. Even the cricket news failed to hold him. He turned to the financial columns and looked up City Corporations. The statement

City Corporations............1/9 –/3

conveyed nothing to him. He would go to see godfather Hallett in the morning; that would be the best in the long run. Like going to the dentist's. No, dash it all! it would be fine to see his godfather in any case, if he were at the office.

A telephone bell rang nearby. In a minute or two the waiter came in as if to clear up odd glasses and tidy tables. There was only one other in the lounge—a civilian—and it was to Wrentham that the waiter spoke.

"Have you heard the news, sir?" he said.

"I'm afraid I haven't," replied Wrentham. "What is it?"

"Plumley's dead, sir. Henry Plumley. We just got the news over the 'phone. Suicide they say it was. Anything else you want, sir?"

"Thank you, no," said Wrentham, if it were he, for it seemed to him that it was another who spoke. On the heels of the waiter he followed to the office and claimed his key.

"You might see I'm called at eight sharp," he said to the clerk. And in ten minutes, in spite of the traffic and the afterglow that still persisted in the sky, he was sound asleep.

CHAPTER III
THE HERO APPEARS TO BE UP AGAINST IT

MESSRS. HALLETT & HALLETT, those old-established solicitors of Giles Street, Norwich, had, in common with most provincial firms of their standing, London offices and agents. It was the custom of Wortley Hallett, the senior partner of the firm, and, to achieve an anti-climax, the godfather of Geoffrey Wrentham, to attend at Bloomsbury Square twice a week, on Tuesdays and Fridays. Ask me not why. Although I cannot, upon the ways of lawyers, express myself with the flippancy of Hamlet or the downright accumulative abuse of old Rabelais, that is not to admit that I like them more. And, to be charitable, let such misliking be ascribed to ignorance.

Between Wrentham and his godfather there existed, however, a feeling that was far closer than that somewhat vague relationship implied. The lawyer had, beneath a morose and dismal exterior, a nature that was almost fierce in its attachments and boyish in its unbendings. It was soon after the death of his mother that the boy had first visited the old house at Cantley, and it was the lawyer who taught him his first nature lore and the way of handling a boat; for in our village there is small chance of sailing anything anywhere unless it be upon a duck-pond. Thereafter had come many a holiday on the Broads, often, too, with Ludovic Travers, the latter always more student than athlete, a finder of nests and a gatherer of promiscuous pets.

It was ten o'clock when Wrentham wandered into the meandering passage-way of the offices, to be met by Jewson, the head clerk, who was sincere in his handshake. "You're looking fitter than I ever saw you, Major," said he. "I told Mr. Hallett as soon as he came in that you had 'phoned us. He'll see you at once."

Whatever the years had done to Wrentham they seemed to have stood still with Wortley Hallett. He was the same as when his godson had last seen him; his hair no greyer and his shoulders unbent. You would, perhaps, have sworn to a suspicion of moistness in his eye. To their first conversation we will leave them. It concerns neither us nor this story. But it was out of these intimate things that the leading question came.

"Now, my boy, having seen a little more of the world at the Government's expense, what are you going to do?"

On that topic Wrentham had so much to say that he had difficulty in expressing himself. "I hardly know," he explained. "You see this business of Plumley has rather messed things up a bit."

The other was surprised. "But surely you got my letter!"

"What letter?" said Wrentham, equally astonished.

"Extraordinary! Most extraordinary! I wrote to your regiment at Cairo, as I had done previously, about two months ago. Your father assured me—I took the precaution to inquire—that the address held good."

But further consideration—the moving to Alexandria, then to Kantara; the week's stay in Taranto and further halt at Boulogne after a fortnight's journey—all this put a different light on the matter.

"What was in it, in any case?" asked Wrentham.

Here the relation became temporarily the lawyer. He cleared his throat and took a minute for due consideration.

"You must know that news reaches us through various channels. It is especially difficult in a case like this—*sub judice*, as it were—to speak more than guardedly. At the time of the new issue of City Corporations, three months ago, we had occasion to make an inquiry on behalf of a client. We were not very satisfied. We regarded their commitments as far too heavy. I wrote to you, wholly unofficially, that it would not be inadvisable to realise most of your holding, and suggested that your banker, at the same time, would give you a list of suitable reinvestments."

"Yes, but don't you remember that great-aunt Mildred's legacy, to us as to all her host of relations, was in blocks of shares.

She distinctly stated that although she had made no proviso (if that is what you call it) she would prefer that everybody should hang on to the shares as they stood."

"I certainly didn't handle the business at all, nor do I call to mind such a proviso. Still, I've no doubt you're perfectly right. Irrespective of the question whether such a proviso would have stood, the fact remains that property was left you which you were meant to enjoy. Necessary realisation was a matter of common sense."

"Look here, godfather," said Wrentham, determining to get hold of the case as far as it affected him. "I expect I'm an awful fool about these things, and what I know about them wouldn't cover a dud threepenny bit. Do you mind if I put the matter in my own way?"

"Go on, my boy," replied Hallett, swivelling his chair into comfort, and preparing to hear, not for the first time, law and finance shorn of their jargon.

"What can I do? Can I realise the market value of the shares?"

"The shares have no market value in fact. The offices of City Corporations are closed. If it was an order of the court that was to arrest Plumley last night, it is almost certain that a liquidator is about to be appointed by the court."

"Then what do I get for my ten thousand?"

"That we cannot say. The usual procedure will doubtless be followed. We will, if you desire it, act as proxy for you at any meetings called by the liquidator, who is bound to act in accordance with the wishes of the majority of the holders. A dividend may ultimately be declared. Whatever the dividend is will be, I fear, all that you will get." The lawyer was genuinely distressed. "Leave it to us, my boy," he added. "There is no need at present to be unduly alarmed even if the case does look sufficiently serious."

"I'm not worrying about biting the bullet," said Wrentham with a grin, "and it's jolly decent of you to offer to do so much. It's myself I'm annoyed with. If I'd taken that tea-planting job instead of going on that trip to Uganda with Prestwich I should have had something at my fingers' ends." He thought a moment and then, "You see I can't very well attach myself to the guv'nor."

And, whichever way they talked it over, the door by which they came out was the same as that by which they went in. There was nothing definite that could be done. But when Wrentham left the office he was much more settled in mind. What a thundering good sort his godfather was! And what a good thing it was to have a man like that to take hold of things! Whatever could be done there wasn't a doubt would be done. It was a brain-wave, too, asking that nothing should be mentioned to his father, whatever happened. There was no point in worrying anybody unnecessarily, and, after all, the whole business might turn out trumps in the end. The death of Plumley, as they had discussed, need not mean the collapse or even the ultimate weakening of those financial activities wherewith he was connected. Then, again, he could easily slip up to Norwich any morning and see how things were getting on.

Only eleven o'clock. What about ringing up Ludo? He could do that at the club. As he hailed a taxi, the thought hit him sharp as a blow that he ought not to be taking taxis. Seven hundred and fifty a year—City Corporations had certainly paid well—and, during the war, pay, allowances, and precious little inducement to spend, all seemed untold wealth before the prospects of what might be left if there was a mess. Still, why worry? He settled back in his corner. Thank whatever gods there be that the guv'nor was all right. There was the living—a bare five hundred—a small amount of private means, about a couple of hundred, he thought, and the five thousand that had come from great-aunt Mildred at the same time as his own legacy. Apex Motors ought to be sound enough. Everybody seemed to be buying cars now. Look at the thousands of fellers like himself with gratuities to burn. Of course there would be his own gratuity; he had forgotten that. There would be a pretty fair lot at the bank too. That pension to poor Holland's wife and kids would have made a hole in it though. Still, why worry? There he was, off again. What was the use of making up his mind to go quiet and then going right off the deep end? So his thoughts as the car moved on.

By an amazing coincidence Ludo was the first person he met as he mounted the club steps.

"Hallo, Geoffrey! Who would have thought of seeing you here?"

"Why not?" laughed Wrentham, taking his arm; "come along in."

If the best friendships must be those of opposites there was cause for the friendship of these two. In their boyhood one took the risk of the trespass, the nest, or the spoil, with like enthusiasm; for the other interest began and ended with the adventure. At Halstead, Ludo had been the worshipper and Wrentham the hero. At Cambridge, their ways had first really diverged. The story of one read: history for a pass degree, games, lectures occasionally on military science and tactics and, of course, the O.T.C. On the field and in the market square he led men as by some natural right. For the other: a first in the economics' tripos, lectures, and dinners at the Temple.

When Wrentham arrived it was always in the thick of it and generally in the van; Ludo never appeared to be arriving anywhere until you found he had got there. Wrentham exhaled an obvious belief in his fellows and in the joy of living. Travers generally looked unutterably bored. His was rather an assured aloofness, a detachment of personality and an extreme nervousness of manner which might to casual observance seem fussiness. Yet, more than the other—and it might have been due to the rare whimsicality of the man—he had the happy faculty of appearing perfectly at ease, whether in an adult-school meeting, a university society, or those places where men most do congregate. So with their faults: Wrentham's a blazing temper, mad impetuosity and an over-confidence in the trustworthiness of mankind; Ludo's a hint of laziness and a superb disregard of conventions. The end of the war had found each with a D.S.O., but whereas one had escaped with a couple of flesh wounds the other was left with impaired sight as the effects of a prolonged exposure to gas.

It seemed as if Ludo were reluctant to re-enter the club, not that his delight at the unexpected meeting was feigned, but that, as he explained, that had been the devil of a day. He didn't know whether he was on his heels or his elbows.

"Well, a quick 'un won't make all that difference, my lad," said Wrentham, and pushed his protesting companion into a chair. By Jove! it was good to see old Ludo again, he thought. There he was, just as nervous and fussy and keen as ever, and true metal down to the very soles of him. Ludo took off his spectacles, polished them, put them back, and then laughed boyishly.

"I've a good mind to toss up—heads, 'Tell me all about it,' and tails, 'Off I go.' Seriously, Geoffrey, I must get back to Bellingham House at once. Look here. What are you doing the rest of the day?"

"Catching the two thirty-four from Liverpool Street."

"I say, that's devilish awkward. Wait a minute though," and he again took off the spectacles and rubbed them vigorously with a handkerchief from his breast pocket. His eyes blinked as an inspiration seized him. "I think I've got it. Everybody wants me, but if I get clean away and have enough sense not to leave word where I've gone I don't see how they're going to get hold of me. What about meeting me at twelve sharp? The Haymarket side of Piccadilly Circus station? I know a little place where we can get quite a good meal."

"The very thing," Wrentham assured him.

Ludo finished his drink and rose to go, but again the other pushed him down into the chair.

"I don't know if I ought to repeat this, Ludo," he began, drawing his pew in closer, "but your guv'nor last night hinted there was something remarkably queer about—about—Plumley." He faltered over the phrasing. Leaving out *de mortuis* and all that, it was difficult to discuss the dead man, and especially with Ludo. But the reply staggered him.

"As a matter of fact, that was one of the very things I wanted to speak to you about." He, too, hesitated, while Wrentham waited expectantly. "Don't misunderstand me, old chap. What I should have said was that I've got something on my mind, and the sooner I get it off the better pleased I shall be. And I don't know anybody I'd rather talk it over with sooner than you. I suppose, by the way, you're not affected by all this bother?" he added casually.

"Only to the tune of ten thousand or thereabouts," replied Wrentham cheerfully.

"Good God!" exclaimed Ludo, with wholly unusual vehemence, and, for him, blasphemy. Neither of them spoke for a minute. Then Ludo again got up to go. His face was like that of the immortal thane—a book whereon one might read strange matters. Wrentham was struck by the thought that rarely before had he seen him look so serious and never so perturbed.

"Twelve o'clock, then," said Ludo, again starting to polish his glasses.

"At the cubiculo, my lad," answered Wrentham soberly.

CHAPTER IV
A STRANGE TALE IS RELATED

THE ALCOVE in which they sat was perfectly suited to the purpose, and there were, moreover, few patrons of the restaurant at that particular hour. Ludo insisted that Wrentham should first tell his side of the tale. It took some time, ranging as it did over three years and a still longer twenty hours. And over the coffee the other began his part of the matter—a story that, as it was unfolded, became more inexplicable; and yet a story that made the listener find, at its end, his coffee cold and untasted.

"You've heard from the guv'nor, Geoff, how I came to meet Henry Plumley. But, before I go on with my tale at all, I must say, however ludicrous and irresponsible the statement may sound, that Plumley was, as far as I am concerned, a jolly decent sort."

It could not be said that he glared or that he looked apologetic; perhaps it was a blend of the two.

"That's all right, old chap," said Wrentham. "You should know."

"The offer that he made me was eight hundred a year. There were three of us secretaries, but how the others stood I don't know. Moulines, the financial secretary, was at the head office; Hollister, the political *walla*, also had an office at Kingsway, but both he and Moulines often had to come round to Bellingham House, where my head-quarters were. I was designated private or social secretary. From what I gathered when I took the job on my chief work would be correspondence dealing with personal matters and charities, administrative liaison between the agents of the various estates and Plumley himself, and any research that was needed for purely social speeches and functions. For the first three months things went along perfectly smoothly. I had my rooms at Bellingham House. There was a small staff for such a large place, not more than eight servants in all, including the butler and the housekeeper. Breakfast was at eight-fifteen and work began at nine in the morning. At about nine-thirty I took into the chief's room everything with which I did not feel myself absolutely competent to deal. Just before ten I reported to him again and received back the correspondence with instructions pencilled on it. If it was involved or of sufficient importance we had a pow-wow on it. At the same time I received a list of special daily instructions. Generally there were sufficient to last well over the day; on rare occasions there were none at all. At six p.m. I was supposed to be in my room. If wanted, I was called up on the telephone; if not, I was free. I don't remember a single occasion, except at the dedication of Michester War Memorial (when, of course, I accompanied Plumley) that I was ever called upon after five in the evening, except by telephone messages which I have just mentioned, and then never more often than twice a week. He was most considerate. I don't know what caused that dreadful business of last night, and I don't know the charge which would have made necessary his arrest as he left the platform, but, looking back, I can see little in him that was not natural-born courtesy and kindliness of heart. He was a bit flamboyant, I admit, and even occasionally hectic, especially in public, but I'd rather have that than some of those damnable old fools you and I ran up against in the army."

He stopped and Wrentham forbore to break in on his silence.

"Well, all this went on until February. You know young Plumley? Never heard of him? Well, I don't know that I should have done except for the sequel. His mother died when he was a baby and the old man seems to have absolutely doted on him. Like most children in such circumstances, there's no doubt he was made a fool of. He was kicked out of his school, and after raising various sorts of hell at Oxford was sent down just before the war. He had a little money of his own, and as far as I can gather fell in with the last people on God's green earth you would have expected him to—some Chelsea crowd or other. At any rate he used to be seen in the West End with a velvet coat, Spanish hat, and all that sort of rot. Whatever you say of old Plumley, he was intensely patriotic. That was the first shock he had, when his son was run in as a conscientious objector. From what Hollister told me once it shook the old man up pretty badly. Then, about a year ago—I should say he was released for health and various other reasons—he married a girl out of the chorus and turned up with her at Bellingham House the same night. From all accounts there was the devil of a scene. All that is known definitely is that they left the house and the old man was found in some kind of fit on the floor.

"That brings us to last February, when it was discovered that Master George had forged the old man's name to a hefty big cheque and had collected the money. Moulines had the handling of the affair, and devilish unsavoury it was. There isn't any point in raking over other people's garbage heaps. Still, as far as it concerns us, that's what started the trouble. That's when Plumley started going mad."

Wrentham scarce withheld an exclamation, but the other went on without a pause, seeming to anticipate the unspoken query.

"You might say, 'Why didn't they shut him up?' Well, you see, it wasn't that kind of madness. It was just a sort of inexplicable eccentricity. Everything he did was so contrary to what he had, as far as my experience went and as far as allowances for human fallibility will stretch, ever done before. He blackguarded me like a fishwife one night because I wasn't in when he arrived unexpectedly at nine o'clock. Often when I used to speak to him he didn't reply. Once or twice he came and spent the whole of a morning in my room, sitting there and doing nothing at all. Then, again, some days he would get a fit of chattering and run on as aimlessly as a washerwoman. At this stage I don't see how I can be more explicit. All I want to convey is that the things he did were diametrically opposed to all opinions I had ever formed of him, and some so grotesque that I would rather hint at them than describe them in detail. Some of the things might have been explained. For instance, he announced that there was to be no more entertaining at Bellingham House, and his niece, Miss du Frene, was sent away. Then he said he would sell the place, and Hindhead also, and dispose of the Hainton lease. Then he would forget all about it. Then he would suddenly demand why the devil I hadn't made all the arrangements for it, and then again say that things were to remain as they were.

"I tell you, Geoff, if I hadn't thought a lot of the old man and sympathised with him, I shouldn't have stuck it and be damned to his eight hundred. Then the extraordinary thing happened which made me stay on in spite of myself, out of curiosity if you like, or else cussedness. If you didn't know me I wouldn't insult your intelligence by asking you to believe these things. As it is, all I ask is that you try to put yourself in my place.

"The first was one morning after he had been sitting for some time in my room. 'What would you do, Travers,' he suddenly said, 'if you were asked for a couple of hundred spot cash?' 'Go to the bank,' said I. 'No you don't,' said he. 'Spot cash,' I said. 'Here and now, find me two hundred pounds.' He saw that I was surprised, and before I could make any comment he went on with, 'Why not consult the venerable Adam Smith?' The way he said it was a sort of order, he waved his hand like that. I felt a bit of a fool, but I got up like a schoolboy and hunted over the shelves until I found the 'Wealth of Nations.' The book opened, marked with two one hundred pound notes. He laughed and clapped his hands and looked as pleased as Punch. One note fell to the floor, and when I picked it up he was gone. He refused half a dozen times afterwards to take them back, and finally I handed them in with some correspondence. Then came the second week in March.

"One morning before nine o'clock, when to the best of my knowledge he had not even come down to breakfast, the bell rang for me. The first thing he said took me clean in the wind. 'I think, Mr. Travers, you are a man of honour.' Well, what could I say to that? What would you have said? Probably what I did— nothing at all. However, he didn't wait for an answer. He told me to sit down. 'If I hadn't thought so, if I didn't know your antecedents and record, I should never have employed you in your present capacity. I expect from any employee of mine, humble or exalted, the most implicit obedience and the completest subordination to my interests. I am going to ask you to undertake for me one or two tasks which may seem to you to be peculiar. When you undertake to do them, which you will do by leaving the room with this list I am now going to give you, it will be an acknowledgment on your part that what you are going to do will never be spoken of except in the event of my death.'

"I can tell you I pricked up my ears at that. It probably sounds to you a sort of comic opera or melodrama, but the old man was as precise and serious about it all as if I were his solicitor. I read the list; I read it two or three times. 'There is only one comment I have to make, sir,' I said, 'and that is that with some of these matters I do not feel myself very competent to deal.' 'That is my business,' he retorted, with, as I thought, some asperity. 'What I require more than competence is discretion.' Well I took the list and went. I have it now," and he handed it over to Wrentham. "What do you make of it?"

It was a double sheet of foolscap, on the outside

"INSTRUCTIONS FOR MARCH 18TH"

Inside it proceeded as follows:

"(*a*) Prepare a monograph of about 50 ll. on Southern English conifers with specimens of needles and cones.

"(*b*) Obtain descriptions, and a 7 lb. tin, of the best waterproof cement.

"(*c*) Obtain three dozen of the best tennis balls.

"(*d*) Précis to an easily followed essay, the best method of rendering transparent glass absolutely opaque.

"(*e*) Obtain the gardening catalogues of the three leading English firms, with special reference to hardy perennials.

"(*f*) Obtain 30 ft. rolls of copper, and aluminium wire, of the handiness of ordinary twine.

"(*g*) Obtain specimens of bitumen damp-coursing and discuss the advantages of this over ordinary slate.

"(*h*) Obtain three second-hand suit-cases in perfect repair and with good locks.

"(Complete within seven days, please.)"

"Well, what do you make of it?" asked Ludo eagerly.

"Damn all!" was the pointed reply. "Can't make head or tail of it."

"That's what I thought. However, the instructions were implicit enough and I saw no reason to query them. (*c*) and (*f*) were settled in a few minutes by 'phone to the stores. (*h*) took an hour in Tottenham Court Road. (*a*) cost me a morning at South Kensington, an afternoon at Hindhead, and a night's hard dissection of an encyclopaedia article. (*b*) and (*g*) I got by consulting with two of the biggest building firms in town. (*d*) stumped me entirely and finally cost me two days in Exeter, interviewing the firm of a former subaltern of mine, interested in stained glass windows. (*e*) I got by a judicious tip at Kew Gardens, and thereafter by reference to the firms themselves. At any rate, by the end of the week I had the whole lot ready and laid out on the old man's desk. I tell you I mounted guard over that collection until he arrived. 'Thank you, Travers! Thank you!' was all he said, but he rubbed his hands and settled down to it like a Scotsman at a free meal. And that's all I ever heard about it, and I never saw one of those exhibits again.

"The next thing was two days later. I received instructions to draw on the private, house, or 'B' account, ten thousand pounds in one hundred pound notes, every other day until I had withdrawn the sum of a hundred thousand pounds. These notes I handed over personally and the matter was not referred to again. All the time I was feeling like some comic assistant for the conjuror at a village bazaar.

"A day or two later I received a further commission. I pass over the fact that when I saw him that particular morning he was squatted on the carpet working a clockwork engine on a set of rails. Otherwise he seemed perfectly all right. At any rate, he handed me over a passport fully made out and a hundred pounds for expenses. If you tried from now to doomsday you'd never guess what my instructions were. Well, I had to go to Toulouse and Carcassone and report on the number of restaurants in these towns the proprietors of which had actually been on service during the war. It took me a fortnight, and I should imagine I made more enemies during that time than during the rest of my life. When I returned I handed over my data, which, I flattered myself, were most complete. He just shoved them in a drawer. I'm as certain as I shall ever be certain of anything that he never looked at them. I made a rather diplomatic query of Moulines on the same point, and from that and my own observation I knew it couldn't be what I had thought it might be—the floating of a chain of restaurants, sort of multiple-shop business, in southern French towns. In any case, why didn't he give the job to Moulines? He is a Swiss and speaks the language better than myself. Besides, it was his pigeon."

Wrentham bethought him of the secretary he had seen at the meeting. "Was Moulines a fellow of medium height, with a rather Latin appearance; thin moustache and all that?"

"That certainly sounds like him. Where did you run across him? At last night's meeting?"

Wrentham explained and Ludo went on with his story.

"Before I'd been back a couple of days the old man was chasing me again. This time it was Plymouth. I was to make a list of vacant plots, near, or likely to be near, residential districts, with an account of their frontages or possible frontages, and with prices per plot or foot. Thank God it wasn't war-time or I'd have been shot at dawn. That job of work took me ten days, and jolly hard going at that. On this occasion, when I gave in my account to Plumley, he seemed remarkably interested. As a matter of fact, he distinctly commented—I forget his exact words—on the likelihood of there being money in it. I wasn't feeling any too pleased about it myself and remarked, perfectly bluntly, that Moulines would have made a better job of it. He didn't pay the least attention.

"I don't know what happened to those figures. I never saw them afterwards, and they were not removed this morning from the library. Perhaps the funniest thing of all is that, after all this haring about was over, things settled down to much about what they had been before. The old man would moon about or have fits of keeping to himself. Then, again, he would be his keen and incisive self. As far as I know he never slept out of London, although on one or two occasions he took the car down to Newmarket and Hindhead. As to last night's events, I had no more concern than the man in the moon how things stood with him financially. All I do know this morning is that there's the hell of a rumpus and I've already had what amounts to a couple of cross-examinations."

That seemed to be the end of the story. Wrentham straightened out his back and frowned. Then he looked at his watch—nearly two o'clock! There were hundreds of things he would have liked to go into, but he must catch that train whatever happened.

"Look here, Ludo. What about coming down for the weekend?" he asked.

"Not a hope!" was the despondent reply. "I shall have to carry on here until I hand over to some court or trustees or other, and then I shall be a man out of a job. I'll tell you what I will do," he added. "If anything happens that affects your case I'll wire you at once."

"That's jolly decent of you, Ludo," said Wrentham. He hesitated as if scarcely liking to ask a further favour, then, "Will you lend me the paper, that list you had? I'd rather like to look at it.

It shall not go out of my possession, and it will be as safe with me as you."

"I don't see why you shouldn't have it," replied the other, handing it over. "All I can say is, that if you can knock sense out of it you're a dashed sight brainier than I"; then regretfully, "though that isn't saying much."

"Oh, I don't know," said Wrentham, stowing the paper away in his pocket-book. "Something's bound to roll up."

CHAPTER V
A QUESTION OF DAYLIGHT
OR DRIVEL

As WRENTHAM WAS settling his bill the desk telephone rang. To his surprise the clerk handed the receiver to him, with "Somebody asking for you, sir."

"Yes, speaking. . . . Yes. Bushels of time. . . . The luggage *walla* is holding the fort over a corner pew."

"There's something happened I think you ought to know. Inspector North has just let fall to me the information that George Plumley was at the meeting last night. What do you make of that?"

"Where was he sitting?"

"Somewhere in the front at the side. North had something to do with withdrawing the warrant issued after that forgery case we were discussing."

"Thank you, Watson."

Must be something good, thought the clerk, or the Major wouldn't be grinning into the mouthpiece.

"By the way, old ferret, you don't intend to say a word to a soul about that list?"

"I'm answering nothing at present that I'm not asked. The matter of the notes is bound to come out, but I don't see how the rest can be known to anybody but us two."

Now Wrenthem had determined that during his journey nothing of the *affaire* Plumley was to cross his mind. The telephone conversation with Ludo had cut somewhat athwart that; but armed with the "Sportsman," and all other papers barred, he still felt that with the disappearance of London the feverish events of the last twenty-four hours would pass gradually from his mind. The journey to Cambridge is always a pleasant one, even when it brings memories of those whom Cambridge and the green fields of England will never see again. The Lady of Shalott had not a better picture of our countryside than that which flashed into his moving mirror: the elm clumps, the rich meadows, the red of tiles, the sweep of a yellowing field, and the rise of ancient spires against the airy architecture of heaven.

The long wait outside Cambridge was trying, the more so since it was to Wrentham a novel one. Some day, somebody will write the story of the train that wouldn't stop—how, in spite of sidings and signals, a certain train refused to pay any heed, knowing that everybody at Cambridge had got so used to stopping trains that it was just a silly habit. So off it darted and the excitement grew unbearable. The fireman and driver chanted a maddening Vachell Lindsay song. One by one the carriages came off—to halt, poor debris of the line. The engine at last slowed up near Hackney Marshes, to be found by the managing director of the line, himself, and a special train full of inspectors, grazing, as it were, peacefully by the side of the way; the fireman sound asleep on his little seat and the driver digging away like billy-o on his allotment.

During the wait Wrentham fell back on his "Sportsman." He had already read and dissected the cricket news and was turning over the sheets somewhat casually, when a heading caught his eye:

THE PLUMLEY STUD
LIKELIHOOD OF DISPOSAL AT JULY SALES

The devil fly away with it! Was there no means of escaping Plumley and all his works? Then the thought struck him that in going home to Hainton he would be going where nothing else would be talked about, and where the Hall was doubtless already being photographed for the morning papers. He couldn't help laughing. It was really rather funny. Jolt went the train and the soft cushions took the shock. The last railway voucher he would get and no more first-class for him after that trip. Then, when Cambridge was left behind and the tedious journey over the fens begun, he found himself drawing from his pocket that extraordinary list which Ludo had given him.

For some time he puzzled over it. Why not make in the margin possible suggestions? The conifers—why shouldn't Plumley have been going to restore some of the shrubberies at Hindhead? Rather too obvious, that was all. The cement, the damp-coursing, and the glass all seemed connected with building. Possibly Plumley had had in mind alterations which involved the use of these things, as, for instance, a watertight and damp-proof cellar. But why opaque glass? Of what use was glass that was not at least partly transparent? Tennis balls—for use or a present? He jotted down a note to ask Ludo for any possible connexion between Plumley and tennis. Wire—why the two kinds? Note—to ask somebody the resemblances and differences between them. Gardening catalogues—just as much too obvious as the other. Then the three cases in good condition and yet looking old. Something had to be put in them or there wouldn't have been the special reference to locks. Again, the very obvious thing, sticking up about a mile high, was that Plumley had intended doing a considerable amount of travelling and wished to keep each case ready packed, possibly one for Hainton, one for Hindhead, and one for Newmarket. Yes, but surely Plumley's valet or personal servant should have seen to all that.

He contemplated the pencilled margins and read them again. Somehow they didn't seem satisfying. None of these would require a protestation of secrecy; the binding of a man and the mention of death. Perhaps it was that Plumley couldn't do anything without pose of some kind. Wasn't there somebody who was once said to be incapable of stirring his tea without a stratagem? Or was Plumley just stark, staring mad? If so, the whole thing might be torn up and thrown out of the window. Or, again, was there something crooked in it all? Why not make another margin on the right and put in motives less obvious?

But the slowing train and a glance assured him that this was Thetford and almost the end of his journey.

So a short wait and then the local train and the leaving behind of fen and heathland. Just like the old days, coming home from school, thought Wrentham, and boyishly poked his head out of the window as they ran into the station. He could see the wagonette—the same old green-lined wheels—and a car, too, a Ford by the cut of it, that seemed to be waiting for somebody. And there was the guv'nor on the platform.

But when their first greetings were over it was the car that the vicar turned to.

"What's all this?" asked Wrentham facetiously. "Been launching out, pater?"

He did not wait for an answer for, as he spoke, two figures came by the narrow exit, apparently mistress and maid, and mounted the wagonette. Wrentham recognised the driver, a lad when he last saw him, but one who had been doing his bit or else usurped the uniform he wore. Wrentham could not tell you to this day why he did it, but he watched the wagonette turn and roll away up the hill towards Hainton. As for the car, the luggage was already in place and they got in. He bethought him of his question.

"Well, pater, what about it?"

"About what, my boy?"

The vicar regarded his son half fearfully as if he suspected some hidden joke.

"This travelling in state and so on, and who are the people in our wagonette?"

The vicar laughed, the laugh of a big man and a big boy. He looked quizzically at his son as if to see whether the joke were worth prolonging, and then both laughed, like two people who are so happy that they can laugh at laughter itself.

"I sold the wagonette," he explained. "There didn't seem to be any reason for keeping it. I go to the station so very rarely that I thought it would be much cheaper to hire. Rummage has this car now and charges very reasonably. Burt bought the wagonette, but I'm afraid he got rather a good bargain." Then very apologetically, "He only gave me four pounds for it."

The car certainly ran well; they passed the wagonette some few hundred yards from the station and young Burt touched his hat as they flew by.

"Who did you say those people were?" asked Wrentham again.

"I don't think you know them," said his father. "She's a Miss Forrest; an artist, I believe. She has the old Lodge Cottage where the Masons used to live. She seems to be down here most of the time. That was her maid with her, I think. I've called once or twice but they've never been in."

"They've been to church, then?"

"Well, I don't know," said the vicar, slowly and charitably. "I believe Miss Forrest did come one evening, but not recently."

"They've been here some time, then?"

"About six months now, I should think. Let me see," and the vicar went into comparison and reminiscence to dig out the date of arrival. But his son had already forgotten the subject of the inquiry, which was really the strange event of the wagonette. They were passing the cricket field, too. "Have you a match on Saturday?" he asked.

"I rather think they're expecting you to play," said his father. "Harris stopped me yesterday and asked if you would be down. He said he's put your name down in any case. I thought you'd be keen on playing. It's Great Bidwell."

"What about you, pater? Surely you're turning out?"

"My boy, I haven't had a game now for nearly four years. I don't suppose they want an old totterer like me," said his father regretfully, stealing another look at his son.

"What! Not call on our brainiest bat! Good heavens, pater, what are you driving at?" Then as he caught his father's eye: "Besides, you're simply bursting to play," and again they both laughed.

What an evening that was! Everybody seemed so jolly glad to see him, from Emma the housekeeper to Tango the Sealyham. Then there was getting out the things he had brought home.

And how topping everything was looking, in spite of the war; the roses as brave as ever and the beds ablaze with bloom. So Wallace was back all right. There would be merely the garden to do now there was no horse kept. He and a boy ought to manage well. A rattling good show of fruit in the orchard and cucumbers hanging in the cold house as thick as the fingers on your hand.

"What have you done with the stable, pater?" asked Wrentham.

"I let that and the back sheds to Jerlingham," was the reply. "He has the paddock too. If we want any manure for the gardens we're to have it. I hope you agree with all this, my boy?"

"I think you ought to be estate agent as well as vicar," smiled his son. "I think everything's simply splendid. By the way, what about an arm-loosener on the tennis court?" So up went a couple of stumps and for a good half-hour they tried curly ones and wrong 'uns and all a slow bowler's repertoire, as if it had been fifteen years ago. Yet with all the things they had to talk over Plumley was never mentioned.

For once the vicar had neglected his paper. Maybe the "Church Times" had claimed him first and left him scant leisure for aught else, especially with the excitement of the day. Then, as the dusk approached and the air grew heavy with the scent of stocks and honeysuckle, the father suggested a game of billiards. It was a three-quarter table they had, picked up at a local sale. Twice a week there was open house and the village players would drop in for a game. Wrentham noticed that all the cues were tipped and the cloth showed up bravely the effects of the day's ironing. He smiled as he thought of the preparation, and a surge of affection rose within him at the thought of the old man to whom he was so much and who was so much to him.

His father was early to bed, though later than usual. Wrentham announced his intention of sitting up a bit in the small study, to clear up one or two things which he had to see to in the morning. What, of course, he really had in mind was to revise that list. Bit of a feather in his cap if he could do the Sherlock Holmes act! He must write to Ludo also, so as to catch the morning post. When all the house was quiet and his pipe going steadily, he got to work.

For a long time he studied the pencilled notes. He lay back in his chair and went over in his mind the events of the previous twenty-four hours. Finally, after much cogitation, he took a sheet of paper and wrote down the few ideas that had occurred to him. Roughly they were as follows:

(1) P.'s allusion to buried money:

(*a*) Was it genuine?

(*b*) Was it for the benefit of his son?

(2) L. certainly handed over to P. money in a suitable form for concealment.

(3) L.'s journeys to France and Plymouth:

(*a*) Were they for the purpose of getting L. out of the way?

(*b*) if so, what was P. doing in the meanwhile?

Then, with a kind of bravado, he added another:

(4) Assuming all the above, what has it got to do with me?

The last was the ticklish point. What indeed had it got to do with him? Putting aside the solving of Ludo's comic conundrum, just how was he interested? If Plumley, in some mad or eccentric moment, had seen fit to scatter round caches of notes, they were the property of his heirs—that was to say, that young squirt, his son; or rather, perhaps, of the liquidator of the Plumley concerns.

Then from the back of his mind Wrentham produced and faced squarely the idea which was already born and which he knew had been there, however vague and embryonic, since his conversation with Ludo. If City Corporations had gone west; if he, Wrentham, had by Plumley's incapacity, mismanagement, or roguery, been done out of a very large sum of money, was he not justified in helping himself if chance and sound scheming should give him the opportunity? He knew the position in law— findings are not keepings. He supposed the correct thing to do would be to hand them over to the creditors. That, he cynically calculated, might work out at twopence more apiece.

Then, again, that was running it a bit far. The whole thing was most likely utter drivel. Even if it were not, why not find something before worrying about its disposal? Lord, what a muddle-up the whole thing was!

That, then, was the result of an hour's meditations. The mountain had been in labour and had produced a monstrous little mouse. Even the night, he felt, was against him, with its hints and suggestions that the light of day would make absurd.

As he moved his arm on the desk something fell to the floor—a small, leather notebook. He picked it up, open as it was, and could not but read the heading: "God's Poor." Followed a list with many names. He closed it, one might almost say with reverence, and replaced it. That was where the wagonette went doubtless, and the rent of stable and paddock. His father had not altered a bit. Any tale was for him the opportunity, and never a regret when the rascality stood revealed.

As Wrentham lay between waking and sleeping he at least made up his mind about one thing: if he came anyhow clear out of the business there should be a full-sized table at the vicarage. What about a small car, too? Then there was that trip to Greece that had always been one of the pater's ambitions. He had forgotten about writing to Ludo—well, there would be plenty of time for that in the morning. But what the morning was to bring forth was of all things farthest from Wrentham's mind. And had he known what the week was to bring it is doubtful if sleep would have claimed him at all.

CHAPTER VI
ALARUMS AND EXCURSIONS

THE MORNING DAWNED cloudy and with a hint of rain. The sun peeped out too furtively and too flattering to last. The first beams that caught Wrentham roused him from his bed, and by seven o'clock he was out smoking a pre-prandial cigarette. The noise of a spade in the walled garden drew his attention and he was glad to recognise Wallace. The man was as pleased as the master. All his life, save for the chances of war, he spent in that garden: first as odd boy straight from school; then, graduating through rough digger and assistant, arriving at the dignity of gardener with a boy under him.

"Don't think it's going to last out, sir," was his comment on the weather.

"You never know, Tom," replied the Major. "So long as it keeps fine for the game to-morrow that's all that matters. You in form?"

Wallace was the fast bowler of the side, tireless but magnificently erratic.

He grinned sheepishly. "Haven't had much practice, sir."

"That reminds me," said Wrentham. "Is Gordon all right for to-morrow?" The thought was natural. Gordon was a wicket-keeper above the average in village cricket, and the liaison established between the two had caused the undoing of many of the unwary.

"Gordon! He's left, sir."

"Left! Left the Hall! When was that?"

"Well, you see, sir," explained Wallace, "he and Mr. Plumley fell out last spring; had a few words and Gordon left all in a hurry. Some say Mr. Trent of Bidwell got him to leave. I don't know nothin' about that, sir; all I know is he left the Hall on the Friday and started at Bidwell the follerin' Monday."

"I say, that's bad, Tom." Wrentham was distinctly upset. "Who's going to keep wicket?"

"I don't know, sir. They're been trying young Frank Ward. He can stop 'em all right, but I don't think he'll ever stump anybody."

"I really can't understand about Gordon"—this almost to himself. "Why, he must have been at the Hall all his life."

Wallace ventured some more information. "They do say, sir, that he had some words with Mr. Plumley over the gardens. You know what some people are like, sir. Now if you or Mr. Wrentham was to come to me and say, 'Wallace, put them roses where the celery trenches are or make an onion bed on the front lawn,' well, that'd be all right, sir, because we know each other, in a way. They say Mr. Plumley he interfered with things and wanted to do a lot of the work himself, and Gordon up and told him he couldn't expect the gardens right when visitors came down if he didn't do them in his way. That's all I know about it, sir."

"When was this, Tom?"

"As far as I can calculate, sir, about the middle of April, 'cause I remember thinking at the time what an orkard time that was for everything. Allus a lot of work to do at that time o' year. Howsomever, Mr. Plumley he got another man down in a day or two"; then, despondently, and somewhat scornfully, "he ain't no cricketer, sir."

"Well, Tom, we shall see," remarked Wrentham, a trifle distracted as he moved away. How amazingly things were beginning to fit in! The middle of April would be during Ludo's famous expedition to Toulouse. If Plumley wanted to get up to anything no wonder he let Gordon go. One of the cleverest gardeners in the county, too—always judging at shows and that sort of thing. Yet again was a doubt. Why shouldn't Plumley want to work in his own garden? Surely hundreds of people did it. Didn't Gladstone go cutting down trees? Still it was odd how it all kept coming in.

He loosed Tango and strolled on along the Farm Road. As he got back to the main gate the postman rode up. Another warrior returned, was the thought of each, though not perhaps in the same words. It is one of the excitements of village

life that each knows each, and that few things about any of
us are not revealed, even unto babes. Yes, Francis was playing
to-morrow. He hoped the Major would make a lot of runs. He
had heard Bidwell had one or two new men. Thanking you,
sir, if you wouldn't mind. So Wrentham took the letters. Only
one for him—from Ludo. He stuck the rest in his pocket and
opened it.

DEAR G.,

There are one or two things I would like to talk over
with you and I hardly like confiding them to the post. As
you may not get this until the midday post, I refer to the
afternoon train. Go up to Norwich to-morrow (Friday)
afternoon. Uncle Hallett is on the 'phone. I will try to
get a trunk call through to you as near four as possible.
Wait for me in any case until four-thirty. There is an un-
holy muddle here and to-morrow I start with an inven-
tory of the House. Am afraid I cannot get down before a
fortnight at the earliest.

In great haste
Yours
L.

P.S.—Official receiver appointed for C/Cs. Various ru-
mours in city. Blacktons and Apex Motors said to be
heavily involved.

He crushed the letter into a ball and thrust it into a pocket
as he saw his father standing at the door, regarding the lawn
and the sky as if there were not a care in the world.

"Sleep well, my boy?"

"Like a top," said Wrentham, smiling. "By the way, Francis
gave me these," and he handed over the assortment of circu-
lars and letters. What in heaven's name was going to happen
next? He called the dog, loath to return to kennel, shut him up,
and walked on to the orchard. What was best to do now? There
needn't be any necessity to say anything to his father at all.
Why not kill two birds with one stone—see Hallett & Hallett
and the bank at the same time? Lucky getting Ludo's letter so

early. Why not catch the ten and lunch at Norwich? Good. He hailed Wallace and scribbled a telegram for the solicitors.

"Get this sent off at once, Tom, will you, and ask Rummage to have his car here at nine-forty sharp." And so to breakfast.

"Anything you want from Norwich, pater?"

"I don't think so," replied his father. "When are you going?"

"Going up by the ten—one or two things I want to do. I ought to be back by the six with any luck." He hesitated a minute. "I suppose you've heard about Plumley?"

"Plumley? Is he at the Hall?"

"No," said Wrentham. "It's all rather tragic. He's dead."

"Dear me! Dear me! I had no idea he was ill."

To the surprised vicar Wrentham told the story, or at least a pale ghost of his real adventures. In a way he used the event to cover his visit to Norwich.

"When people like Plumley die there's bound to be an upset, more or less, in the markets, so I thought I'd run up and see the bank and godfather Hallett and make out how everything's going."

The vicar agreed. The reception of money was to him much of a mystery. That he generally found something in the bank when he was there was enough for him. If not—well, something was bound to happen. All that he mourned most, for he had met Plumley but twice, was an excellent subscriber to parish affairs, and for this, had he known, Ludo had often been as much responsible as the other.

Things were not very busy at Norwich. Compared with the rushing city of a Saturday it was quiet as a village. Percival Hallett was unfeignedly pleased to see him but had no news of any sort. The senior partner was in town and wouldn't be returning, in the ordinary course of events, before the last train. Would the Major like to leave a note? Wrentham, however, was determined to go to the bank first, and said he would drop in again.

At the bank a surprise awaited him. Margetson had died some four months previously and the present manager was his second successor. He was received, however, as if he were known to be a customer. The manager thought everything was in order. They checked back pay. Yes, the gratuity had been received. The matter of the pension for Mrs. Holland? Yes, that had been arranged through Messrs. Hallett & Hallett. A general statement? Yes, no trouble at all; only a question of a minute or two.

"You might let me have Major Wrentham's pass-book, will you, absolutely to date?"

Wrentham broached the question of City Corporations. An extraordinary business, the manager agreed. He hinted, with a touch of wisdom, that there was always danger in those multiple corporations. Now, if one wanted a really sound and at the same time promising investment, he would recommend — And so on. A clerk entered.

"Thank you, Mr. White." The manager scanned the totals. "Approximately fifteen hundred pounds, Major," he remarked, with the least suggestion of unction.

"Or thirty bob a week for life," said Wrentham cheerfully as he received the book.

The manager made as to rise, but the other kept his seat. "I want to ask a favour of you," he said. "Hallett & Hallett, as you know, manage our affairs and I am seeing them also this afternoon about the same thing. I have reason to believe that Apex Motors, in which my father, another of your customers, is interested, is in rather a bad way. What I want you to do is not to communicate with my father on any account about money matters. When dividends become due pay into his account, from my own private account, the same amount as last time. And I should be more than grateful if you would let me know personally anything that transpires."

The manager thought he saw the point. Perhaps not quite as things should be done. However, if the Major would send instructions in writing during the week he thought it could be managed.

After that Wrentham felt much more cheerful. A bit of lunch at the "Royal" seemed clearly indicated. Things were not so bad. Suppose City Corporations declared any sort of dividend, that would be something. Apex Motors, too. Put the whole bag of tricks together and if the worst came to the worst the wolf could be kept from the door! And thinking away as he was he failed to look exactly where he was going, and nearly came a cropper over a roll of wire-netting outside a shop. A high-class ironmonger's evidently, judging by the display in the immense windows. The roll of wire gave him an idea; he made up his mind and entered the shop.

He was fortunate in that at that moment a partner in the firm, who had come to the ground floor for some information or other, happened to catch sight of him. The lean, athletic figure and the tanned face caught his eye and he came up inquiringly.

"You'll probably think me either very ignorant or a bit of an ass," said Wrentham, "but I should be very grateful if you would give me some information about something."

"Not at all, sir; anything that we can do—"

"That's very good of you. What I want to know is, what are the resemblances between copper and aluminium wires?"

The other thought for a moment. "I don't know that there are any resemblances, except that both conduct heat and electricity. Of course both are unaffected by damp, though in different ways."

"Would you mind telling me how?"

"Well," was the reply, "copper wire would never actually corrode clean through if left in water. It might—it probably would—have a harmful effect on the water. Now, aluminium wire would have no such effect. It might be called permanent in water. A lot of rose-growers use fine aluminium wire for fastening name labels to their roses."

"I think that helps me a great deal," said Wrentham; "but, if you don't mind, would you be so good as to answer another question on the same point. Suppose a man ordered a quantity of such wire of the thickness—"

"Excuse me. 'Gauge,'" interrupted the other tactfully.

"Gauge of ordinary twine, what would he most likely be wanting it for?"

"That I couldn't say for certain, sir. But most likely for tying something, possibly under water or where weather and damp were likely to be in operation. Brass wire, now, of such a gauge—we sell a lot of that for hare and rabbit snares."

"I am very much obliged to you," acknowledged Wrentham gratefully. The other escorted him courteously to the door.

"Quite a decent chap, that," each thought, and, strange to say, each was pondering the why and wherefore of it all, Wrentham was recalling a scene he had once witnessed near Gaza, when an Arab had hauled up from the side of a deep well the half of a goat, which had been kept in that cool refrigerator. And as he lingered over his lunch the scene recurred with intensity, until he could picture himself winding in an almost interminable coil of aluminium wire with which was tied an ancient chest—except that it wouldn't be a chest but a small box made of special concrete. Almost he cried "Eureka!" so sure was he that he had it. And in another few seconds he was equally sure that the idea was rubbish. Well, he would visit the Hall and see the roses. If the labels were tied with aluminium wire that was all there was to it. If not, there might be milk in the coker-nut and there might not.

He turned up again at the office at about three-thirty. Here he left a note for the senior partner. He also confided to a certain extent in the other member of the firm and was assured that everything possible would be done, and immediately necessity arose he should be communicated with at once. No doubt Percival Hallett wished to be helpful, but Wrentham could not but smile ironically when he was given a copy of the Companies (Winding-Up) Act of 1909.

He did not have long to wait for his trunk call. Extraordinarily prompt and lucky Ludo must have been, he thought. At a minute or two after four he was talking to him, and the gist of what he had to say was as follows:

Late the previous evening Moulines had called at Bellingham House. After a few generalities he had asked one or two pertinent questions. Had Travers noticed anything peculiar about Plumley during the previous three months? He

(Moulines) gave instances of his own, and wondered if the other could duplicate them. What had Travers been doing during that long absence from England? Did he know Plumley had been away from London most of that fortnight, chiefly at Hainton and Hindhead?

"Of course," said Ludo, "I gave him answers as vague and unsatisfactory as possible. He's a queer specimen, and I can't say I ever cottoned to him much. However, I should guess that not only was he not satisfied but smelt a pretty hefty rat into the bargain. What do you think about it?"

"I think," said Wrentham bluntly, "that if anybody will only read the obvious into the last dying words of Henry Plumley the whole of Hainton and Hindhead will be buzzing with treasure seekers. I shouldn't be surprised if the damn places get torn up by the roots."

There was a slight pause at the other end of the line, then: "So that's your idea too."

"Good God, Ludo! give me credit for a little brains," was the reply, somewhat tersely it seemed to the other. "But, look here"—the line buzzed and it was a few seconds before the conversation could be resumed. "Are you there? Oh, yes. Why not write to me direct if anything rolls up? If you're afraid of anybody tampering with your correspondence be as vague as you like, so long as I can read between the lines."

He was about to ring off when another idea occurred to him.

"Are you there? Oh, could you tell me if our friend was doing any building alterations at that particular time?"

"Building alterations!" The other was evidently surprised. "There seemed to be nothing else. The whole of the entrance to the 'Metropole' was remodelled for one thing; then there was the new brick and oak pergola at Hindhead. The dining-and morning-rooms here were knocked into one and a girder put in to carry the stress. The old well at Hainton was restored and an art top added to it—one of those ideal home antique things. I dare say there were some more if I could think of them. Oh, yes, the stables at Chalton were enlarged."

Wrentham could scarcely keep the satisfaction from his voice as he answered. "That's enough to be going on with. Tell the quartermaster to put you down for proficiency pay."

"What a damn silly thing to say!" he thought as he rang off, looking round as though expecting, in so dignified a building, to be reproved for his levity.

He had to rush for his train, but he felt very pleased with life, after all. The way old Ludo reeled off that list of building alterations! Pretty plain he'd been putting in some overtime at this sleuth business himself. Well, stout work had undoubtedly been done; stout work, that was it.

That night as he lay in bed—perhaps the sound of a threatening wind crying in the trees recalled in some intangible way the idiotic past—he thought of a day at Newmarket. He had run up from Cambridge with a few select spirits, and in the cheap enclosure he remembered an enormous bookmaker, clad in unmistakable checks and surmounted by a herculean umbrella. The rain poured down, but nothing damped his ardour or quenched the stertorous echoes of his raucous voice as he bellowed, "What a day! What a day! Five to one the field! Five to one Popgun! Seven to one Goldfinch! What a day! What a da-a-a-y!"

CHAPTER VII
GARDENING AND ONE OF THE FINE ARTS

THE MORNING BROKE bright but treacherous. As they made their way to the cricket field, there was almost an April feel to the air and the clouds ran free across the sky. The post had brought no news and the vicar was settled down to his sermons. Wallace was pushing a barrow containing lawn-mower and fork, since there was an unwritten law against preparing pitches except on Saturday mornings, and then the work was done by those who happened to be free. This particular morning the village schoolmaster, Harris, was already there and at work.

"Well, Harris, what do you think of it?" asked Wrentham.

"Very fiery, Major. I shouldn't like to stand up to anything fast on it," was the verdict.

"Perhaps you're right," agreed Wrentham.

So they decided that all they could do would be to raise any holes, cut short, mark out, and run the big roll over for appearance' sake. The Major, who spoke of having business at the Hall, was to lend a hand with this on his way back.

Having managed to get so far with a perfectly good excuse, he made his way round the churchyard and into the kitchen garden of the Hall. Here he had no particular reason for his presence, but he did not anticipate that the need for excuses would arise. In any case there was always Martin and cricket the ubiquitous. As it happened, he ran full tilt into a short, sturdy man, with close-trimmed beard. His shirt-sleeves were rolled up and he was carrying a cucumber basket. He touched his hat, gave a "Good morning, sir," and waited.

"Are you the head gardener, by any chance?" began Wrentham.

"I am, sir; name of Tait."

"My name's Wrentham."

"That's right, sir," answered the other. "I've heard of you, sir."

"How are the gardens looking now?" inquired Wrentham tactfully. Gardeners and antique dealers, who both have business in matters of beauty, have another thing in common— each loves to talk of his work and each is a grateful listener. Tait speedily put on his jacket and led the way.

"Anything particular you'd like to see, sir?"

"I don't think there is anything special," Wrentham assured him. "Perhaps I take more interest in flowers than in vegetables or fruit. What are your roses like this year?"

The roses, as a matter of fact, were not at their absolute best. A month earlier, as Tait remarked, and the blooms would have been finer.

"What is this called?" asked the visitor, looking down at the metal standard which indicated the name of a superb yellow bloom. Tait needed no reference.

"That's 'Mabel Morton,' sir. I don't fancy that rose is even on the market yet. Mr. Plumley was a great experimenter, sir, and we had orders to discard at once any old roses which were not up to catalogue descriptions. Not that they ever are," he added pessimistically.

"Don't you ever use labels wired to the bushes?" asked Wrentham. "Somebody told me the other day that that was a very common method."

"Well, sir," Tait explained, "I have been in places where it was done, but I don't like it myself. It never looks very tidy, and if the wire is put on too tight it's liable to cut the bark."

"You put a lot of new roses in this year?"

"I should think not as many as usual, sir. Masters, the second gardener, tells me there often used to be as many as a hundred new bushes every autumn. There aren't the new varieties now, on account of the war. For all that, I suppose there were about forty fresh bushes put in last spring."

"What did Mr. Plumley like best in the garden?" Wrentham recognised that in Tait he had not only one who would talk for ever, but who also would see nothing remarkable in being questioned.

"That's hard to say, sir," was the reply. "Now look at these penstemons. I was going to move them from round the summer-house this spring, but Mr. Plumley he says, 'What do you want to move them for?' he says. 'They're sheltered enough to stand any winter. Let 'em grow into clumps.'"

They eyed them a minute. "A bit straggly," suggested Wrentham.

"That's just it," exclaimed Tait emphatically. "That's exactly what I said." Wrentham felt that his reputation was being established.

They paused before the border, so rare in its riot of colour that it seemed to catch at the heart of the beholder. So beautiful it looked as to be unreal; like the gardens of catalogue covers or those water-colours of Mrs. Allingham's. Peering over clumped delphiniums were the tall verbascums and hollyhocks, growing to nobility. The yellow helianthus stood compact against the straggling masses of blue anchusa. Here were last lupins and columbines; gaillardias glowing with orange and gold; flaming poppies and white achillea. Thrift ran unchecked to the stone path and dusty miller worked a stealthy way beneath carnations and the shy aubretia. Everywhere was colour, from the flaunt of a scarlet geum to the scarce discerned velvet of the pansy.

"Beautiful! Beautiful!" was Wrentham's only remark. He could find nothing save the trite to express it.

To Tait it was all in the day's work. "It'll be better next year, sir. We shall discard one or two weak varieties and let the healthy clumps get out a bit more. That's what gives the effect, sir, not a lot of little things."

Diplomatically Wrentham agreed. Then: "Mr. Travers was telling me you had had the old well restored."

"Yes. This way, sir," said Tait. Wrentham followed the familiar cut through the rhododendron walk, and they came out on the west quadrangle with its turf and flagged paths. The well had indeed been altered. The brickwork had been raised and the top was now very like a lich-gate, with tiles old and mossy. But against the green of the house creeper it stood well—far better, thought Wrentham, than any piece of pretentious statuary. He made some banal comment and then thanked Tait for his trouble.

"No trouble, sir. It's a pleasure to talk to a gentleman like yourself who understands things."

The pentstemons, thought Wrentham, had stood him in very good stead; then aloud, "I rather want to see Martin about this afternoon's match. I shall find him at the house, I suppose;" and: "You don't play cricket?"

"No, sir. I'm no cricketer, sir. Not that I don't like to watch a game. Thank you very much, sir. Good day, sir."

But it was not to see Martin that Wrentham was anxious. As they had come through the rhododendron walk he had caught a glimpse, and scarcely that, of a figure seated on the south lawn, and of an easel. It was not until the connexion of art and the well that he had guessed who it might be. Whoever she was she had chosen an excellent position from the point of seeing all there was to see. She might have watched his progress from the time that he entered the rose garden. An impulse made him retrace his steps. He moved along the hedge to where the tall bushes concealed his height—luckily there was a gap where an undersized plant had succumbed to the summer heat—and through into the walk, with dense rhododendrons and the drooping boughs of a lime before him. All round was the hum of honey-bees in earnest labour and, save for them, the walk was as deserted as a crypt. But in front of him, not five yards away, was the lawn and the artist.

She was sitting on, or rather leaning against, a shooting stick, and before her was a tall and spidery easel. She was dressed in some kind of browny tweed and, though the month was July, had round her neck a wrap of furs. Her face, almost in profile, showed clear-cut against the distant green. Composed it looked, thought the watcher—the face of an attractive woman and an intellectual one. The wind blew a small shiver and the sun came out from behind a galloping cloud and caught the gold tendrils of her hair. He was not conscious that he was spying, so intent was he on nothing but the moment. He wondered what her work was like. Beyond the edges of the board he could see nothing. And then it suddenly struck him that she was not working at all. She seemed rather to be watching—sweeping steadily, as it were, a green field of fire. Like the beam of a lighthouse her gaze moved regularly from the far edge of the sunk lawn, across the beds, and away over the roses to the back margin of the border. Then she would make a motion with her pencil as if that were a thing that had to be done, and again, for the time spent on that, bestow ten times as long on her watching.

Something told him he must see that sketch; must see the woman and everything from a different angle—in the open and not as through a green curtain. He backed quietly again on the turf, moved west some twenty yards, once more crossed the walk, and emerged, light as bird from bough, not the length of a cricket pitch behind the sketcher. As if on business bent he made for the sunk lawn and the distant cricket field. His tread was as soundless as a mole's and he must have passed her ere she was aware of him, so fixed was her gaze before her. He passed on down the bank, over the plank bridge, and, bearing left, came again to the kitchen garden. What he had gathered filled him with perplexity. He had passed within a foot or two of the sketch, and though he appeared scarcely to observe, yet he had looked closely. The sketching board was bare of mark. It was as white as the day it was made!

How long had she been working? That would not be hard to discover. He pulled out his watch—eleven-fifteen—and went in search of Martin. Fred Martin and his wife were the caretakers. When Plumley had come down to the Hall the servants travelled also from Bellingham House. In his absence there were simply the rooms to keep aired and clean. Quite a boy was Martin, but they marry young in the country.

"Oh, Martin," said Wrentham, "I heard from Mr. Travers yesterday and he wondered, as I was down here, if I would drop in and see whether any people from London had called with authority to see the Hall."

"No, sir," replied Martin. "Nobody's been that I know of. Come in a minute, won't you sir?"—for a sharp shower was blowing gustily in the door and Wrentham was coatless. As he spoke the rain came down with a rush and he was only too glad to bolt inside. It was pleasant in the stone-floored kitchen with its diamond panes and chintz curtains. He settled down in the Windsor chair and pulled out his cigarette case, always a sure putter-at-ease.

"I thought I saw somebody sketching out there," he remarked casually. "I'm afraid she's going to get wet."

"I expect she'll get under a tree," was Martin's opinion.

"Well, let's hope she's finished," continued Wrentham, "because she won't do much more to-day."

"I think she got here about ten"; then to an elderly woman, whom Wrentham did not recognise, and who looked into the room and bolted out again at the sight of the Major, "What time did Miss Forrest come this morning, Clara?"

An indistinct reply was heard which Martin interpreted as ten o'clock.

"She had permission from Mr. Plumley to go anywhere on the estate, sir," volunteered Martin. He went to an old bureau, evidently his own property, and after some rummaging found a paper which he handed to Wrentham. A sheet of parchment writing paper it was, stamped with a black "Bellingham House, W." in the corner. It read:

Miss Sylvia Forrest has my permission to go anywhere on the Hainton estate.

That was all, save, at the bottom, a sprawling "Henry Plumley." There was no date, but he thought it as well not to inquire into that. Moreover, as soon as he had taken it, he wondered why he had read it. Martin must have known that it was no concern of anyone who was not in authority. Perhaps on the strength of his first remark about Ludo, Martin had so regarded him. Still, it was the peculiarity of villagers to be offerers of fortuitous information. After all, what would life be but for the cheap amenities of gossip? He handed back the paper without comment and changed the conversation. "Doesn't look much like cricket this afternoon, Martin."

"That it don't, sir. And the old cone was shut up this morning too."

"Cone?" Ah! he remembered the country weather-glass. Hanging before the window was a large fir cone. He got up and examined it through the panes. "Surely this is a very large one?" he remarked.

"That ain't so big as some of them, sir. This one come from the shrubbery, if you want one, sir."

The rain persisted. Once or twice they consulted the sky. Not a bit of blue to be seen. The heavens had closed to a dull grey and the rain maintained a steady beat. Finally Martin suggested some covering, and an ancient oilskin was found—a bit tight, but any port in a storm. Not that Wrentham cared a couple of straws about his appearance. Home, therefore, at the double, by the back meadows and the rain harder than ever. All the way was the thought of the morning's happenings—the new well and the virgin sheet of paper. Was that letter a forgery? It didn't look so, and, in any case, why shouldn't it be perfectly authentic? What was the woman looking for? Why that intent searching? And why that pretence of sketching and actually doing nothing? Over an hour and never a stroke! In the classical words of Little Tich, these little things wanted watching.

What about a little scouting? Night operations would certainly have to be put down in battalion orders. And the rain still came down.

CHAPTER VIII
NIGHT OPERATIONS

IT WAS OBVIOUS that the rain had set in for the day. At two o'clock it was coming down with a steady and merciless monotony. Wrentham could not but speculate on what would have been his feelings when a boy had such a deluge swamped a match. He looked out of the long window and suddenly laughed. The vicar glanced up inquiringly. "Thinking of the day we went to Little Beldham in the wet," he explained. The vicar laughed also. They had set out for an away match in just such a blinding rain. Seven miles it was, and the old green wagonette had to have its cover on. When they got there they waited in a big tent on the field while the rain lashed down on the sides. The vicar, keen as mustard, peeped out at the sky and then appealed to the village umpire—a palpably gross man, with a fringe of whiskers and scant respect for little save his office.

"Don't you think it's clearing up?"

The ancient had a peep, spat disgustedly, and then ejaculated, "That's what the devil said to Noah."

The vicar started on the paper which the post had just brought, and the other betook himself to the small study. He restoked his pipe and groped round for a book. Not a thing in his line. Sermons and meditations all the way and so-and-so on this and that. What about a bit of putting practice on the carpet? Dash it! he must get some golf in somehow during the week. There seemed no time for anything nowadays. What a restless sort of devil he was getting! And by these channels he came back to the inevitable subject. Precious little to do in the wet, so why not get down to it? He took his notes from the drawer and looked at them. For the best part of half an hour he looked and thought and thought and looked. Then he set aside Ludo's list and the copy of the Companies Act and started all over again.

The sight of the official-looking document gave him a further idea. He went for the paper. The vicar apparently had not worried much about the devasted match; he was asleep and the paper had slithered down his knees. Wrentham smiled to himself as he moved away over the deadening carpet with his spoil.

Nothing about Plumley. He scanned the financial columns—still nothing. Then the heading "Apex Motors" caught his eye. "Stormy meeting," "Directors resign," "Drastic reorganisation" were other phrases that stared at him. Well, Apexes were at any rate alive and kicking lustily, that was one consolation. He turned over the pages of the Companies Act. How involved all this jargon was! People talked about the army and its stereotyped phraseology, but that was plain as the way to the parish church compared with the sort of drivel those lawyer blokes could produce when they really got going.

One thing, however, emerged from his meditations: some sort of order was absolutely necessary. He helped himself to a sheet of writing paper and spread it lengthways. This he ruled into four columns, and after experiment headed them FACTS—DEDUCTIONS—QUERIES—URGENT. Then he stoked his pipe yet again and settled to it. He filled one or two sheets with rough notes and then set about achieving, for the first time in his life, a really advanced précis. So absorbed was he that this time it was his father who peeped in unobserved and left him to it.

Finally he arrived at this:

FACTS.	DEDUCTIONS.	QUERIES.	URGENT.
P. changes the course of his speech after receipt of the note. His son was present; mention of treasure and gardens was forced	P. was sending a final forgiving message to tell his son where money was		
P. experimented with Adam Smith	P. undoubtedly hid money	As a nest-egg after possible imprisonment ?	1. Interview Gordon *re* P. and garden
L. gave him the notes. L. was then got rid of		In case he wanted to bolt ?	2. Get verbatim report of P.'s speech and test for clue
Re List	*From List* money		
If P. proposing to bolt, money hidden where accessible. If P. merely mad, then anywhere	(a) In new wall or damp-course (b) Under water (c) Under roses	If under roses or water, how except in cement box ?	3. Get fullest information *re* G.P.'s marriage
Miss F. at Hall under false pretences	Something to do with the P. business	Was she G.P.'s wife ?	N.B.—Test the well at once

By the time this was done tea was on the table. He fastened together his sheets. Almost like going back to the adjutant's office, he thought. Jolly business-like and all that. More stout work; and he nodded his head approvingly.

Then, after tea, to the old workroom, to see about a gadget for testing the well. His eye lit on an old fishing-rod. The top section was not very strong but the other two were sturdy enough for his purpose. Ten feet of rod ought to be ample. With a brace, he bored a hole through the top section, within two inches of the end. Through this he stuck a tightly fitting four-inch wire nail. He bound this so as to keep it securely in place. He tested it on the floor and found it to his satisfaction. Apparently at that very moment, with that annoying irresponsibility that makes our weather, the rain stopped, for a belated beam of sunlight cut cheerily athwart the workbench.

That was bad luck, in a way, for a rainy night would have been much better suited to his purpose. It was true that neither Martin nor his wife was likely to stir out of doors; indeed, they would probably be sound asleep at the time he proposed starting operations. Still, nothing like making assurance doubly sure. It would be devilish awkward if somebody blundered across him in the very act. He would have to pretend to be looking for something lost in the morning. Still, why worry? At any rate, the fine weather would allow of a bit of exercise before dinner. He must remember, too, to ask Emma to make enough coffee to fill his thermos. Better give her the tip at the same time not to parade it.

· · ·

It must have been nearly half-past ten when he slipped unobtrusively out of the french window. He thought it best to leave the lamp burning low and the window unfastened. It was a moonless night and chilly and the wind still blew gustily. He had put on his old trench-coat and pulled his grey fishing hat well down over his ears. The tennis shoes he had found in the workroom were grimy with age. There was certainly no fear of their whiteness betraying him. His fishing-rod gadget he carried at the trail. As he moved across the meadows he felt as excited as a schoolboy. The back way to the Hall would be decidedly the best. Work at the cross-roads was going to be somewhat murky. What about footprints? There wasn't any need to worry about them. It was at least fifty thousand to one against anybody in the wide world having the least glimmering idea of his whereabouts. Nevertheless, he tiptoed across the road and, instead of taking the drive, made for the shelter of the plantation.

The unexpected sight of a light caught his eye. It would be at Lodge Cottage, and not upstairs at that. Somebody must be ill. Except at Christmas and rare holidays the village was always dead to the world at ten o'clock. Still, perhaps Sylvia Forrest, having been little used to country ways, had other views. A lady with such questionable methods of sketching might prove capable of anything. He almost laughed aloud—perhaps it was her bath night! All the same, he was rather uneasy. Something seemed to be a bit peculiar in the state of Denmark. For some time he watched the cottage, but no movement could he detect and no alteration in the intensity of the light.

He reached the outskirts of the orchard, and, having reconnoitred carefully, shinned over the five-barred gate. The grass was long and dripping wet to the feet. The low boughs got in his way and he had to walk as delicately as Agag. Then a black figure scurried away as on all fours. He halted, still as a rock, every nerve keyed up. Good God! A goat! Martin's, he supposed. The night appeared to be darker here, and he could scarcely see half a dozen yards before him. He moved noiselessly through the small gate, along the path of the kitchen garden, and so through the latched door into the west quadrangle.

The Hall showed no light and, from where he halted by the well, was nothing but a deeper blackness in an enveloping gloom. Not that he felt the pressure of this darkness; if anything he felt rather like a boy playing some magnificent game of Indians. Almost as good as stalking the old Turk, and no chance of a crack on the pate either. Ludo would rather have enjoyed all this, he thought.

There was no sound to be heard except the quiet swish of boughs in the casual wind. Already his feet were feeling like ice, and as he made a slight movement they squelched and he felt the water oozing. A final look round and then to work. With infinite care he raised the wooden flaps of the cover until the well yawned open to its roof. He leaned down, grasping his top section of rod, and with the nail to the sides scraped methodically the circle of the well, course by course. The nail slithered and scratched with never an obstacle. He had expected at least that it would have been caught occasionally in some of the joints. Perhaps the bricks had not been laid in mortar. He got out his knife and, leaning over as far as he dared, tested one of the joints. It was as hard as rock. Cement, evidently. Was it waterproof cement? He had no means of finding out. Well, on with the good work. He scraped away at the sides until the full arm's length of seven feet had been explored.

He screwed on the other section and again leaned down. To his surprise, another foot found water. Rather ticklish work that would make. Nevertheless he persisted. Course by course, as far as he could judge, he paid out the rod, but never a bit of taut wire could he catch. So much for that then. He replaced the covers with the same care and then stretched his tired arms. He was feeling a bit cramped too. Better be moving along again. His feet and ankles felt desperately cold and his shoes went squelch-squelch as he moved. Why not cut out the orchard this time and go back by the road? It would be as safe as houses anyhow. So he bore to the right-hand fork and emerged at the drive.

He stopped for a moment at the gate and listened. The wind seemed to have dropped a lot and the night was as still as death. Then a rat whimpered and rustled in the hedge, and away in the woods an owl hooted. Somewhere far off, at the back of the village, a dog was barking and then was quiet again. He moved open the gate and by instinct took the narrow grass margin close to the open ditch, whose shallow, black ribbon was scarce perceptible. And, before he was aware of it, he went full tilt into a motor-cycle standing in the damp bottom beneath the thorns.

The most blasé habitué of Maskelyne and Devant would probably then have been mystified. Compared with what followed the vanishing lady was a trick for rubes. In the minutest fraction of a second, so it seemed, he disappeared, noiseless as a sand lizard and folded as invisibly within the enveloping shadows. On the other side of the road he lay crouched beneath the beech hedge, twenty feet away, almost before he knew what took him there.

Who should have a motor-cycle at the Hall at that time of night? It carried no light and the position alone, without anything else, was sufficient cause for suspicion. It couldn't belong to Martin or any of the gardeners. They would have pushed it under the open shelter a bare fifty yards on. After the excitement of the headlong dive to the hedge he was beginning to feel cold again, yet for some minutes he did not move. There was no way back except by the orchard or straight out by the drive. Either way he might run straight up against the owner of that bicycle. Then two sounds—one the distant striking of a clock, the other the faintest padding of feet, as on a runner, rubber-shod like himself.

The runner dropped into a walk. The feet were now passing over grass. Then he discerned the figure of a man, short, broad, muffled in some kind of coat or waterproof. His boots, too, were squelching as if he had been among long grass. Wrentham could hear his quick breathing—the breathing of one who was near exhaustion. The watcher could see no farther. Cramped as he was he dared not move his head and the dark figure had already passed out of his sight. But not out of sound: there came the noise of the lowering of the bicycle from its stand and the click of the replacement. In a minute or two, so near that he could have touched them, man and bicycle passed in front of him. The bicycle was being pushed, not on the path, but on the uneven margin of grass. Yet there was no great pressure on the part of the pusher. Indeed, so easily did it run that the chain must have been removed.

And now Wrentham did not hesitate. The moving portions of darkness—they were little else—must be about thirty yards in front of him, breasting the brief incline towards the village. Taking the risk of a fall on the uneven grass he sprinted as fast as he dared. At the top of the small hill a bare ten yards separated them, and Wrentham was behind a tree. Then the other mounted the machine and, with the action of a hobby-horse rider, gathered speed down the sharper slope. It was not more than two hundred yards to the foot, but Wrentham dared not follow fast. By the time he reached the road the rider had vanished, whether in the direction of village or station he could not tell.

At the same moment Wrentham remembered the cottage. In a flash he was across the road and in the hedge. Here for several minutes he waited. From the cottage there was no light that he could see. The bordering trees threw over the road shadows so dense that the road itself was hardly discernible. Away to the east, beyond the village, still sounded the hoarse barking of a dog, and at his back, in the meadows, cows moved heavily and cropped their food. But of that rider there was neither sign nor sound. The night had swallowed him up as though he had never existed.

The hedge was broken and gapped—rude traces of the passage of bird-nesters or the gatherers of summer cowslips. He backed into the meadow and made his way over the short-cropped grass. At Farm Road he found the gate, and so made his way to the vicarage.

Everything was as he left it, save for that faint smell of oil that rooms will take when lamps have been long burning. He fastened the window and pulled off his drenched shoes and socks. From behind the books where he had hidden it he took his thermos and poured out the hot coffee. It tasted good. Not for nothing had he gone campaigning. One o'clock and a Sunday morning!

In a quarter of an hour he was in bed, feeling as if it were twenty years ago after a party when the long night was over. How perfectly mad he had been to think there was anything in that well! How could Plumley have put it there, that is to say, with any sort of wire? And the wire must have been visible had it been there. That man with the bicycle might have been anybody, after all. Yet it was puzzling where he had been. Why from the village and hide the cycle at the Hall? Had he been at Lodge

Cottage? Was he a friend or relative of the pseudo artist? Still, why the cycle at the Hall? He could not get past that.

Somehow he felt a bit dispirited. Had there been the least thing that was tangible, or even comprehensible, he could have seized it; had action been demanded he would have leaped into it. Almost he was determined to have nothing further to do with the whole affair. Buried treasure! Bats in the belfry! Platoons of them! So night, which brings counsel, advised him, but the day was to bring in its revenges.

CHAPTER IX
A SECOND CURTAIN

To LIE LATE abed in summer is a species of indulgence that commends itself but rarely in England, nor has it yet been vaunted by our essayists. The army had no use for it, or on any other morning for that matter, holding that drill and daylight are synonymous. Indeed, many a man, having finished with the day, found it all he could do to escape the fell clutch of that other school which held that darkness was solely designed for operations.

From a boy Wrentham had known that Sunday was as other days. It seemed rather as if the Wrenthams, after two centuries of experiment, had framed the meals at Hainton Vicarage so that the week accorded with Sundays. Breakfast was always at eight-thirty, and an hour before that the house was well astir. Wrentham was minded to continue his early morning cup of tea, an army inheritance, and a cigarette after his tub. Then a sharp walk or half an hour in the paddock with his mashie.

This morning, however, as he was surveying from the porch a dull, if rainless, sky, a man came running down the short drive. Wrentham recognised him as Clark, one of the under-keepers who lived away at Big Copses. The man arrived panting at the iron gate, and then, seeing the figure at the porch, came to the front door, not, as he had obviously intended, to the back. He touched his cap. "Can I see the vicar, sir?"

"The vicar's at the church, Clark. He won't be back"—consulting his watch—"for another twenty minutes."

The gamekeeper was evidently in a state of considerable excitement.

"You're not a magistrate, sir, but you'll do just as well. There's a man laying dead in Puddle Pond!"

"Good God!" ejaculated the other. "What sort of a man?" Then, without waiting for an answer, "Here, you come back along with me."

They started. "By the medders was the way I come, sir. That's the quickest way there."

Wrentham agreed. "Tell me all about it," he suggested.

Clark needed no inciting. "I was just walking along this morning, sir, round Clay Hill and the Little Copses and I thought I'd go along to the Hall and get a buttonhole off of Martin, as I was going out this arternoon. I come drawing along by the wood, sir, and when I got to the pond the old bitch she went nosing in and started to bark, so I look in, sir, and there was the man with his head all blood and his motor-bike laying with the front wheel in the water."

"A motor-bike!"

"Yes, sir, laying half in the water and half out. I didn't know what to do, sir, and he looked dead enough to me, so I left the old bitch on guard and run to the vicarage. I thought the vicar, being a magistrate, would know what to do, sir."

"The very best thing you could have done."

They crawled under a rail and moved in single file along the furrow of a ploughed field. Two hundred yards brought them to the pond. A quiet and much-shadowed spot it was, overhung by oaks and at its margin by tall willows. Last year's reeds waved forlorn among the new, and the water-weeds lay undisturbed on the surface, save where in one spot a rustic fisher had made a way for his hook. A grassy path now brought them to the road. The setter rose and snuggled a cold nose into her master's hand, and they could discern the still figure of a man.

Wrentham stooped down beside him. Face downwards the figure lay, sprawled out as one might fall who stumbled unawares. A greyish tweed suit he wore, but no hat. This lay a little to the left among the reeds. He felt the icy pulse and found no movement. Then with his fingers he drew the long grass from around the head, and, stepping across the body with his foot on the water's edge, looked at the face. He recognised the man; the question of doubt never entered his head, so sure was he. Moulines, Plumley's financial secretary!

They stood in silence for a minute or two—Clark because he thought of nothing to say in the presence of the unexpected, and Wrentham busy with his thoughts. He motioned Clark to remain where he was, and, treading carefully on the grass, came to the bicycle. He caught an overhanging willow and leaned over it. There it was, in the water as Clark had described it. Two other things he noticed—that it looked intact and that it had no chain. He signalled to the other to join him at the top of the grassy bank and peered through the ragged hedge. Nobody was in sight.

"This is a bad business, Clark," he said; then, seeing the man's face fall, "not that you haven't done splendidly. Now I want you to pay the strictest attention to what I am going to tell you to do. Sit with the bitch under that elm, a hundred yards down the road on the left. Pass the time of day with anybody who goes by in a perfectly natural manner, but don't say a word about what is lying in that pond. It is a thousand to one that nobody will have any occasion to go there, but if anybody should—boys, for instance—stop them at once. You'll have to be there for an hour or two, but there's not likely to be anybody along the road before people start coming to morning service. If anybody should ask you what you're doing tell them anything you like. You're sure you've got that?"

Clark thought he had.

"Right-ho!" said Wrentham. "You hang on here and I'll have some breakfast along for you in half an hour."

So, leaving the keeper on guard, he made his way quickly to the village. Rummage was having his breakfast, and him he dispatched direct to Norwich in the Ford. The best way, he thought; no use troubling about the local police. He hastily scribbled two notes, one for the doctor at Longham and the other for the Norwich police.

"If your old bus breaks down, Rummage," he was careful to add, "stop the next car and make them take you on. Get to Longham or Windley, open the note and telephone the message to Police Head-quarters, Norwich. If you can't use the telephone find somebody who can."

He supposed there wasn't much fear of the bus breaking down, but it was as well to be on the safe side and allow for any contingency. So, having dispatched the obviously inquisitive and wholly unsatisfied Rummage, he strode out home again. The vicar had finished breakfast. Still, he got Emma to boil a couple of eggs, and with these and the full thermos set off again by the back meadows. He found Clark at his post, looking like one who holds temporarily a position of astounding trust. So back to his own meal.

He realised that in giving the news to his father there would have to be many things kept back. The problem craved wary walking. And yet it turned out to be very easy. Henry Plumley's tenure of the Hall explained to some extent the presence of Moulines in the village, and the general term "met him in town" covered the recognition. What the vicar seemed really worried about was that such a thing should have happened in Hainton. It was inconceivable that so remote and quiet a spot should be the scene of what was bound to make it notorious. He persisted in his view that there must have been some mistake; it was an accident and no murder. Wrentham was rather relieved when the church bell rang out and he was alone in the house.

Before the bell had made its last hesitant call a closed car drove up the drive. Two men descended from it. The taller, and a man of magnificent physique with it, introduced himself.

"I'm Inspector Delane. Major Wrentham, I take it?"

Wrentham shook hands; a very business-like sort of fellow this. All part of the day's work to him. The other was then introduced—Detective-Sergeant Burrows, a quiet, unassuming sort of chap who dropped at once into the background. Wrentham noticed how his eyes went wandering all round, and couldn't help smiling. He caught the inspector's eye.

"Mr. Burrows reminds me of an aunt of mine, Inspector. She was one of those collecting fiends, and as soon as she got into anybody's house, even while saying 'How do you do?' her eyes would be all over the place on the look out for antiques. Used to make me feel devilish embarrassed sometimes."

Even the detective laughed and the ice appeared to be well broken.

The car was left behind and they set off the back way. The two officers were in civilian clothes, and although publicity was not to be avoided, there was no point in courting it at that juncture. Wrentham explained everything and told all he had to tell.

"All I can say, Major," was the inspector's comment, "is that if there were more about like yourself and this man Clark our job would be twice as easy."

Arrival at the pond saved Wrentham the necessity of replying.

While the inspector was despatching Clark to find the village constable, the detective set to work. He pulled out a notebook and sketched rapidly the position of the body relative to the pond. The inspector joined him. Wrentham feared to intrude on their conference and watched from the far bank. The experience was a new one for him, and, after the quantity of detective novels he had read, a fascinating one. He could not but admire the sureness with which the two worked. The body seemed to be studied from every angle and the ground was searched foot by foot, within the boundaries of a stretched-out line. Wrentham had but one remark to make and that he thought sufficiently urgent to warrant disturbing the searchers.

"If you should see on each side of the body the impressions of sole marks, Inspector, they will be those I made this morning when I straddled over it."

"Thank you, Major. Were you wearing the same boots?" He came over and had a good look at the soles and apparently found no difficulty in tracing out the marks on the ground.

Not wishing to appear too interested or be in the way, Wrentham went through the hedge to the road. It was some minutes later that a car drew up, piloted by the indispensable Clark. Dr. Ware, well known to Wrentham on the cricket field, got out with a "Hallo, Major! Sorry I couldn't get here before. What's it all about?"

With them was Maxwell, the village constable. Both were escorted to the inspector, and Wrentham took advantage of the opportunity to ask what was to be done with Clark.

They moved away to let the doctor make his inspection.

"As a matter of fact, Major, you're the very fellow I wanted to see. Sorry to trouble you again, but where can we put the body? What about the school?"

Wrentham suggested the vicarage room; quite handy, and would disturb nobody. How was it going to be got there?

The inspector soon settled that. Clark was sent to the other end of the field to fetch the shepherd and a hurdle. Burrows remained behind; his work was only begun. The four of them managed the laden hurdle, and behind came the inspector wheeling the cycle, apparently undamaged except for the water in the engine. A trestle-table was fixed up in the little, tin-roofed room. Leaving the doctor to go on with his work, the inspector took Clark on one side.

"I want you to know, Clark," he began, "that we are extraordinarily pleased with what you have done this morning, and, depend upon it, you won't be forgotten. I'm not going to ask you to keep your mouth shut; just the opposite. Talk to everybody you can about this morning. You a teetotaller?" Clark shook his head emphatically. "All the better," continued the inspector. "Go along to your favourite pub and talk about it. Remember the dead man was about six feet tall, probably a foreigner, dressed in grey and with a red and black necktie. His motor-bike was a Douglas. You got all that?"

Clark thought he had.

"Now, Clark, I regard you as a man of extraordinary intelligence. Don't talk too much, but as soon as you have started the ball rolling let others talk as much as they like. Keep your ears open and learn all you can. Maxwell will already have that part of the pond railed off to keep people away, and so there's bound to be a lot of talk in any case. But you're the one everybody will want to listen to. Come back here after your dinner at about two o'clock."

Wrentham moved off indoors. He recognised that in this show he was a subordinate. It was up to him to get out of the way until he was wanted. He would doubtless be fetched soon enough. And, indeed, by the time he had finished a pipe the inspector came for him.

"If you can spare a minute or two now, Major, we shall be very glad of your help."

The body was covered with the dust-sheet of the piano. At the end of the table was a small heap—money, penknife, pencils—evidently the contents of the dead man's pockets. The doctor was apparently writing some sort of report, using the top of the piano as a table. The room was scented with the tang of the firs that brushed idly against the window and overhung the open door.

"By the linen marks and certain other indications the deceased appears to be the André Moulines of your acquaintance, Major. Can you tell me anything more about him?"

Wrentham mentioned the dead man's connexion with Plumley; more he did not know.

"No relatives? Nobody who could identify him?"

"Yes," said Wrentham deliberately. "I think I can help you there." He mentioned Ludo's address and the mutual connexion with Plumley.

"Capital! The very thing! Where is your post office, by the way?"

Wrentham told him, and then, "You'll come here for lunch, Inspector, if you have time? One-thirty. And you too, Ware?"

"Sorry, old chap," said the latter, "but I shall have to bolt as soon as I've seen the Inspector. I shall be back again this afternoon, however, when I've fetched some things I want."

The inspector accepted—"If it won't be giving you too much trouble."

"Not at all," Wrentham assured him. "Bring Burrows too. We'll find your man a bite in the kitchen."

By lunch-time the forces were once more assembled, nor was the meal as depressing as one might have imagined. Wrentham himself was braced by the news that Ludo had been located and would be down by the evening train. The inspector turned out to be a churchwarden of St. Witholds and by way of an expert on early Staffordshire ware, both of interest to their host. Burrows discovered that his nephew had served under the Major in Palestine. The Stilton was good, and afterwards from somewhere was produced some excellent port. Wrentham found the detective a most likeable sort of man—one who, though evidently self made and educated, could carry himself with that natural and homely dignity of manner that are often found in the country. A pleasing fellow, too, to look at: hair just greying, moustache close-clipped, and cheeks like a November russet. However, immediately after the conclusion of the meal he disappeared unobtrusively. The vicar and Delane were still carrying on their argument, until Emma announced that Clark had been waiting for some time. The vicar, too, looked at his watch with a "Dear me!" Sunday school was imminent. "Shall we see you for tea?" he asked, and the smile implied the welcome.

"If you don't mind us coming in at all sorts of hours, Vicar, we shall be very grateful."

So off they went their several ways, business of souls and bodies. Wrentham, who found himself alone with his thoughts, was too restless to remain with such mad company and betook himself to the heath with his dog.

CHAPTER X
MEETING OF THE GENERAL STAFF

A MORE UNLIKELY conspirator than Ludovic Travers could hardly be imagined. He did not possess that keenness of manner and that incisiveness of speech which appear to be the distinguishing marks of a human bloodhound. As his colleague might have expressed it, he didn't look as if Sherlock was his middle name. All the same, had he been picking a side out of all the men he knew it is more than likely that he would have been Wrentham's first choice. The thing was that you never knew just what he was capable of doing or when he was going to do it. Such was Wrentham's faith in him that he would have consulted him on anything, from toothache to tattooing, and have been sure of an answer.

It must have been ten o'clock when they had their first chance of being together. The inspector had gone and the detective had taken up his quarters at Rummage's inn. The vicar had retired at his usual hour. The day had told on him very much, and at his age it is the mental stress that tells.

Ludo had news to impart that seemed to join up some of the loose ends. He had seen much of the police department in their inquiries at Bellingham House, and one bit of information had reached him which appeared childish in its conception and grotesque in its execution.

The proprietor of the Hôtel du Lac at Geneva had staying at his hotel for one night, about a year since, a man and a woman. The register had been signed Mr. and Mrs. Bellingham, England. A day or two later he had seen in an English periodical, left behind by an officer, a picture of Henry Plumley and had recognised his guest. A month ago he received an amazing letter, enclosing a sealed letter of instructions. The covering note, which was unsigned, asked him, upon receipt of a telegram consisting simply of the word "Bellingham," to open the enclosed letter and act in accordance with the instructions contained therein. A hundred pound note was enclosed as a sort of retaining fee. Upon reading, however, of the sensational death of Plumley, M. Klotsch was in some trepidation. He finally decided to open the envelope of instructions, and had found that they were simply that he should have in perfect readiness a high-powered car. The writer would give the word "Bellingham" as proof of identity and would arrive within twelve hours. Having no wish to become involved in any suspicious affair, M. Klotsch thought it as well to communicate with the police.

"Looks decidedly as though he were preparing to do a bolt," remarked Wrentham. "Furthermore, I wouldn't mind betting my shirt that if inquiries were made there would be exactly two other hotels similarly warned."

"I think I follow you," said the other. "You think the three suit-cases would be at three different termini, leading to the Continent: say via Dover, Harwich or Hull, or Southampton. Certainly, if we assume that Plumley did want to abscond, the idea was not a bad one. What are you proposing to do?"

"I hardly know. We might advise the police to check the cloak-rooms at all termini. If they did, unless the information were anonymous, the question of the connexion of the suit-cases and your famous list would be bound to get out. I don't think we're quite ready for that yet, do you?"

"Moreover," suggested Ludo, "we cannot definitely assert that we are dealing with facts and not suspicions. Still, if they are true, there's one matter that should be inquired into, and that is, what was the object at the back of Plumley's mind? Even if he were mad, we must not necessarily assume that he was without method. If he were preparing for a getaway, the matter of the cases must have been—at least to my mind—preparation for it."

"But why three cases and—"

"Just a minute. I was coming to that. First of all, let's go back to your theory of suit-cases at three termini. Have you considered what a small place London is and that termini are equally accessible?"

"You mean he could get to one just as easily as to another?"

"Quite so. Therefore why have them there? However, if you don't mind, we'll leave that for a moment, because I rather wanted to refer to it in another context. Let's deal with the simple question of concealment of money. To carry that to its obvious limits we must assume that there were caches wherever he might be—caches handy so that he could disappear at a moment's notice. They would therefore have to be at Hainton, Hindhead, Chalton, Newmarket, the Central and Metropolis Theatres, Bellingham House, and the City Corporations offices."

"Ludo," said Wrentham with a grin, "when you get wound up I know why we won the war."

The other was imperturbable.

"The message handed to Plumley before his suicide was recovered by the police. It was something scrawled in copying pencil on a sheet of ordinary paper torn from a notebook. Plumley had so wetted it with his fingers that it was practically undecipherable. All it looked like—I say that deliberately—was 'Moving,' and if so it was probably a code word. It is not too much to suppose that Plumley had certain sources of information and had made arrangements that any urgent message should reach him anywhere and at any time. The regrettable thing for him was that the police moved when he was in the one spot where there was no preparation for decamping and where there was no egress. His precautions were useless and the game was up. But—and here again I allude to the suit-cases—might he not have arranged that warning should reach him, say at Liverpool Street on any return from Hainton or Newmarket, at Waterloo on return from Hindhead, and at King's Cross on return from Chalton? I think that really would account for suit-cases at the termini and give us the termini themselves. Far-fetched, I admit, but logical. Bear in mind those were the only three stations which Plumley was in the habit of using frequently."

Wrentham had nothing to say. It might be fantastic but at least there was logic in it. He changed the subject. "What did Delane tell you?"

"Nothing much except that they are convinced that the murder did not take place near the pond. They are quite prepared for the inquest to go forward on the evidence they have. Whatever they know, therefore, unless they press for an adjournment, it is bound to come out to-morrow."

Wrentham slowly filled his pipe; then he got out his file of notes. The other was gazing at the ceiling as if Hainton and his thoughts were as far removed as the poles. "Here's something may interest you, Ludo. Listen to this," and he repeated in meticulous detail the events of the previous day. "Now what about it?"

Ludo grunted and said nothing. Wrentham tried another line of approach. "Didn't Moulines come round to you and ask all sorts of questions relative to Plumley's eccentricities and your absences? In other words, didn't he suspect something?"

"He must have done more than suspect. The matter of the hundred thousand pounds must have come to his notice. My accounts were in the hands of the police the morning after Plumley's death. Moulines must have had access to them in his official capacity."

"The thing is, who pipped him?"

"As far as the police are concerned, I grant you. As far as it concerns us, what was he looking for? The missing chain and the concealed bicycle show that he was there on no public matter."

"I admit all that, but what's worrying me is, who was our friend who cleared off with the motor-bike? My own particular impression is that it was a case of thieves falling out and the devil getting his due. What was the Forrest girl looking for? What do you think about that mysterious damsel, Ludo? Is she George Plumley's wife?"

"Order is heaven's first law," remarked Ludo sententiously. "Let's take the girl first. I know that George Plumley's wife was in the chorus of the 'Metropolis,' and I naturally know Callender, the manager, very well. If you like I'll take up that and get a full account."

"Splendid, Ludo! Then there's another thing that's intrigued me. If we had an exact copy of Plumley's last words we might test it for a further clue."

Ludo was diffident. "Don't you think that the making up of such information as he conveyed to the listener, quite on the spur of the moment, mark you, was a sufficiently difficult feat? Surely anything like a cryptogram would have been too incredibly difficult and miraculously spontaneous."

"Watson, you're right," admitted the other, "but you're the devil of a chap for throwing cold water on my pet theories."

"Still, there'd be no harm in getting a verbatim report. Do you know anybody likely?"

"A subaltern of mine had a very good job on the 'Daily Wire.' What was his name now? Crook. That's it—Crook. What about writing him in your official capacity, mentioning my name. Use your well-known suavity."

"Well, I'll have a shot at it. But why not come back to Town with me to-morrow?"

Wrentham had his chance to be mysterious. "If the weather holds, I may. If it is wet, probably not."

"I don't quite see—"

Wrentham laughed. "Here's the scheme. The inquest isn't until eleven. What about my strolling along to the Hall in the morning? If it is fine our fair friend may be at work. If it is wet I ought to hang on for a try the next day. Honestly, Ludo, that lady interests me enormously. I haven't got much use for them generally, but something tells me that this is the lady we've got to search."

"Not a bad scheme. If I were sure of being in time for the inquest I'd come along and form my own impressions. Now a word in your ear." Ludo here looked more solemn than usual. "What exactly are you going to tell the police—I mean about your night's adventures? Doesn't it strike you, young feller, that if everything is put together you might appear in an awkward position?"

Wrentham was ready with his answer. "I thought over all that this afternoon. At present—nothing. If I could explain my reasons for being at the Hall at heaven knows what unearthly hour I wouldn't mind. Do you think I should make a good diplomatist, or, in the vulgar, liar?"

Ludo grimaced. "I expect you would pass muster."

"Seriously Ludo, we don't want, at this particular moment, the country flooded with headings like:

EX-OFFICER SEEKS TREASURE FINDS
TRAGEDY INSTEAD

and all that sort of tripe. All the newspapers in the world can't bring Moulines to life, and if treasure-seekers grub Hainton up by the roots it won't mend matters. I know it's everybody's duty to help the police, but—"

"Specious, my dear chap. Specious. And yet in a way I'm inclined to agree with you. At least, there's no harm in waiting for the inquest."

There fell one of those unaccountable silences that come to all conversations. Each felt perhaps that mere adventure had receded from the presence of that pitiful shell lying but fifty yards away. The influence was vague and yet disturbing.

Wrentham roused himself. "Look here, Ludo, let's get down to brass tacks. Put all speculation on one side. All this business is serious enough for me and it's likely to be more so before I'm through. Do you believe Plumley concealed anything at Hainton?"

The other answered without hesitation. "I do; and at Hindhead too."

"Of course, you don't believe that, as far as I'm concerned, findings are keepings, at least to the extent of any loss the pater and I may suffer through Plumley?"

"Geoffrey, don't ask me that." It was Ludo who smiled now. "Let all that take care of itself until the necessity arises. But if you ask me if I'm with you to find what there is to find, I'll say I'm with you every time."

"That's good enough for me. Well, we're in it up to the eyeballs already. When will you be free, Ludo?"

Ludo shook his head. "Not for a fortnight at the earliest. You've no idea of the mass of stuff there is to clear up. I am employing a fair amount of outside help; and the auctioneers are doing most of the inventories. All the same, there might be heaps of things to do in Town while you are running this end of the show."

"Still, it's no use just at present drinking to 'Conspirators Ltd.'!" laughed Wrentham as he poured out a couple of nightcaps.

"You never know," remarked Ludo. "To use your own deadly remark, something's bound to roll up."

"True enough. In any case, there's no need to waste these excellent drinks, so here's to us!"

. . .

Suppose Henry Plumley, invested now with "that deity in his nature of here and everywhere"; suppose him on some ghostly tour, revisiting the glimpses of the moon and watching that hour the personæ of this our play. What would he have seen in his shadowy wanderings?

The vicar would have been sleeping, a trifle uneasily, his fine old face like the profile of a great actor, clear-cut against the pillow. The killer of André Moulines would have been superintending the slow burning of a Burberry on a heaped-up fire. Doctor Ware would have lost twenty-nine shillings at shilling a hundred bridge, thanks to persistent overcalling. Inspector Delane would have been writing odd sentences on sheets of paper and regarding them contemplatively. Sylvia Forrest would have been awaiting the drying of a sheet of Whatman paper, stretched on a frame. Fred Martin would have been cycling to Hollingham as fast as his legs could pedal to fetch the doctor to his young wife. Detective Burrows would have been comparing a paper, cut in the shape of a footprint, with the sole of a shoe and then staring amazed at the result. George Plumley would have been reading a book on gardening and finding it desperately uninteresting. Wallace would have been sleeping with no more dreams than the dead. Clark would have been on his back, potations loud and deep and much unwonted meditation proving too much for him. Tango the dog would have had nightmare. His master and he that afternoon had played a strange game on the heath away among the brakes. Two or three sticks had been stuck in the ground and another stick supporting a coat behind them. All one had to do was to shake the coat and be called a good dog. As for Rummage, he would have been sleeping soundest of all, his face unfurrowed by any care. Business was thriving!

CHAPTER XI
THE LAW HAS AN INNINGS

IF IT BE TRUE that nothing is so rare as a day in June, whereby doubtless the poet meant some idealised day wherein all perfect Junes should be epitomised, then it might also be asserted that nothing is so miserable as July turned October. Perhaps on that morning the rustic genius of the groves, incensed at so unwonted a disturbance of his solitudes, was minded that mortality should at least share in the derangement. The air was cold and the rain steady. Only when beholding the oaks would one have said summer; to turn and look at the firs was to meet the sadness of early winter.

Wrentham, consulting the ancient glass in the hall, was joined by Ludo. "I think I'll change my mind after all," said he. "If I know anything about weather this is going to last more than a day or two."

The other turned to greet the vicar who was coming down the stairs.

"Morning, Uncle Peter. Just in time to give us your authoritative opinion. How long is this going to last?"

The vicar tested the glass. He smiled affectionately at the pair of them. "Sooner or later youth is bound to defer to age. Even I am a stripling compared with this fellow. I should say two days at least. What were you boys planning to do?"

Wrentham took his father's arm and they passed into the breakfast-room. "The fact is, pater, I have to go to Town on one or two matters of business, so why not go while it's wet? After all, the weather doesn't matter so much in Town."

"I think that's very sensible," replied his father. "He'll be company for you, Ludo. And when are you going to spend a real holiday with us again?"

The unusual sight of Emma, and not the maid, bringing in the coffee interrupted them. She said "Good morning" to the vicar and received with comparative equanimity the jocular greetings of the others. "Twenty years ago I'd have boxed your ears for that, Master Ludo."

She took up her position with arms folded across the amplitude of her waist. "There's a message for you, Master Geoffrey. I didn't get the chance to give it to you yesterday as you were out, and after church I clean forgot all about it. It's about those tennis shoes of yours you left in the study on Saturday night."

The first he had thought of them. What a damn careless thing to do!

"I dried the socks in front of the kitchen range and made Wallace give the old shoes a good scrubbing and put them to dry too. And yesterday afternoon, Mr. Burrows, or Sergeant Burrows, or whatever he is, came into the kitchen and we had a little chat. You see, sir, he comes from my old home." Emma now included the vicar in her remarks. Wrentham knew better than to interrupt. Emma at the flood would take some stopping.

"He asked me whose the shoes were and I told him yours, Master Geoffrey, and how I expected you'd forgotten them. So he said, 'Do you think he would lend them to me?' You see, sir, he'd got all the skin off his heels with tramping about the roads. I came to find you but you'd gone and he said he'd probably see you himself. He said, sir," again addressing the vicar who was obviously taking no interest whatever in the matter, "that he thought a change of shoes would be as good as a rest. So I thought, Master Geoffrey, that if Mr. Burrows said anything to you about the shoes you'd know."

"Oh, I'll probably know all right, Emma," was the reply. He glanced at Ludo and they both laughed. Emma laughed too—she didn't know why—and departed. The vicar, who had been preoccupied about the weather, poured out the coffee.

The talk fell naturally to the inquest. When was the last one? Wrentham didn't remember. The vicar bethought him. "Fairly recently," he said, "about two years ago. Old Western was found at the bottom of his well. Didn't I write you about it, Geoffrey?"

Geoffrey didn't remember; or probably one of those letters that had got torpedoed.

His father went on. "Jensil, who is coming to-day, was acting as coroner. That reminds me of a curious coincidence. Jensil's father was coroner when I was a boy, and the first case of the kind I can call to mind young Jensil came with his father and we had lunch in this very room." The vicar shook his head. "Nearly fifty years ago. Your grandfather told me at the same time what I had not previously been aware of, namely, that not only is a coroner concerned with matters of sudden death but also in all cases of treasure-trove."

Ludo gave a sudden start, and Wrentham, regarding him, misquoted maliciously:

"Thus conscience can make cowards of us all."

"I don't quite see the point," said the vicar, looking round and fearing as usual some pulling of legs.

"There isn't one, Uncle Peter."

Wrentham decided to switch off on a new tack.

"I seem to remember that name 'Jensil.' Is he a man something like old W. G.: huge beard and so on? If so, it was when I was quite a small boy."

"That's the man," said his father. "What you remember, Geoffrey, is when the Society of Antiquaries came here to lunch. They were tracking out the original Peddars' Way, and when they got as far as Hainton they spent the day here. There were some interesting things at the Hall in those days—I mean before it was rebuilt."

And so to talk of priests' holes and moats and Kett's rebellion and Socialists and even, as wines accord with courses, of Jaffa oranges over the marmalade. As they got up from the table the vicar harked back to treasure-trove.

"If I should forget it, Geoffrey, you might remind me to ask Jensil about that discovery I was mentioning. If I recall the circumstances correctly, a farm-labourer, clearing out a ditch, turned up some coins, mostly Elizabethan. I think I saw some of them the other day at the Castle Museum."

It was certain that Wrentham's expedition to the Hall would have to be put off. No cause that for alarm, as he pointed out to

Ludo. As long as it rained there would be no sketching, or, as he summarised the situation, "The balloon will not go up."

"My dear fellow," said the other, "if you scatter round this hamlet many more traces of your Saturday's exploits something will get strung up."

Wrentham was slow in the uptake. He looked interrogatively.

"Strung up!" repeated Ludo, giving a pantomimic illustration. "The indefatigable Burrows knew of Moulines' connexion with Plumley, and Plumley's with the Hall. If he could not trace back from the pond he would be bound to start at the other end. It's practically certain that by this time he has fitted your enormous shoes into the equally Brobdingnagian tracks, so that the side AB coincides with the side CD. Honestly, Geoff, I envy you."

"Envy me! Good Lord, why?"

"Well, the only way I can put it is probably a bit over your head, but Bacon has it that there is nothing in the world equal to surveying the errors of mankind from the hill and vantage ground of truth. You, my dear chap, will have all the thrills of the suspect and at the same time wear an invisible halo."

"Perhaps you're right," agreed the other complacently; "but what about doing the surveying from the end of the billiard-table? There's bound to be a bit of a rush on soon, and it strikes me we should be well out of it."

Just before eleven, however, they set out for Jerlingham's barn, a walk of two or three hundred yards. On the way they picked up Rendell, the agent-bailiff of the Hall estate, a breezy, horsey-looking sort of sportsman, since Wrentham's time, but evidently known to Ludo who hailed him familiarly.

The barn had been swept and garnished. Benches and widely contributed chairs were crowded and quite a number of the unlucky were standing at the back of the building. It appeared to be as warm as any other place though not too well lighted. The vicar spoke to Jensil and took his seat at the side of the table where the coroner sat. Wrentham recognised Ware, Delane, and the detective; and among the jury Harris and Tait. For himself he refused the offer of a seat and moved to the back, where, with the advantage of his height, he could easily survey the whole scene. The end of the barn had been screened off, and behind this recess the body doubtless lay.

Most of the preliminaries appeared to have been concluded. After acknowledgment of inspection of the body by the jury, Ludo gave his evidence of identification. Questioned by the coroner, he knew no enemies of the dead man. His acquaintance was a superficial one and due only to the occasional overlapping of their departments. No, he could not give any reason for the presence of the deceased in Hainton. He admitted that he might have had some commission from the late Mr. Plumley, but that was extremely unlikely. Everything connected with Hainton passed from the hands of the agent, Mr. Rendell, into his (the witness's) hands, and the accounts were entirely separate from the other activities of the late Mr. Plumley. Asked for elucidation of this, he explained that the deceased was financial secretary. As such he might be instructed to place a certain sum of money, say ten thousand pounds, to the credit of the private or estate account. Thereafter the money passed entirely out of his control.

Dr. Ware was then called. There was a movement among the crowd, who thought apparently that something really interesting was about to take place. The doctor described how the message reached him and his arrival at the pond. He gave the impression of absolute capability. His tone was assured, so much so that you would have said he courted cross-examination rather than feared it.

"I found upon examination that the deceased was a well-nourished adult male of good development. On the back of the head was a large contused wound of recent origin, and no other external injuries were found.

"The internal examination revealed that all the organs of the body were in a normal condition and no disease was evident. The examination of the head and neck resulted in the disclosure of a severe dislocation of the vertebrae of the spinal column in the cervical (neck) region, resulting in a complete laceration of the spinal cord in that region. The brain and skull were found to be normal."

"What, in your opinion, was the cause of death?"

"The injuries which I have described—that is to say, laceration of the spinal cord in that vital region just below the brainstem—resulted in interference with those important nerve centres which control respiration and the heart's action, and thus death would have been almost instantaneous, from sudden failure of respiration."

"Might these injuries have been caused by some weapon of offence?"

"I could not say. From the jagged nature of the wound such a weapon would have to have been wielded with extraordinary strength and precision."

"How long had the deceased been dead at the time of your examination?"

"As rigor mortis was firmly established the man had been dead about twelve hours, speaking roughly; this phenomenon usually taking from ten to twelve hours in its development."

"So that death must have occurred between the hours of ten p.m. and midnight on Saturday last?"

"That is so."

Clark, brave in his velveteens, gave an account of his dramatic discovery. It was noteworthy that the coroner, a man with vast experience in the ways of rural witnesses, let him have his head, and there was consequently little that Clark omitted. He was praised for his promptitude of action and complimented as an excellent witness. That day certainly flashed meteor-like across the black centuries of the Clarks, not that he didn't deserve every word of it.

The inspector unobtrusively placed a chit before the coroner. He and the vicar whispered together for a minute and then the coroner rose.

"At this stage of the proceedings the police do not propose to call any further evidence. The inquest will be adjourned until Wednesday week. I must further warn gentlemen of the jury that it is not improbable that at our reassembly there may have to be a further adjournment."

All over in three-quarters of an hour; and quite enough, thought Wrentham, to keep the gossips going for three weeks.

When the barn was comparatively empty he moved up to the table. Jensil was a man of considerable charm of personality; one who had seen much of things. He showed his pleasure at meeting the son of his old friend. He couldn't afford the time, he said, but he was coming to lunch. Wrentham had a word with Delane, who told him they had got hold of a relation, apparently an aunt, of the dead man and he was just rushing to Norwich to see about the burial. The detective was apparently busy elsewhere, but as the two were strolling quietly back to the vicarage, leaving the vicar and Jensil to follow, they saw him waiting at the drive gate.

"If you will keep your ear trained on the bloke that owns the vantage ground," said Wrentham, "you'll hear something to your disadvantage." He hailed the detective cheerily. "Hallo, Burrows! How's the heel?"

"You must have thought it a cheek on my part to—"

"My dear fellow, I only hope they were some use to you. In any case, they were very little use to me so hang on to them as long as you like."

"That's very good of you, Major." His limp became very noticeable. "You staying down here long?"

"As a matter of fact, I'm going to Town with Captain Travers this afternoon, but I ought to be back the day after to-morrow. Is a layman permitted to ask, by the way, why you adjourned the inquest?"

The detective smiled. "As we often have to say to the Press, Major, you may ask whatever you like."

Ludo here took a hand. "That reminds me. Did I ever tell you the story of the pushful subaltern? We had one in the mess—a most objectionable sort of swine. One day the mess president announced a meeting of the messing committee and this chap gets up and says, 'I believe anybody can attend a meeting of the mess.' 'No,' says the M.P., 'what you mean is anybody can *try* to attend a mess meeting.'"

"Burrows," observed Wrentham, "if you will kindly allow Captain Travers a few seconds to change he will have great pleasure in relating a few further episodes from his highly sordid and adventurous life." They had reached the porch. "Well, what about a drink?"

"Sorry, Major. I haven't a moment to spare. I may drop in for a minute or two when you get back. And with regard to the question of the adjourned inquest, I don't mind confiding to you gentlemen that this is the idea in the back of our minds: people will talk now more than ever and something's bound to come out. As a matter of fact," looking straight at Wrentham, "I shouldn't be surprised, between you and me, if some people in a short time, having had time to think it over, were coming to me and giving information."

But Wrentham was not to be drawn. "Perhaps you're right." Then, changing the subject, "How's that brigand Rummage treating you?"

"Very well indeed. Couldn't wish for a better dugout than the 'Bird in Hand.' Good food and plenty of it."

"Well, drop in when I get back. Any time will suit me," was Wrentham's farewell.

Ludo was more ceremonious. "Good-bye and good luck, Burrows. And if things don't go according to programme, remember the oft-repeated remark of the Major: something's bound to roll up."

"A stout fellow that!" was the Major's comment, "and a damn shame your rotting him like that! Which reminds me. I wonder Ludo, if when I'm in Borstal, or wherever they put scoundrels like me, they'll allow me to read your reminiscences?"

CHAPTER XII
STILL MORE INQUIRIES

As WRENTHAM LEFT once more the offices of Hallett & Hallett after an interview which left him no wiser as far as concerned his financial position than when he entered, he realised that it was exactly a week since he arrived in England—a week that, even compared with the events of the last five years, could fear no rival in its thrilling output. If they included battle and sudden death, at least they laid no claim to murder. And yet some of the fellows last night were lamenting the absence of action. Courtney-Pyne was off to Rhodesia and Hippsley joining a cinema circus up the Amazon. He chuckled at the thought of the possibilities of his present enterprise from the point of view of the cinema. What about having a chap turning a handle in the rhododendron walk? And fancy taking Ludo unawares into a movie show and letting him discover himself strolling with an air of serenest detachment through blood and gore.

At the "Melton," where they lunched, things were very quiet. "Very little to report on the Western Front to-day. What's the programme, Ludo?"

Ludo reported everything as satisfactory. The previous night he had secured Wrentham's man at the "Daily Wire" building. Crook thought it might be done and hoped to send the necessary information round to Bellingham House sometime during the day. Furthermore, Ludo had got hold of Callender. The "Metropolis" was closed at the moment for rehearsals and Callender had been run to earth at his house. He had said he was meeting another fellow at the Medley Club that night at seven-thirty, and if Wrentham would see him there he'd do all he could. "I hinted," said Ludo, "that you were not unconnected with some insurance groups and that everything was in strict confidence."

"The devil, you did!"

"Dash it all! You had to be accounted for somehow. In any case there's no need to refer to that again now the way is clear. These theatrical chaps are by no means averse to hearing themselves speak, and I've no doubt you'll get everything you want from Callender. He's a bit loud, but quite a good-hearted chap. Spent most of the war in France, too."

Ludo departed to his labours, and as the rain showed but scant signs of abating the other was soon endeavouring to earn an honest penny. The cards ran exasperatingly—not that his hands were bad; rather they were so good as to lead to disaster since the others had better. And if he held a stumer, his partners found themselves with hands whose value was in consequence grossly exaggerated. However, after tea, the swings compensated for the roundabouts and a few shillings was the extent of his losses. Then he tossed Porter double or quits and won.

The Medley Club, a product of the war, was situated in a basement in the Haymarket. Impeccable in its affairs, it possessed a strange British Bohemianism of its own. A good lady was housekeeper and cook and her daughter did the cleaning up. A small dancing-room led to the bar and the smaller kitchen. Back of this, distemper decorated by a reasonably sane Cubist, was the dining-room. From here a ladder led to a wholly inadequate, wicker-furnished lounge above.

At first Wrentham thought he must be mistaken, but the notice "Medley Club" and an arrow pointing downstairs invited exploration. At the foot of the stone steps was a door and the repetition of the club's name showed him he was right. Inside was a tiny office and at the desk a man so mild in appearance that he might have been a missionary.

"Is Mr. Callender in the club?" he asked. "My name's Wrentham. I have an appointment with him."

"That's quite right, sir. Mr. Callender 'phoned up. He's just coming along. You'll find the cloak-room there, sir," indicating a small curtained recess off to the right.

Having deposited his gear, Wrentham made his way again to the office. The chap at the desk turned out to be the secretary, and at his suggestion he strolled into the dance-room. Some sort of exhibition seemed to be on, as the panelled walls were hung with pictures, priced and with occasional "Sold" labels. Wrentham himself was a bit of an artist, as one might have predicted twenty years previously from the margins of his school-books, but he found little to please him. A mauve "Zeppelin Attack" was certainly original, but most of the others looked as if they had been built up with a palette knife. By the time he had completed the circuit of the room he was joined by Callender.

Over a gin and bitters they discussed things generally. Callender seemed a very sound fellow. Whether this was due to the artificial atmosphere of quiet Wrentham did not consider. The dinner itself was decidedly novel—just a plain roast and some fruit tart, both excellently cooked. Of the five other diners, one was a well-known writer of ghost stories. At another table by themselves sat a black-and-white illustrator and his wife. At the far end were a couple of girls, discussing a cocktail and chattering noisily.

"Not many people here to-night, Major," explained Callender. "A lot of them away on holidays. It generally fills up about ten. Dancing starts at nine. What about a trip in the sausage—the upstairs room," he explained.

He secured some coffee and having left a message with Mrs. Green, showed Wrentham up to the deserted room. Under the electric light it seemed a rather cheerful sort of place.

"Now, Major, I gathered from Mr. Travers that you want information about Pamela Price."

"If that is the girl George Plumley married, I do."

"Well, how will this do for a start?" He produced two photos. They showed a face of no particular character, just like any dozen of those photos of young actresses one may see in shops or the illustrated papers—in the latter with the probable title, "A Winsome Picture of English Girlhood." Teeth, fluffy hair, and a *retroussé* nose, the latter at least individual and of importance.

"You may hang on to those, Major, if they're any good to you. They were taken about eighteen months ago, when we were doing 'Monologues.' You remember 'Monologues'? What, you don't remember that show! Not—

Lum tiddy, um tum, lum tum;
Tiddle um, tiddle um, tum.

and he hummed the air of that song which in its ephemeral existence set all England singing—

"Tell me you love me on the telephone
And I won't tell a soul what you said."

"The idea was that Miss Price was to have a speaking part in our No. 1 Company. I didn't know her very well at the time, having just taken over after being invalided out. Then there was the devil of a shindy one night, a regular fight with Delia Devine's dresser, and, between you and me, we weren't sorry to get rid of her altogether. I think the fact that she was friendly at the time with George Plumley—some lad that!—made her a bit top-heavy. It was her or Delia Devine, so you can guess which had to go. The last time I heard of her was her marriage."

"I'll tell you how you could help me enormously," said Wrentham, "if you don't mind my putting it that way. Suppose she were missing and you had to produce an advertisement, supplementing a photograph. What would you say?"

Callender thought for a minute. "Well, I should call her a blonde of average height and sturdily built. The hair was very fair, though Gawd knows what colour it is now. Complexion highly coloured, like a girl from the country. Eyes, I can't say—"

A voice was heard below. "That's Raimont," said Callender, "the chap I was meeting here. He's a weird bird. Wears an imperial, pretends to be a Frenchman, and poses like a performing ape, but a damn clever fellow at his job. If you sit tight you'll hear something."

Wrentham duly sat tight. A hand clutching a tumbler appeared above the opening and was followed by a head. Callender lent a hand and rescued the whisky. Raimont was assured that he need not trouble to keep up his foreign nationality among the party, but Wrentham was greeted in terms which he had always supposed were either purely Victorian or survivals in the humorous press. M. Raimont, whose acquaintance with France was probably less than his knowledge of New Jewry, was not a very likeable sort of soul.

"It's a curious thing, Percy, but the Major and I were talking about the old days at the 'Metropolis'"—Callender winked significantly at Wrentham—"and Pamela Price happened to crop up. What colour were her eyes, do you remember?"

"Ask me another, dear boy," was all the information the conductor could supply. He added, however, certain comments on the lady's antecedents and spiritual home, which were more virile than polite.

"If I were a detective, Percy, I should say you didn't like that girl," laughed Callender.

"Well, it might have been worse. I always reckon she had designs on old Henry, and if she'd hooked him our occupation would have been gone. By the way, speaking well of the dead and all that, did you ever see a man alter like the old guv'nor? They say his affairs are in one hell of a state. Ah well!" and he sighed with simulated heaviness, "all I know is that the jury who brought him in as of unsound mind were the only ones who were ever right."

He noticed a look of interest on Wrentham's face. "Tell the Major about that night, laddy."

"I don't know, Percy. Doesn't seem the thing to talk about the old boy now he's gone."

"If I know anything," the other asserted, "you'll find the book of his life on sale at the kerbstones in a week or two, give you my word."

"What Raimont is alluding to, Major, is one night—how long ago?—oh, yes, about three months ago—the guv'nor came in one night and insisted on taking Wittle's part—you know Willy Wittle?"—("cleverest man in London to-day," interrupted Raimont)—"wanted to go on for him in the policeman scene. Gawd, what a night! We quietened him down after a hell of a shine and got him home, but the whole show had to stop—you'll understand, Major, there hasn't been a word of this got out."

Wrentham nodded. "Where's George Plumley now?" he inquired as nonchalantly as he could.

"That's what one or two would like to know," answered Callender. "If I could lay hands on him there's a little matter of twenty quid I might collect. You may safely bet your life there are two places G. P. won't be seen at, here and the 'Metropolis.'"

Raimont finished his drink and suggested a renewal. "Not for me, thanks," said Wrentham. "I must cut off now." They descended the ladder and went through to the office, leaving Raimont at the bar. A few couples were dancing to the music of the piano. Quite charming people they seemed. And quite a jolly little place. Of course there were bound to be a few bad eggs in every nest. He thanked Callender warmly at parting, explaining that he was leaving town early in the morning, but would he come and lunch somewhere next time he came up? And so, as the rain had at last ceased and the stars were visible in heaven, on foot to the hotel.

It was still far short of ten when he arrived, to find Ludo in the lounge, legs extended almost to the danger zone, and watching as one fascinated the famous parrot before the desk. He kept back the obvious greeting and up they went to his room, feeling, as he expressed it, like a second-hand Guy Fawkes. It did seem rather absurd, as Ludo admitted, with the traffic of the Strand in one's ears, to be talking seriously of murders and loot.

Wrentham told his evening's doings without comment. Nor had the other any questioning to do. "There's one thing about all this, Ludo," added Wrentham, "and it sounds too silly for words. You know when we were kids, if we wanted to make up our minds about something we used to say, 'If so and so happens I'll do it, and if not I won't,' and so on. At one time this afternoon I was losing about a tenner. Thinks I to myself, thinks I, 'If by seven o'clock I rise all square we're going to come well out of this job of work, and if not I'm not so sure.' When I tossed up with Porter I'd have bet my shirt on tails turning up as it did."

"The way of the world. Nero gambles while Rome is burning. Have a look at this," and he handed over a copy of the famous speech.

"You read it, Ludo?"

"In a way I have. I typed you out that copy," was the reply.

"Right, my lad. Do you agree about the extraordinary break in style, after the part where Peterloo is mentioned and where I said the messenger came in?"

"Yes, I think you are perfectly right about that. But with regard to a possible cryptogram in the last part, I'm afraid I'm not with you."

"Well, you know more about that than I do. Let's have a look at the last part again." They read it through word by word, with as much care as a hen consuming a bowl of water, drop by drop. "Tell me what you make of it, Ludo."

"I'm implicitly satisfied that it contains nothing beyond a hint. Let's put ourselves in the same situation. Here's Plumley, faced with a desperate crisis in his life, so desperate indeed that he actually carried poison on him. He sees in front of him his son—his only son, remember. In that second or two Plumley had a chance to right whatever wrong his conscience confronted him with. He probably knew that his son, if not in actual want, could at least do with the money; but, more than that, I think it was the act of reparation that counted."

"You think then it's no use testing this, word by word? It couldn't have been prepared for an emergency?"

"I think I follow you there. You mean just as kids prepare French phrases and drag them in by the scruff of the neck into their French essays. No, I really don't think Plumley had this peroration prepared. Given the necessity for such preparation, what was the necessity of preparing for other eventualities—flight, for instance? And again, if it was prepared for anybody it could only have been his son. If he had wished to forgive him there was only to make a paternal gesture or send along a cheque. No, I think the gist lies in the one phrase, 'Here before your eyes is money,' and, 'There to your hand and for your taking.' How do you interpret that? and in conjunction, mark you, with the reference to trees and grass and flowers."

"And order and gardens."

"Granted. The suggestion is, I take it, that at Hindhead or Hainton, and for the present we will consider the latter only, there is money in some form to be found. It is not necessarily present to the eye, but the acute should discern a clue. That clue concerns order and trees (say shrubberies) or gardens. You agree as far as that?"

Wrentham nodded. "If you recall the rough notes I got out on my ideas, you'll remember that I marked off Gordon as the likeliest man to help us there."

"Right-ho, then! Gordon's your pigeon. Now about Moulines. What clue had he in his possession that led him to the Hall? For the life of me I can't imagine any except his deductions from the speech."

"And," suggested Wrentham, "the almost certain fact that he recognised George Plumley."

"Yes, there's that. A further thing is, that if we made certain deductions from Plumley's acts, why shouldn't he have had similar facts and have made similar inferences? However, as Moulines is dead the dangerous thing is not what he knew but what he communicated."

"Or what the third man knew—the man who killed him."

"If I know anything about Moulines he would have kept his own counsel about anything he discovered. I suppose that if we had the money to spare and wanted to do the thing thoroughly we should employ private inquiry agents and really ferret out all Henry Plumley's history and antecedents, the whereabouts of his son and his son's wife, the nature of and necessity for all building alterations to the various properties during the last six months, the exact whereabouts of Plumley during my absences, and so on. You see the loose ends in the case, how involved it is, and yet what a lot we could do given unlimited time, money, and patience." Ludo flourished his glasses in the air as he concluded with, "And yet, I repeat, all the inferences lead me to one main idea, that the centre of everything is the killing of Moulines."

"You imply that, given that man, it will be easy to find out the rest?"

"Not necessarily, Geoffrey. I admit I'm a bit tedious as far as conveying my ideas goes. In my own mind I have no doubt that unless we find the man or men who killed Moulines we shall find the rest much more difficult. Take your own case, for example. If you go on any more night operations round the Hall there will probably be something found in the famous well that won't have any wire on it."

"Jolly good luck to him!" Wrentham seemed quite enthusiastic. "He may not reckon with my practice against the old Turk, and one thing I'm certain of: unless the whole world, including yourself, has been in a conspiracy of lying, my skull will take a damn sight more cracking."

"Thickness is not of necessity density," remarked Ludo dryly. "However, you do what you can about Gordon and let me know how the battle is raging. Above all, tell me the result of the identification parade with the lady. I'll keep you posted at this end. If necessary you can always run up here, whereas I can't get down to you."

But that was to be Wrentham's last visit to Town for many days. The question of thickness of skull was also to be settled at first tentatively, with Wrentham himself as the only begetter of the said experiment. But that, to be prophetic and proverbial, was to be between him and the gatepost.

CHAPTER XIII
THE PLOT THICKENS

"Mr. Gordon, sir," announced Helen. "Come in, Gordon!" cried Wrentham from the comfort of his chair. The gardener greeted his host with a mixture of respect and camaraderie. When you can interpret the cunningest wiles of a slow bowler it is not difficult to recognise the fact that you are meant to be made at home.

"I see you got my letter all right. What about a spot of whisky?"

"Don't mind if I do, sir," said Gordon. A spot—more or less—he got and the choice from the Major's cigarette case. Not till his man was settled properly did Wrentham open his light artillery.

"I expect you've been wondering, Gordon, what I wanted to see you about. The fact of the matter is, I was very upset, on coming home again, to hear about your leaving the Hall. If I may put it that way, the Hall seems a curious place without you, to say nothing of the cricket team. Just imagine if you had turned out for Bidwell last Saturday!"

"I shouldn't have done that, Mr. Geoffrey," declared Gordon emphatically. "I don't mind owning up to you that the chief reason I was upset about going to work elsewhere was that I shouldn't be able to play cricket. I haven't played this year, sir, and I ain't going to."

Wrentham let this settle for a second or two, then: "I can quite understand how you feel about it, Gordon, and devilish rough on you it is. You remember Mr. Travers?" Of course Gordon did. "He thought a lot of you, Gordon, and after I told him all about it yesterday we put our heads together to see what could be done. Mr. Travers is really in charge of everything now Mr. Plumley is dead. It was suggested you might like to tell me all about why you left the Hall so that we might see what could be done."

"Well, I'm very much obliged to you, sir, and that's a fact." Gordon was so genuinely grateful as to be upset. "I don't mind telling you, sir, because you understand it, that the day I get back to the old job will be the happiest since I left it."

"How are you getting on at Bidwell?"

"Oh, all right, sir, for that matter. Mr. Trent pays well enough, but money ain't everything by a long chalk. He's a good master too, sir—one of the best."

"Well now, Gordon, you must regard this chat as confidential, but I want you to give me a full account of what happened. Don't be afraid of being too detailed. Just bring in the whole bag of tricks." He spake, as the epic poets would have it, and thus encouraged Gordon began, not without a certain amount of diffidence and with the aid of a fill from the other's pouch.

"Mr. Plumley allust used to take an interest in the gardens, sir, and if any of the gentry were staying at the Hall he used to cart them round as pleased as Punch, as the saying is. He knew the names of everything better than I did. He used to go to all the big shows in town, and when he came down he allust had a lot of notes about things he wanted to try. Not that they was allust suitable, sir."

Wrentham nodded sympathetically.

"Mr. Plumley liked doing a lot of things himself, sir. He often used to say, 'Are the roses here yet, Gordon?' and if I said they were, he'd say, 'Well, don't put them in till I come out.' And it'd have been as much as my place was worth to have made a start before he did come out, sir. He didn't like digging, or at least

I never saw him do any. Planting was more in his line, so to speak."

"What did you think about that? I mean his working?"

"Well, sir, that's all in the day's work. Mr. Evesham of Morton, he'd know if anybody touched a single carnation in either of the big houses. I didn't mind that, sir, if it was a bit trying at times. After all, it's a poor thing if an owner can't do what he likes in his own garden when he's paying for it. And them as does can appreciate work better than we do; that's my opinion."

"A very excellent opinion too. Now, tell me, Gordon, what did Mr. Plumley like best?"

"You mean which part of the garden, sir? Well, he hadn't much use for either of the greenhouses or the ornamental beds on the lawn, except one he allust had filled with begonias, as, it was sheltered. The big bed, sir; you remember. He was very fond of the roses and the border; I think the border best. You see there isn't anybody who knows all about a border, sir, and what with the new sorts they're getting out every day it takes a bit of doing to be able to explain all about them as Mr. Plumley could."

Wrentham quietly renewed the glass.

"Then what happened last April, sir, struck me all of a heap. As you know, sir, I'd allust been most respectful to Mr. Plumley and ready to do anything he wanted. Well we did the border in October as usual, except some of the late stuff, and that we did the latter end of November. Anyhow, it was all ready by April, except for a bit of extry mulching and puttin' in annuals in one or two gaps where the frost had killed off. Then what do you think, sir?" He paused for his host to show incredulity, which he did as well as he could. "Mr. Plumley came down in April, and the first thing he did was to tell me that he was going to replant the whole border at once." He nodded his head as if to ask what the other thought about that.

There was no need for the listener to simulate surprise. His, "You don't mean it!" was spontaneous enough.

"Yes, sir; he ordered a lot of new stuff, and it all come down with him. He sent word for me to meet him at the border the first day he come down and then he sprung it on me. I own up, sir, I didn't look best pleased about it, but I didn't say anything. All I did say was to tell Mr. Plumley that he couldn't expect me to have the border looking as usual in the summer."

"What did he say to that?"

"He didn't say anything—at least not then, sir. He told me what he was going to have in. As far as I could make out, all I had to do was to get all the men and take up everything in the border and lay it on one side, ready for replanting if necessary. We got that done in the morning, sir, and the ground all re-dug, ready for planting. In the afternoon he gave me the idea of what he was going to plant, starting with the edging. 'We'll start off at each end,' he says, 'with a two deep of uvularia.' I could see from the way he looked at me he didn't expect me to know anything about that, but, as it happened, when I was over Colonel Hillyard's place, sir, I saw some in his rock garden."

"What exactly do you mean by two deep?" inquired Wrentham.

Gordon started to show him by the use of matches, but a piece of paper and a pencil made the illustration more easy.

"You see, sir, most people think a border runs straight up in a steady and regular slope from front to back, from pinks to hollyhocks as it were. If it was like that it'd be too regular, too stiff like, and so we break it up by running groups of stuff from one row back into the next. That's what we mean by 'two deep.' I don't mean there isn't a slope from back to front, but it isn't too straight, sir."

"Well, what happened to the—whatever it was you were planting? What is it anyway?"

"The uvularia? Well, that was where I slipped up Mr. Geoffrey. 'Don't you think, sir,' I says, 'that the uvularia is too mean a plant for a prominent place like this?' I spoke very respectful, but you can imagine what I felt like. Suppose your missus, sir, if you had one, was to put a pot of dandelions on the drawing-room table. What would you think about it? At any rate, sir, that's where I slipped up, as I was saying. Right in front of the men he let out. 'Damn you, Gordon,' he hollered right out at me, 'take your damned interfering face out of it!' It was pretty bad,

I can tell you, to put up with that, sir. And when I started to explain his face went absolutely red. 'Will you get to hell out of it?' he hollers. That's all there was to it, sir, and I goes back to the potting-shed. I didn't see no more of him, sir, and went home as usual, and Mr. Rendell, he come round about eight o'clock and told me Mr. Plumley had given orders that I was not to go near the place again. 'You can tell Mr. Plumley,' I says, sir, for I was that furious I could hardly speak, 'I wasn't going to set a foot in his damn garden anyhow.' After him speaking to me in front of the men like that I knew it'd be all over the village. And so it was, sir; at any rate, Mr. Trent sent for me the next day and I started in along with him the Monday follerin'."

"Surely it was most unlike Mr. Plumley to speak like that, Gordon."

"I couldn't understand it, sir. It fair knocked me all of a heap. He used to be a bit sharp now and again, but I tell you, sir, you could have knocked me down with a feather. I've thought about it a lot since, and if he wasn't drunk, sir, I've lost my mark."

"Surely not, so early in the morning. Still, I think you've been damn badly treated, Gordon. There's two sides to every question and we shall never hear Mr. Plumley's, but I must say, from what I knew before and what you have told me, that you haven't had a square deal. There's just one thing more I want to ask you. What happened to the border, after all?"

"Mr. Plumley he finished it himself, sir, with the under-gardeners, so young Masters told me. Tait come the week follerin'. They don't any of 'em understand anything about that border, sir. I allust did it myself with one of the men only."

"Now don't you worry about this any more, Gordon. I'll give Mr. Travers a full account of what you've told me and I'm sure he'll see you put right."

It did Wrentham good to notice the change in the gardener as he saw him out. He was as one who has been reprieved. If Wrentham should ever need a friend to go with him to the last inch there he was, ready to hand. Nor was there need for Wrentham to feel any reproach for his share of the conversation. Whatever happened, he made up his mind that if his influence could do anything Gordon should be put right. What a fine chap he was, and as straight as a gun barrel! And how decently he spoke about Plumley, though the Lord knows he hadn't much cause. Well, things were moving. How about the time? Nine-thirty.

The vicar was not yet back from a sudden call to the village so he decided to write Ludo a full account of the interview with Gordon. He got out his file of notes and jotted down the results of his visit to Town. He also filed the two photographs. Then when he was about to start on the letter he thought of making a copy. He was getting rather attached to that file of his. Looked like some army correspondence that had been circulating for a week or two. It would be a sound idea to keep everything together, and you never knew when you might have to refer to something. What about using an old army message book? There ought to be one handy upstairs with carbon paper all complete.

He sprinted up and found a battered survival of the war, much out of shape but quite good enough for the purpose. Rather tickle old Ludo—this pencil business, what? 'From our Seat of War,' made a good heading, and he settled down to it. So engrossed was he that he did not hear his father enter the room.

"Well, my boy, burning the midnight oil?"

Wrentham felt guilty. It is bad to hoard a secret, especially when one is not naturally secretive. Not that his father would ever notice anything unusual or, if he did, comment on it.

"Hallo, pater! I'm afraid you'll soon be thinking me either very industrious or very dissolute with these late hours."

The old man smiled. "Remember your 'Kim.' There's always the middle way."

"How did you find Wharton? He must be getting very old."

"I think he's in a bad way. Seventy-six next week, so Fred tells me. They don't think he'll last out the week. Yet those old people have perfectly wonderful powers of recuperation. I've known them almost dead one day and about again the next. By the way, did you know that Martin has a son?"

"Martin?" Wrentham did not see the connexion.

"Yes. He married Jane Wharton. I expect you don't remember that. The baby was born on Sunday morning." He stooped and made a note in his small book. Then Emma came in with some coffee and the vicar protested that there was a conspiracy to keep him out of his bed.

It was late when the letter was finished, and Wrentham yawned as he put away the thickening file. He felt very certain now that the balls were going to break well. That information from Gordon was the very thing needed. Plumley at work on the border, and practically alone for best part of a week! That could be checked up by a few judicious inquiries at the Hall. He wondered if Ludo knew anything about borders. A quiet bird, Ludo. You never knew how much he did know until it came out. He seemed to have the knack of assimilating all sorts of odd information. He could probably make his own clothes at a pinch! Typing out that copy of Plumley's speech, for example. Lord knows what he hadn't picked up during the course of the last year or two.

He yawned again. Pity there wasn't a book on gardening in the house. He ought to have asked Gordon for the loan of one. Hold hard, though. Wasn't there one in the spare room? He went up with his candle, quiet as a mouse. Yes, there was the book—"Gardening Made Easy."

When he was in bed he propped the candle on the chair and looked through the grubby volume. He was not to know that since the day when it was first published gardening had moved on like a bicycle from a boneshaker. However, he found a section, "Perennial Borders," and read of anchusas and hollyhocks, pinks and columbines. It conveyed little to him. Moreover, there was plenty of time for that in the morning. He gave a final yawn, blew out the candle, and snuggled into the bedclothes.

Outside, Burrows observed the extinguished light. He stepped from behind the giant elm and made his way across the paddock and out on the road. He moved carefully in the dark, and yet he had no limp. He stood for a minute, watching from the distance the intense shadow that marked the house, and then, keeping to the grass of the roadside, made his way towards the village.

CHAPTER XIV
A BATCH OF LETTERS

THIS IS TO HOPE you are quite well, dear fellow-blood-hound, as it leaves me at present. The attention of all ranks is drawn to the para, in King's Regulations concerning the saluting of superior officers, we being now appointed, with seniority of this date, detective of the first class, together with the grand order of the penetrative eye.

To cut the cackle, old scout, and come to the hosses, I expect my letter of yesterday showed you up a bit and awoke in your senile bosom some spark of that adventurous spirit which was yours ere you fell into your present state of mental torpidity. (Strictly copyright.) However, as I remarked before, to cut the cackle, etc., I cut off this morning, accompanied by one dog, Tango to wit, for the Hall. Clutched tightly were the photos of Mrs. G. P. An ostensible reason for the visit was to take Martin to inspect the cricket pitch and incidentally to congratulate him on the birth of a son and heir, said arrival on the strength reporting Sunday morning last. As a *quid pro quo* for your seconding me to the insurance business with Callender, I thought seriously of putting you up for godfather.

First, with my usual uncanny skill, I found out what the fair unknown had been up to in my absence. I told Martin I expected Miss Forrest was pleased to hear about the new arrival, women always being interested in babies. "She hasn't been here since Saturday," he informed me sheepishly. "Well, why don't you tell her now?" I asked. He didn't say anything to that; probably thought I was pulling his leg. Anyhow, he didn't say she wasn't there. Good that—what?

I asked him where Tait was. It happened that he was away with Masters, tracking down briars. It appears, and this will shed light on your abysmal ignorance, that although briars are not dug up until November it is usual to hunt them up in the summer in the hedges, and put a tape or some such distinguishing mark on them, to keep the other enterprising lads of the village gardens off the grass. Anyhow, it was a bit of luck for me, not that I couldn't have coped with it in any case, but there you are.

I tied Tango up to the gate, and it would have done your blasé heart good to have seen me doing the Red Indian act round the rhododendrons. I ran the lady to earth in the same old place and took up my stance by the sweetbriar hedge under the cypress; catching her half in profile and getting my excellent glasses well focussed. Then I pulled out the photos and started checking up. Result: washout—nothing! The nose had a suspicion of a turn-up and the hair was a topping gold and all the rays of the spectrum made it appear, through the glasses, like a halo. (Also copyright.) In other words, I was up a gum tree and the photos were about as much good as a top hat. She had the same fur on and the sketching paper was absolutely blank.

Well, sergeant-major, I stuck it for a quarter of an hour and all the time she was watching like a lynx and not even troubling to pretend to sketch. Then when I thought of giving it a miss in baulk—hold your breath—she opened a satchel, put the paper in it, pulled out a finished sketch and put it on the easel!

That was a bit of a staggerer, but there was more to follow. She opened the paint-box, fitted the water container, and wetted the sketch all over—to make it look as if just completed. Quite right, Watson. Go up one! Then she went on with the patience stunt, just sitting there and sweeping the horizon.

Now we have what I shall always consider my *chef-d'œuvre*. I don't mind revealing to you, old scout, that this part of the proceedings took me a few hours' practice with Tango. By hook or crook I had to see that sketch. Why? Perfectly obvious, my dear Watson. Show me the sketches you do, as Confucius remarked, and I'll show you the sort of woman you are. I loosed Tango and carried him to the hedge. Then I set him on. I admit things didn't turn out according to Hoyle. The first objective should have been that the intelligent animal was to seize the lady's skirt and I was to rush up, full of apologies and curiosity. I expect Tango was only human; anyhow he started well and then got the wind up. But what he did do was beyond my wildest dreams—he knocked the easel over. Enter on his heels, or paws, courteous officer and gentleman.

I grabbed that sketch like a streak of lightning and cussed several kinds of hell out of the dog. All the lady did was to draw herself up and clutch her fur with her gloved hand, not at all scared and about as frigid as a she-bear. I was full of apologies, but whether she was not in a coming-on disposition I cannot say. I do know she accomplished a hitherto unheard-of feat—she made me look and feel a fearful ass. She didn't say anything but "Thank you" and "Really it's quite all right," in a rich contralto voice. And her eyes! As our American brothers have it, "Oh, boy, her eyes!" Well, I put that sketch on the easel and bowed in my best manner and hopped it. Lord, what a fool I felt! A blind man could have seen through anything so obvious.

At the same time I don't mind adding that I have rarely felt more pleased with myself in my life, and that's saying something. The sketch was a thundering good one, and yet there was something fishy about it. Everything was there all right: old, red bricks, shadows on the lawn, and masses of green at the back where the beeches stand up (I know because I'd often thought of trying that bit myself), and yet, as I said before, there was a feeling in my mind that everything wasn't as it should be. When I got to the cricket pitch it dawned on me. Lord, I nearly kissed the dog!

You remember that match against Morton, when that slogger of theirs hit me for two sixes in one over, one into the garden under the old elm. Just as the fielder retrieved the ball, a bough, the biggest on the tree, fell off and scared the life out of Tom Smith. You know elm boughs have a nasty habit of doing that. Well, that's what was wrong with the sketch. She'd painted in a bough that hadn't been there for ten years!

Now to a person of your discernment, my dear old brother in crime, I need not hint that one thing stood out as clearly as an adjutant's wine account: that the lady was masquerading, and further, that the sketch must have been done from a photograph. "No time like the present" being the motto of us detectives, I went back by the village and called in to see Bevan the photographer. The *suaviter in modo* you can imagine for yourself. "An old friend of mine, Bevan," I said, "has asked me to send him a photo or two of the Hall. He particularly wants some of about ten years ago, or even longer. Now you've been here as long as I can remember. Did you ever do any?" He said he had done two, one the very view our friend was taking. Unfortunately he hadn't got the plate left. I asked him if he knew anybody in the village who had a copy. "If you can get hold of one," I told him, "give anything in reason for it and bring it to me."

(Vicar of Bidwell just arrived to tea. Am bolting upstairs.)

Now all I have to add is the sad *denouement*. After I had been in about an hour Bevan called to see me.

"After you'd gone I thought over who had some of those photos, and all I could think of was old Mrs. Mason, because I framed them for her." The chap was bucked as blazes. "I knew Miss Forrest had taken over all Mrs. Mason's things when she moved into the cottage, so

I ran down on my bike straight away and asked her if she would sell them."

He was apparently loath to continue. "What happened?" said I. "She shut the door in my face. However, she might let you have them if you asked her."

Now if that doesn't put the fat in the fire, what does? You'll admit the sequel to a brilliant morning's work was distinctly unfortunate. And as I've taken about three hours over this damned epistle I'll shut up.

(Signed) G. Wrentham (Lt.-General)

P.S.—Very urgent. I want to get an exact plan of the Hall border, and with that four-eyed sleuth abroad I don't feel like risking it. Will you do us a low-down service? Send an anonymous telegram to S. F. from Chelsea, asking her to meet a friend at Thetford, three-thirty to-morrow. That should make the coast clear.

P.P.S.—As Lodge Cottage is not under the Hall estate you can't help me. Suggest approaching Roberts, Hare's steward, for news as to how exactly the fair S.F. got possession.—G.W.

St. Giles' Chambers
Norwich

Personal.

Dear Geoffrey,

The news I have for you is not, I fear, very satisfactory. All we have been able to gather is that after realisation there will be a tremendous deficit. The most optimistic prediction is a dividend of five shillings. Even that I should not build on.

With regard to Apex Motors, proceedings have been instituted in the courts for reconstruction of the company. It is rumoured that the total deficit may amount to two million pounds. There is no uncalled capital to be called up.

In spite of all this I hope in the very near future to have some excellent news for you. Developments are taking place over the Hainton estate, which is likely to be in the market. I think we may with confidence say that your very natural worries will soon be over.

Come and see me some time next week. We are always glad to see you, my boy, even if there is not what we call business to talk about.

Your afft. godfather,
WORTLEY HALLETT
BELLINGHAM HOUSE

DEAR G.,

Still up to the ears in work, but a ray of light is coming through the gloom, namely, that I hope to be turned finally adrift from this highly desirable West End mansion inside the week. Chalton affairs were disposed of yesterday, and I expect, with your knowledge of the sporting Press, you have seen the announcement *re* disposal of the stud. As it has been advertised extensively abroad and time is being allowed for foreign buyers to get to the sale, there should, Warlingham tells me, be some sensational competition. To be sordid, the exchequer ought to flourish. Hindhead will be settled by Saturday, provided you continue to remain in the front line, which I imagine is a remarkably sound dug-out.

Your news about Gordon was splendid and represents some excellent staff work, almost as good as you appear to think it. We shall have to do what we can for him. Seriously, the news is tremendously important. If the advice is not too late and you haven't waded in already, get a perfectly accurate plan of the Hainton border, as near scale as possible, and send me a copy. The little knowledge I have of gardens is not likely to be of much use, but I am tremendously interested.

A bit of news that will interest you is that the liquidator is regarding the unexpired lease of the Hall estate and the shooting rights as an asset. This lease does not expire until Michaelmas twelvemonths. Hare, however, is now in a position, by virtue of a disentailing deed, to sell the whole estate outright, and it is expected that our part will be put up with the rest, so that the property may be acquired as a whole. Some argument as to values will doubtless go on before final settlement, but some sort of composition will certainly be arrived at. The importance to us is the comparative imminence of the sale. In other words, the motto seems to be, "What thou doest, do quickly."

As to the P.'s, I can get little information. Saw C., who reported a very jolly meal with you. He says Mrs. P. was seen recently at the "Good Intent," and a day or two later G. P. was seen at the "Blue Cockatoo," having tea with a lady unknown, so it is possible that there has been a domestic split.

I am sorry to be such an unproductive partner in the concern. In a few days I hope to be full in the fray and making myself the usual kind of nuisance.

To answer by the book, I subscribe myself,

From my hermitage (which may Allah blast!)

L. TRAVERS
(Undertaker. Estates a Speciality).

21, ST. WITHOLDS
NORWICH

DEAR ARTHUR,

You are the man on the spot, and however clear a report may be there is bound to be something at the back of your mind which I cannot see. M. W. is decidedly unlikely, as you say, but then our trade flourishes on improbabilities. Memo, of movements herewith. I should certainly nail him down at the earliest possible moment. I shall be definitely at Langham to-morrow night. Run over between eight and nine if you can.

With regard to the Staffordshire figure called "St. Paul," if it is as you describe it and is only damaged in the tree at the back; sound Rummage by all means. If he will part go as high as thirty bob, but for God's sake don't excite his cupidity. That man has a grasping nature.

Until to-morrow then, and many thanks,

Yours as ever

JOHN DELANE

CHAPTER XV
IN WHICH TRUTH WILL OUT

"A NOTE for you, sir," announced Helen, coming into the break-fast-room.

Wrentham read it and inquired who brought it.

"Young Sid Rummage, sir."

"Ask him to tell Mr. Burrows it will be all right, will you, Helen?" and the maid departed.

He read the note again. Sooner or later, he supposed, the truth would have to come out. Yet Burrows might be perfectly sincere in his desire to have a morning off and take advantage of being in the neighbourhood to visit the heath country. One never knew what those police fellows did in their spare moments. Burrows might be a keen amateur photographer. Look at Delane—forgetting all about bloody murder and discussing Staffordshire figures. The other one, too, showing a sound knowledge of old-time rifles. What a thing it was to have a hobby! Wasn't there a chap whose hobby had been dodging the police? What was his name? Peace—that was it—Charles Peace. How would "Geoffrey Wrentham" sound in the "Police Gazette"? Not very convincing and rather like a burglar from the "Pansy Library." Well, criminals couldn't be choosers. What about a stouter pair of shoes and giving Tango a run? No, that wouldn't do. Too much game about.

There was not much talking done during the early stages of that walk, and the little that was needed was furnished by Wrentham. Burrows was a good listener. He would nip in with a local query or a leading question and withdraw discreetly again for the answer to come. Why was the farm called Harberry? What was the origin of all the honeysuckle? Was it possible to rear partridges? What did the Major think of the British Legion? And so on. The other's was the difficult rôle to play. Amid the medley of information, his thoughts had to be principally concerned with the main problem of the walk; what to tell when the time came and what to conceal.

The morning itself was singularly serene. The faintest of winds made the sun scarce felt, and yet the sun was dominant. Across the fen the birches stood grey, with here and there the flash of a silver stem. Last year's heather retained a faint purple, and the warm brown of dead brakes still lay drowsily at the foot of the new. Now and again came the smell of sweetbriar or the faint, fine perfume of the honeysuckle, high embowered among the thorn. The timid yellow of the faded gorse was clear against the honeycombed warrens. Banks of flaming cankerweed or the winish ragged-robin made flaunting furrows over the flat expanse. Above, the clouds moved scarce perceived and beneath the foot the turf re-sprang traceless.

"What do you think of it? Come up to your expectations?"

"I didn't know there was such scenery in the county, and me born and bred in it. When you were speaking about it the other day, Major, I thought you were piling it on a bit."

"Well, you'll know what to do when you leave the hospitable Rummage. Tell the glad news in the visitors' book, if he keeps one. How long do you expect to be before finishing off?"

"That'd be hard to say. The case has too many unusual features for my liking and too many obvious solutions. You read many detective stories, Major?"

"Read 'em! I've wallowed in them. Whenever a bloke was going on leave he used to bring me a new consignment. Jolly good for passing the time when there was nothing doing."

The detective shook his head despondently. "So have I, and never a darn thing did I learn from one of them. Always seemed to have too much hard graft to do any of these show-man tricks."

The other said nothing. Burrows was not one to angle for compliments, and if half Delane had let fall were true, there was not a better man at his job in the provinces. And while he was ruminating the detective caught him clean in the wind.

"I don't mean we can't all be theatrical at times, Major. Like to patronise a crystal-gazer and learn a bit about your past life?"

"Tell on, provided I can stoke up my pipe and get my back against this tree."

The detective, too, squatted in the pine needles and produced a blackened briar. "On Saturday night," he began, "you muffled your feet in tennis shoes and, by way of the orchard, entered the Hall gardens. You spent a considerable time examining the interior of a certain well and returned by the drive and the low meadows. On Monday afternoon you went to town with Captain Travers, sharing a taxi with him to the 'Somerset.' You did not leave the hotel but telephoned to some friends at the Melton Club. Later in the evening you also rang up Bellingham House. The following day you spent in a solicitor's office, the Melton Club lunching with Captain Travers, and the Medley Club dining with a Mr. Callender of the Metropolis Theatre. You returned to the 'Somerset,' meeting Captain Travers there. You came back to Norfolk by the eight a.m. and the same evening interviewed Gordon, late head-gardener at the Hall, giving him some good news. You were writing until late and fell asleep at about one in the morning. How's that?"

"Out! I mean jolly good!" was the victim's whole-hearted verdict. "I am only surprised at two things: why you didn't tell me what I dreamt and why you chaps should think it necessary to put the bloodhounds on the tracks of a perfectly respectable citizen like myself."

"Look here, Major. Let's drop all this pretence. What exactly were you doing at the Hall and what did you see?"

"To answer the first, looking for truth."

"Looking for truth?"

"Surely you know that truth is said to lie at the bottom of a well!"

The detective smiled, but with a touch of grimness and exasperation. "All right, Major. Produce the lady in your own time."

"One thing you didn't mention about Saturday: that I visited the Hall in the morning and for quite *bona fide* reasons. What you don't realise, Burrows, is that I know every leaf and stone at the Hall, or did do before the war. I went over all the gardens with Tait (I was really expecting to find Gordon there), and had a good look at the new well. Suppose I inadvertently dropped something down it—something desperately secret and important. Why not use the creepers and try to recover it at night?"

The detective said nothing.

"In any case, to come down to brass tacks, I give you my word, as solemnly as if I were on oath, that my business of that Saturday night had nothing to do with André Moulines, and that nobody was more amazed than I when he was found dead. By the way, how did you trace me out, at least through the orchard?"

"Well, in the orchard you twice trod full on some goat dung and across the meadows on more than one mole heap."

"The way of transgressors is hard! Now I'll add exactly what I did see," and he told of the motor-bicycle and the man in the coat.

The detective struggled between anger and dismay. "Good God, Major! Do you know what you have done?" The realisation was too much for him, and if teeth can really be gnashed with rage the detective's were.

The other was aloofly apologetic. "If you'd been absolutely fair and square over those shoes, Burrows, I should probably have loosened up at the time. You got my goat and now I've got yours. Then, again, I was going to tell you all about it after the inquest if you hadn't hinted at my coming to you with information." Yet his better nature somewhat asserted itself. "I suppose in a court of law I'd cut a damn poor figure and get blue, merry hell cursed out of me."

They were on their feet now—the one slowly knocking his pipe out against the tree and the other trying to get a hold over himself, but failing badly.

"Well, if that's all your training and the army taught you about discipline no wonder we nearly lost the war."

Wrentham went white with anger. The two men remained staring at each other like a couple of terriers. The detective gave way first. "Let's be moving, Major. This cross talk won't get us anywhere."

A mile on the homeward journey brought both to their senses, and it was the Major who first broke the silence. "I owe you an apology, Burrows. It was unpardonable of me to keep back that evidence."

The other softened at once. "That's all right, Major. I had a good deal to do with it. But what you fellows don't appreciate is that such business as that over your shoes is perfectly legitimate with us. All the same, I agree that it would have been more decent of me to have questioned you openly. There's one other thing. With us discipline is discipline and the law comes first. My orders are the only things that go with me. In spite of that, I knew more about you than most, and I'll own that your connexion with this business was inexplicable to me. You'll admit that you might have got yourself into the devil of a mess."

"Oh, I know that," was the cheerful reply. "Also, between you and me, I'm not out of it yet."

The detective appeared to agree. "That creeper story certainly sounded too good to be true."

"Perhaps your next bulletin of my movements will manage to untie that knot," suggested Wrentham, and the other laughed.

Wrentham, as he explained on leaving his companion at the straight road to the village, had to see Roberts, and noon would be a good time to catch him. He promised that at any time his services should be available, and so ended, at least temporarily, a business that each felt to be far from satisfactory. Wrentham was by no means happy in his mind. Sleuthing was the very devil for getting a man off the straight and narrow. It was all very well for Ludo and his twopenny vantage-ground, reclining at ease in the seats of the scornful. The fact of the matter was that he had cut a remarkably poor figure, and he was aware of it. And not only a poor figure but a close resemblance to a crooked one. By the time he had got through the wood and in sight of the cottage he felt like washing his hands of the whole affair. Fortunately Roberts was in the garden earthing up celery and had caught sight of him, so that before he knew where he was he was again on the trail.

"Morning, Roberts. Can you spare a minute?"

The steward scraped his boots on the spade and came out of the gate, and Wrentham moved slowly on the back way.

"Mr. Travers was down here last week-end, Roberts, and he was wondering exactly how Lodge Cottage came to be separated from the Hall estate. I wonder if you know all about it?"

"I think I can manage that, sir. If you remember at the time the Hall estate was first separated, Mrs. Mason, the squire's old nurse, was living there with her nephew. There was some talk then that if the estate hadn't been entailed the squire would have given her the cottage, but all he could do was to keep it under the village part of the estate so that she should never get turned out."

"But she isn't dead, is she?"

"No, sir. Young Tom got killed in the war and she went to live with a sister of hers somewhere in the shires."

"Then why didn't it revert to the Hall estate?"

"Well, you see, sir, Mrs. Mason got special leave when she thought of leaving the village, for her niece to come and live there, and the squire agreed to it."

"Her niece! But Miss Forrest isn't her niece?"

Roberts looked surprised. "She is, sir. If I may put it that way, she looks a cut above the Masons, but what with this new education and what not you never know where you are."

"Um!" That cooked that goose then. He thanked the steward and started on his way back through the wood. Again an impulse made him turn round and he saw what some curious kink of mind had started restless within him. Something peculiar about the man there had been which had brought to his mind some formless suggestion that refused to declare itself. He had it! It was the cap!

Common enough these peaked and flapped monstrosities had once been: every steward and gamekeeper had sported one. And correspondingly rare they had now become. He could not recall the last time he had run across one. Yet in a few days he had seen two: this one, and the other on the unknown remover of the bicycle. Roberts himself, too, short and sturdy, the very spit of the other fellow.

And then he had to laugh. Was there ever a peaceable village so filled with sleuths and murderers, crooks and suspects, detectives and disguises! Just because Roberts had a certain kind of cap he had to be added to the noble army of mystery-mongers. What a priceless ass he had come near making himself over that girl! Come near it? He blushed as he thought of the elaborate machinery he had urged into being for espionage in the Sylvia Forrest case. Good Lord! What must that girl be thinking about him? An apology? No, dash it! That would be worse than ever.

Out of this self-castigation there emerged safely one ray of self-congratulation—the border. That at least was no mare's nest. No bats in the belfry about that. He could kick himself about that anonymous letter to clear the girl out of the way for Saturday's inspection. But why trouble about that now? Why not go up to the Hall in the afternoon? To blazes with the woman, in any case.

As he regained the road his father, returning from the village, met him. "Well, my boy, had a good walk?"

"Topping, pater. It's good to be alive this morning."

The vicar agreed. The morning had drawn him out of his study. He stooped down to smell some of the stocks on the crescent bed.

"I've been thinking, pater, we might make a thundering good border where that old shrubbery is. What do you say to digging out those old roots in the autumn and making a good one?"

"I think it's a capital idea. There wasn't much attention paid to borders in those days, but your mother always wanted to make a bank of it and plant annuals there."

"I was looking at the Hall border the other day, pater, and I'm sure we could get quite as good a one here. What do you say to coming along with me this afternoon and having a look round?" The vicar halted between pleasure and regret. "After your nap, that is to say," and so it was agreed.

He was feeling decidedly better. If Ludo wanted hustle he was going to get it. Now there was no need to worry about the girl there was a day saved. There might have been still more saved if Ludo had added the tag about hastening slowly, but that, luckily for him, Wrentham was not to know.

CHAPTER XVI
LILIES AND LADIES

MATURER REFLECTIONS after lunch, Induced by the preparation of a further duplicate dispatch for the sleeping partner, sent Wrentham somewhat on another tack. He recognised that the discovery of Sylvia Forrest's relationship to the late occupier of Lodge Cottage, while going far to exonerate that young lady from any suspicion of duplicity, yet took no account of the episode of the missing branch. It seemed, indeed, that the policy of inducing the lady to abandon temporarily any possible surveillance of the Hall and its grounds was not after all entirely unjustified. There might be a perfectly good and sufficient reason why she should pose as an artist; perhaps, on the other hand, there was not. Was it better then to adhere to the original plan and wait for the arrival of Ludo's anonymous telegram, or, now that matters were *en train*, to run the risk of bringing himself further to the lady's notice?

Finally he decided to let things remain as they were, that is, to accompany his father as they had arranged. After all, if he did go on a Saturday it would mean asking Tait to come up specially, and he hadn't thought about that. Moreover, there was nothing remarkable in two perfectly respectable gentlemen spending a bucolic afternoon among the flowers.

There was his letter to post, and so it was not difficult to go round by the village instead of taking the more obvious shortcut across the meadows. Few people were about, for hay harvest was in full swing; everywhere the air was fragrant with the scent of it. The village drowsed peacefully and, save for the sound of Paygrim's anvil and the drone from the little school, might have been cast in a repose as deep as befell the wanderer from Sleepy Hollow. As they drew near the potting-sheds, however, quite a hum of voices could be heard. Through the open door, seated at ease on boxes, could be seen Tait and Burrows. Lounging against the wall was Martin, and the sole worker appeared to be Masters, who was putting an edge on the long pruners. The voices stopped as the two made their appearance. The men rose courteously at the vicar's salute and Wrentham made himself spokesman.

"I was telling the vicar, Tait, about your wonderful border, and he and I agreed that we should very much like to do something of the sort at the vicarage this autumn. I wonder if you would mind showing Mr. Wrentham round, in spite of the heat?"

Tait agreed with alacrity and was about to put on his coat.

"Don't do that, please," said the vicar. "To tell you the truth, if I was sure the story wouldn't get abroad, I should take my own off."

Burrows here interposed. "Before you go, Vicar, would you mind settling a little argument we've been having. It's about that cap," and he pointed to a gamekeeper's cap, hanging from a nail over the tool rack by the tapes of its unfastened flaps. The vicar and his son regarded it with the requisite attention. "What I say is that these caps are still very common."

To start the vicar on local history or reminiscences was equivalent to winding up a clock. Without more ado he went into the history of such caps: King Edward's partiality for them, their gradual passing out before the war, and, as far as his experience went, their comparative rareness in these parts. "In fact," he explained, "like most unusual things—because, after all, a cap with inventions, or what Major Wrentham would call 'gadgets,' of any kind must be considered unusual—they gradually went out of fashion. First from the master to the keeper, and then to that usual receiver of discarded fashions—the labourer. Whose hat is it?"

"Mine, sir," said Tait, "and I don't mind saying you've told Mr. Burrows just what I told him, except put a bit different so to speak. Now what would you say I have that cap for, sir?"

Wrentham hazarded a guess. "To keep your ears warm in winter; possibly to keep off chilblains."

"No, sir. As I was telling Mr. Burrows, you'd never guess in a hundred years. In my last place we had a very long pergola, set a bit too close. When we used to lay out the roses for pruning we used to have on gloves to protect our hands against them, but in spite of having got one or two nasty tears, nobody thought of that dodge for protecting their face and ears. I used to get laughed at a goodish bit, but what does it matter what you wear as long as you're comfortable?"

"Quite right," said the vicar. "Where shall I hang my coat?" and everybody laughed except the maker of the suggestion who had been in earnest.

He moved towards the gardens, accompanied by Tait; Wrentham, waiting for Burrows, brought up the rear.

"With regard to that cap," said he. "You remember my remarking on it to you this morning. Now it's very extraordinary but it's the second I've seen to-day," and he gave the detective an account of his meeting with Roberts. Whether as a peace-offering or not, the other had also his information to give.

"Between ourselves, Major, Roberts was the only person seen by Martin when he was going for the doctor that night. He insisted that it was Roberts he passed at about eleven, going apparently to his cottage. I approached Roberts discreetly enough and he denied being out of his house after ten. I know he left the pub at nine-thirty." Wrentham said nothing.

"Now it looks as if I shall have a job of searching the district for caps and looking up Tait's whereabouts on that night and the whole of his previous history. Then people expect miracles from us and think we're grossly overpaid."

At the door he stopped. "Aren't you coming in to have a look?" asked Wrentham.

"Afraid not, Major. There's one little job I must do, and then I've to catch the four-thirty for Norwich. I ought to be back in a couple of days at the latest."

"Well, I'll keep my eyes open," said Wrentham, "and you might look me up as soon as you get back." He passed through into the quadrangle and round to the gardens.

His father and Tait were standing before the border, the gardener pointing out, apparently, things of unusual interest. About a hundred feet long and ten to twelve feet deep, the border curved gently to embrace in its ample arc the bulk of the west lawn. Colour ran riot; indeed the foreshortened side view made a great bank of bloom. More to the front the hues dispersed themselves. "If it's looking like this after that April replanting which Gordon was so worried about, what would it have looked like normally?" thought he. Two clumps above all caught the eye—a noble group of palest delphiniums and a mass of white lilies.

He smiled at the enthusiasm his father was showing.

"Well, pater, what do you think of it?"

"It's really wonderful!"

"I was telling Mr. Wrentham, sir," explained Tait, "that the end of July is between seasons for a border and about a week's time will be better. None of the phlox are out properly and they always make a great show."

"What do you advise us to do, Tait?"

"Well, sir, if I were you I'd get my ground dug and manured and then wait till October or November. A lot of these clumps will have to be thinned and you might as well have them. If you send your man up I'll do my best for you. The rest he can get from any of the well-known firms."

"That's very kind of you," said the vicar, and his son endorsed the plan. Then, "Look here, pater; if you really want to see Mrs. Martin, cut along now and meet me here again when you're ready. I want to talk over one of two things with Tait."

And now for it. "I wonder if you would mind if I took down the exact plan of the border, Tait?"

"Not at all, sir. Shall I call the names out to you and you take them down?"

"That will do splendidly." He produced paper and pencil. "Won't it be rather a long job?"

"Not so long as it looks, sir. Mr. Plumley had the border made to meet in the middle, that is, it starts the same from each end."

"Which is the middle then?"

"That clump of lilies, sir, is the middle. It's the only thing that isn't in duplicate."

"Right-ho!" said Wrentham. "Let's make a start here," and he moved off to the end. The list came from left to right as he faced, completing a back row and working gradually to the front. He found it easy to mark off the groups in circles and odd shapes. The difficulty lay in spelling, and he shrewdly suspected in Tait unique methods of pronunciation. Many of the plants he knew already, and in the event of a check being required he could consult an encyclopaedia. Still, he put down with meticulous care everything as supplied—helianthus, anchusa, hollyhock, Michaelmas daisy, helenium, delphinium, and all the long roll of that glorious mass.

"What about sorts, sir?" Tait suddenly inquired.

"What do you mean?"

"Named varieties, sir. Phlox now," and he consulted a label. "This is 'James Sandham.'"

"Carry on," said Wrentham resignedly. "We'd better put down the whole bag of tricks." And on they went, through phloxes, achilleas, pyrethrums, erigerons, and ultimately to the edging. Here violas, aubretia, and the coarse arabis were interspersed with carnations and the heavy scented pinks. "You've left out this chap," Wrentham pointed out.

Tait consulted the label. "Uvularia that one is," as much as to say that accidents might happen with any well conducted inquiry.

"Don't think much of it, do you?"

"Can't say I do, sir. The last time I looked at it I thought to myself, 'You won't have much longer to live.' Penstemons are the things for there, sir."

"They'd certainly make a better show," agreed the other. "By the way, how is it that certain things can be found in different rows—Michaelmas daisy and delphiniums, for instance?"

"That's a question of sorts, sir. Some grow to nearly six feet and others to only two, and so on intermediate. It's the same with a lot of the plants. Some sorts grow much taller than others. Then again there's the question of the time of flowering. Take that erigeron," and he pointed to a mass of mauve running back to a clump of pink phlox. "Just as that gets over its best at the end of August, the phlox will make a show and last out the autumn. The same with the dwarf heleniums."

Finally it was finished. There is no finer feeling than to do a job of work and to look on it and find it good. "Well, I'm grateful to you, Tait." A treasury note changed hands. The vicar had not appeared. "I think I'll be pushing along now."

"Thank you, sir. Any help I can give I'll be only too pleased to."

In the kitchen they found the vicar learning from Masters the whole art of summer pruning. Wrentham cozened his conscience by the solemn dedication of a border and whole avenues of cordon trees if the good ship "Adventurers, Limited" should ever come safe to port.

They returned by the drive at the vicar's request. It was cooler and the trees would make shade most of the way. Wrentham felt remarkably pleased with himself. Everything had gone swimmingly, and there remained nothing to do now but to get down to the cryptogram business. With a bit of luck he might steal a march on Ludo yet. So satisfied was he indeed that at the sight of the cottage some imp of mischief took possession of him.

"Don't you think it would be rather decent of you, pater, to call on Miss Forrest now you are passing by? She might think it a bit peculiar if she saw you."

"If you think so, my boy." The vicar's years were but visits. For him it was merely a part of the day's work. Besides, he had intended to ask her if she would like to lend a hand with the Sunday school. So they turned in at the grass path and came to the cottage door, hung to suffocation with its mass of honeysuckle. The vicar tapped with his knuckles. His son regarded his watch. A quarter-past four.

To his immense surprise a drowsy voice said, "Come in." He almost took to his heels and ran, so sure had he been that the house would have been closed to them. The vicar lifted the latch and entered. Wrentham bent his head and stooped down to the cool, stone floor. His sight was obscured by his father, but he heard an exclamation as of surprise and dismay.

Sylvia Forrest was lying in a Morris chair, a rug round her feet and some sort of white arrangement round her head. She was making as if to rise. The vicar protested profusely.

"Really, Miss Forrest, I'm very sorry. I had no idea. May I call again some other time?"

"No, please don't go, Mr. Wrentham." She moved from the sideways position and sat back in the chair, holding to the shaped arms. "I was really expecting the baker's boy when I said 'Come in.' My maid has gone out for a walk and I had such a splitting headache that I took some aspirin and drew the curtains and went to sleep."

She waved forlornly with her hand. "Please do sit down."

It almost looked as if, by some mysterious foresight, their visit had been anticipated, for two chairs stood handy under the path window.

"This is my son, Major Wrentham," said the vicar, and the Major bowed.

"The Major and I have met before," and she smiled quite friendly.

The vicar looked surprised.

"I'm afraid Tango made rather a mess of Miss Forrest's sketch the other morning," Wrentham explained, relating the circumstances, largely to cover his own confusion.

They remained standing. The vicar was apparently debating how to make a happy exit and Wrentham let his gaze wander round the room. It was a typical country parlour, with rag rugs, polished chairs, and the usual mahogany side-table. Only the pictures were vastly different—fitter for a cabaret or an advanced drawing-room than this quiet, stone-flagged haven. In one corner stood a gramophone and near it the easel. On the large rug before the grate a black and white cat was sleeping, as if in anticipation of winter. On the mantelpiece was an oil lamp, and in a tall, green vase a bunch of carnations, which had probably come from the Hall gardens. His father's voice recalled his wandering thoughts.

"We really must be going, Miss Forrest. No, please don't get up. I can see you are still very unwell. I am very sorry indeed we broke in on your rest. May I call again some other time?"

Wrentham was feeling very uncomfortable: the atmosphere was a most unusual one for him. His father, of course, was quite used to that sort of thing. In his cynical frame of mind it was quite easy to imagine the pathetic tone somewhat overdone.

"Please call whenever you like. I have to go to Town tomorrow for a few days, but perhaps I may send round my maid some time with an invitation for you both, if you are free."

The vicar expressed his pleasure at the prospect and Wrentham mumbled something. She gave them a delightful, though rather wan, smile as they bowed themselves out, and one of the two, at least, was by no means sorry to see daylight again.

Not very romantic that, he thought, as they made their way along the path. But what a finely modulated voice she had! Extraordinary a girl like that being associated with the Masons! The vicar stopped to do up his shoe-lace and Wrentham idly turned his head. He showed no sign of remarking anything unusual.

"Now, pater, show a leg. My tongue is hanging out for a cup of tea."

"Not more than mine, my boy, and if it wasn't too hot I'd take twenty yards and beat you across the meadow."

Wrentham laughed merrily. "If it were a bit hotter I'd take you on. What did you think of your parishioner?"

"She seems a very nice woman—a very nice woman! What was your opinion?"

"I'm not much of an authority in any case, pater, but I'm hanged if I know."

Which was perfectly true. Why had she said her maid was out when he distinctly saw her peeping from the front bedroom window? From there, with a good pair of glasses, it would be easy to see what was going on round the Hall. The stairs had been in his sight all the short period of the visit, and there had been no time for her to get there since. That headache didn't sound any too genuine, and she was either an amazingly plucky soul or a devilish curious one or she'd have turned them out of the house straight away.

On a table by her chair he had noticed a saucer and some lemon, for whitening the hands he supposed. People with splitting headaches don't usually trouble about their hands. Then, if she were going to London, what about Ludo's message? Wouldn't it be just as well to see what did happen and whether she did go to Thetford or not?

They were already going in at the drive before he spoke again, and his father had forgotten about the visit and was planning a personal pruning assault on the orchard.

"Why worry about womenfolk anyhow. Come out to-night and use your superfluous energy, pater, and I'll bowl you twice in twenty balls."

"Done!" was the reply. "If you wait till the shadow gets over the lawn I'm your man."

So off to ask Wallace to come along, and then to tea.

CHAPTER XVII
READING BETWEEN THE LINES

THE MORNING PRODUCED a letter from Ludo, announcing briefly his intention of coming down on the Monday. If everything was satisfactory that is to say; if not, a telegram would meet the case. Otherwise he would arrive on the tea train. Any news could wait until then.

So off Wrentham went to give the glad news to Emma, so that the spare room might be got ready, and to tell his father. That done, and the morning being outrageously fine, he took his file of papers and the gardening book under the elm tree, being minded, from the depths of a deck chair and over a pipe or two, to get really down to an examination of the collected data of the previous afternoon. He had meant to put in the evening at it, but Wallace had come along to bowl and his son to field, and altogether it must have been well past the usual hour for dinner when they knocked off cricket. Then two or three village stalwarts had turned up for billiards, and not being able to resist the click of the balls he had joined them; and it was nearly half-past ten before the house was cleared. Then that walk in the morning and the rest of the day in the air had made him so amazingly sleepy that he had simply crawled off to bed and slept like a top.

It was therefore a very serious and tenacious investigator who set to work, making up for what was really lost time. Where to start he had not the foggiest notion. Perhaps it would be as well to make an inked copy of the half of the border so as to be able to scribble notes on it and then rub them out. He found the top of a cardboard box and copied out his plan, with the cardboard cut roughly to shape. That looked more like business.

What about putting down the rows in order? Or would it be better to check up some of the rows? He decided on the latter and hunted up the herbaceous border in the gardening book. To his astonishment he found that out of a book of two hundred pages a scant two and a half were allotted to that section. Then, too, many of the flowers were not mentioned at all, and as for those named varieties on the importance of which Tait had so much insisted, they didn't exist. He looked at the front for the date of publication—1892. Phew! There was only one thing to do, therefore—to get a book that did have them in. Off therefore in search of Wallace.

Wallace hadn't a book. He took a weekly gardening paper, and that, together with experience, sufficed for all his needs. Wrentham took advantage of the opportunity to explain about the scheme for a new border at the vicarage and expected the gardener to be far from enthusiastic, especially about consulting with Tait. To his surprise Wallace showed considerable enthusiasm. Fortunately, too, young Wallace was profiting by the school-less Saturday morning to get his hand in, and he was dispatched by bicycle to Gordon with a note. With luck he would be back in an hour.

Wallace's real views might have amused the Major had he heard them, for as soon as he had returned to the elm the assistant thought it necessary to comment to his immediate overlord on the additional work.

"When you get as old as I am, my lad," said Wallace, "you'll know that the more work a master makes the less trouble for the gardeners. If the vicar now, or Mr. Geoffrey, come and said we ought to put a pigsty on the front lawn, all I'd say would be that it was just what I'd been thinking and when was I to start on it." So saying he left the other to go on mulching raspberry canes and proceeded to inspect at his leisure the scene of the proposed alterations.

In the meanwhile Wrentham was wrestling with his plan. He tried every row from back to front, or at least such rows as he could make out. Only in the rarest instances did plants form a line in that direction. The fact that they got smaller and closer towards the foreground made that almost impossible. Often a line started well and then broke off with choice of left or right. In any case there was no semblance of a word to be found.

He started working across where there were certainly well-defined lines, especially at the back. He wrote down initial letters, but never a trace of a word could he find. Then he tried wandering anywhere from left to right. This produced "Help" (very exciting that!), "Papa," "Scalp," and other short words of haphazard location and evidently wholly fortuitous.

How about a cryptogram? That would imply the use of twenty-six symbols. He checked the letters. Not nearly enough. Then what about the rows? The front row alone had more than twenty plants. So he took down the names of the front row as if they were an enormous addition sum, first with the left hand letters of each in a straight line downwards and with the rest making a ragged right edge, then with the last letters of each word in a straight line downwards and the left edge in the air. There was not a glimmering of sense to it anywhere.

Just then Joe Wallace arrived with two books. He apologised for being late owing to a puncture. Late! Wrentham looked at the time. Good Lord! An hour and a half he had been puzzling over the damn thing! He groped in his pocket for a tip and then had a look at the books. "Hardy Border Flowers" and "The Herbaceous Border": both of them pretty new too, by the look of them. He turned over the pages of the latter. It seemed full of illustrations.

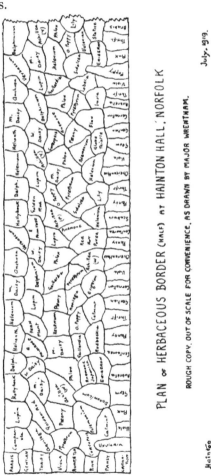

PLAN OF HERBACEOUS BORDER (HALF) AT HAINTON HALL. NORFOLK

ROUGH COPY. OUT OF SCALE FOR CONVENIENCE, AS DRAWN BY MAJOR WRENTHAM.

The list of flowers, too—anchusas, three varieties. He hadn't got that down for a start.

Were all the anchusas at the Hall the same? That would mean another visit. There was going to be more to this gardening business than he had first realised.

Again he set about the plan. Now these twenty-six symbols? Wouldn't there be less if redundant letters were cut out? Well, ignoring that, didn't every cryptogram have "e" as its most frequently occurring letter? Which initial was commonest on the plan? "A" appeared to have it. Then something else struck him. After all, what was the good of trying for a cryptogram? He consulted Plumley's speech:

> I might take you to a certain spot and say to you, "Here is money." There to your hand and for your taking it shall be.

Surely that implied something to be seen reasonably plainly, or to be read by any person of average intelligence. In any case, it ought to put cryptograms out of the question. Names of varieties also. Whereas a well-informed person might possibly be expected to know the names of flowers it would be preposterous to expect any but a super-expert to recognise at sight the names of different sorts of the same species.

His head was beginning to go round. Time for lunch too—within a minute or so. What in heaven's name was the sense of his doing all that brainy work! All he was good for was the strong man stunts and, recalling the comic business with the easel, not much good at that. No. Ludo was the chap. If there was anything to be found out from that plan he was the one who'd be bound to ferret it out. So he decided to leave it over until the Monday. Yet he for once did not trust himself. When one gets hot on a trail, whether he have four legs or two, it is hard to quit it. He felt he was getting a bit stale, and quit it he must, in spite of Ludo's recommendation as to haste. He would go over to Marnham and see the Carews. Frank would be at home and there would sure to be tennis going. Nevertheless, he put books and all in the drawer and locked it, and, to make assurance still more sure, explained to his father that he was doing a job of work that was likely to keep him indoors too much. Would he hang on to the key and not give it up on any account?

"That won't be difficult," said the vicar, stowing the key away in his pocket. "Having a secret mission to perform I thought of going to Thetford this afternoon."

"Good Lord, pater! What on earth next? Out with it and keep it in the family."

"Not a word," laughed his father. "It's so rarely that I get the chance to keep anything to myself in this household that I am going to make the most of it. If you don't mind, I thought of seeing Harland at the same time and coming back by the nine-thirty. What are you going to do?"

Wrentham explained his intentions, which would involve the hire of a bicycle from Rummage, since the vicar was having the car.

Frank Carew was, however, not at home. Pamela, the eldest of the girls, was in, and so was her mother. The menfolk and the other girls had gone to Norwich for golf. All the same, he had quite a jolly time. Women had come but little into his existence, and he was rather shy in their company. Yet he had known the Carew girls since before their school-days, and if he had to pick a mother out of all the women of his acquaintance he would have gone no further than Rosalind Carew. First they had a look at the rock garden, with its small trickle of water mossing the stone steps. There were the new roses to be admired, and then came tea under the beech on a lawn that was good to eyes not yet recovered from endless sand. Then in the cool of the evening a game of croquet, and very merry they were with Wrentham chased hither and thither and hopelessly out-manœuvred.

They pressed him to stay to dinner, but he would not. He promised, however, to bring Ludo over during the week, and also to join them at golf. There should also be a tennis party at the vicarage, and what about an all-day match on August Bank Holiday? As soon as he had said it he realised that the remark was a bit tactless. It was that cricket match in 1914 that had broken up at midday when half the side had been recalled and poor Dennis Carew had to rejoin his ship.

It was a different Wrentham who rode home those eight peaceful miles in the cool of tree-shadowed lanes. The thoughts that flitted through his mind were many, and so varied that at the journey's end he could not have recalled a tenth of them. There were stout fellows who year by year had accepted the Carew's hospitality for that cricket match—gone now as briefly as the echo of ball on willow. There was his childhood and the maze of war and the wonder what the world should hold for the future. Back of it all, urgent and yet unfelt, the serenity of the landscape, the calm of a July evening, and the simple melody of the fields—all that pervading influence that claims us, catches at the heart and is gone ere we are aware.

Then, at home, the mood passed and he was restless again. He had his scratch meal and sat with Tango on the lawn. There the devil, to his undoing, found him with idle hands. Perhaps the remembrance of that night a week ago first suggested the thought to him, or it might have been born of his desire to be doing. In any case, the idea came to him to sally forth and survey the Cottage. Some itch of the mind kept him at it, and the rebound from brain to body found it good. The vicar arrived too, tired but in excellent spirits, and bringing his secret with him. Seen anybody at Thetford he knew? Oh, yes! So-and-so and So-and-so, and Miss Forrest and her maid had travelled on the same train with him, in the afternoon.

That was the deciding point. If there was nobody there, if Burrows had really gone to Norwich, why not keep his hand in with a short night operation? An old cap, a muffler, change of gait, two pairs of stockings instead of shoes—that would find Burrows and his molehills a job!—and a sound use of cover should do the trick.

As a matter of fact, when he set out there was no set programme in his mind. The setting out was, as it were, the crystallising of thought into deed. No schoolboy on nocturnal orchard robbery or daylight bird-nesting felt more full of adventure and life. And had Sergeant Miller been able to follow him here from the time the jaws of darkness did devour him up a new episode might have been added to his repertoire.

Until he reached the road he halted but twice—once when a trap drove by and once when a rabbit cried shrill from the grip of a stoat. The road he crossed quickly, landing in the dry, open ditch. Here he crouched for a minute or two, and then felt his way along to a gap. Had another trap or bicycle come by he would have had to risk the dive into the hedge.

In the shallow wood the darkness was intense. He got down on all fours and, with infinite patience, here avoiding a denser mass of undergrowth and there a tree with feathered bole, made his way in the direction of the back of the cottage. He came to the path, and rising to his feet made for the directer way, but more slowly and shuffling to avoid the cracking of twigs. The sky appeared, a blacker darkness against the gloom, and the myriad stars. Under a clump of young elms, scarce five yards from the kitchen door, he crept. The night was still as the grave.

From his lair the cottage soon showed itself. He could discern the window and door and even the water-butt by the penthouse side. Beyond that—nothing. Roof and chimney stood clear, silhouettes quaint and colourless. His eyes caught the brick path where it circled the shed and the lighter grey of the doorstep. Then his ears caught the faintest of sounds, something that instinct alone could have distinguished. A black shape moved by the water-butt and then stood still while one might count to fifty. It moved again to the door and again halted. Whoever the man was, he stooped and felt below the butt, soundless as a ghost. Looking for the key, thought Wrentham, but if so the seeker was disappointed, for he again stood upright, so motionless that the watcher scarce dared to breathe. Then by some trick of gait as the man turned again, or maybe by some carriage of the head, Wrentham knew him for Burrows.

Next he heard a faint rubbing as of wood against wood. There was a movement before the window, and then the detective's hands went up as the bottom window slowly rose. Again he crouched, and so remained for many seconds. Then something was taken from the window-sill and placed on the ground. The shoulders of the detective disappeared—the legs—and Wrentham realised that he was inside.

For half an hour he lay there, eyes fixed on the window. From the cottage came no sounds, no flash of light—nothing to betray the entrant. In the undergrowth was now and again the movement of life and the scarce perceptible brush of leaf against leaf, but the cottage itself was part of the night and its long reticence. Almost he thought that the searcher had gone out the other way, so incredibly still was everything. Then the shoulders appeared again and the body moved noiselessly to the grass. The flower-pots were replaced, the window was lowered, and again came the chafing noise. Again, too, the slow movement to the shed and then no more.

For himself, Wrentham stood not upon the order of his going. For the moment he knew where the detective was, and for the moment only. He, too, faded into the shadows of the undergrowth, and, careless of discovery, moved as quickly as he dared along the grass track, through the thin tree belt to his right, and so to the meadow. Then he ran. He crossed the road and regained the low meadows and, once more sprinting, reached the path. Then, as secretly as before, he reached the window of the study by which he had emerged and, removing his soaking stockings, made his way up to bed.

CHAPTER XVIII
THE HERO HAS A BIRTHDAY

ON THE BREAKFAST-TABLE by his plate were two packages, a pound of his favourite tobacco and a regimental tie, both with good wishes for a happy birthday. So that was the pater's secret and the real reason for the visit to Thetford! Then along came his father and Emma with their greetings. He acknowledged laughingly that he had forgotten that it was his birthday. For breakfast, too, there was his special grape-fruit. Altogether, with the sun shining and even old Tango dancing with excitement, it seemed like being a very jolly day.

Since coming back it was his first chance also to go to church. It would please his father too, especially the walk there and back. He did not think of it in quite that way, since we do not always see how others see us. Yet, patent for all to see, was the vicar's pride in his son; less noticeable but very deep was the tie that bound the two together, since neither could be called demonstrative.

As Wrentham slipped into his accustomed seat that morning the world seemed a very good place to be in. On the walls were the tablets of those whose name he bore, all for certain years "vicar of this parish," and the same pungency of the pines that greeted his nostrils had doubtless assailed theirs. The sun cut the same sharp swath across the choir, and outside the same twitterings of birds but emphasised the quietude of the ancient place of prayer.

The same, too, were the steps of the heavy-footed worshippers. There would be the loud-voiced conversation to the porch, the decorous shuffle before the door, and the movement to the family seat. The wheezy organ would strike up hesitant in its bass and coy in its treble. The choir would become involved in the intricacies of harmony, with altos a mere hint and sopranos lusty and shrill, while the tenors would prolong a happily found note. There were no nuances; the business was to sing, and the choir acquitted itself as well as its fathers and finished with a palpable flutter of satisfaction.

There are among us two generally accepted classes of parsons—those who read their sermons and those who have no notes. The vicar was of the latter elect; brief, too, and homely, so that a wayfaring man, however foolish, should not go astray therein. The main part of his discourse that morning you shall not be troubled with. It was the text and the preliminary exposition that struck one listener as absurdly apposite and left him with the application unheeded.

"Consider the lilies." The vicar paused to let the text have its effect on the minds of his hearers, to start some train of thought. "That is what I want us all to do this morning; to consider, to think about lilies. But not the lilies that Christ thought about.

Not the fragile, ephemeral lilies of the Holy Land, clad though they were in such beauty that the great Solomon in all his glory was not arrayed like unto them. No! When Christ urges us in the words of the Book to look at lilies, I think He means the urging and the lesson to be applicable to any age and time. There is the same lesson to be learned from the lilies of our gardens as from the lilies of Palestine's fields."

Here Wrentham could almost feel on his neck the glances of the congregation. He felt, too, that if by some strange magic he suddenly produced from his pocket a handful of Palestinian lilies it would be regarded as by no means unseemly by his fellow-worshippers.

"The commonest lily of our villages is the tall, white, Madonna lily, the lily of our Lady, the Mother of Jesus. The Latin has it *Lilium candidum*, that is, the chaste, the pure white lily. This is the lily that the old painters put always in the hands of the Holy Mother. This is the lily that occurs all through their landscapes, whether real or merely the backgrounds for their saints. It is this lily that Shakespeare and Marvell and Milton and rare Ben Jonson talk of. It is essentially the English lily, the one that your grandmothers grew and their grandmothers before them."

And so on to the simplicity of the lily and its lack of pretension; the brevity of its blooming and the sweetness of it; all these with their open hints for the Christian of observation and discernment.

But the lessons that Wrentham was drawing were less spiritual and much more worldly, though none the less apt. There was that central mass of lilies in the border, the keystone, as it were, upon which the whole scheme rested. They were white with, as far as he remembered, black markings, and the fragrance of them came twenty yards with the wind. Why were they so plainly in the middle unless it were to give some indication that ought to be read?

Then another train of thought—the Latin name. Did all flowers have two names? He called to mind an occasion when he had been talking at cross-purposes with Wallace about asters and had found they were really Michaelmas daisies, or was it the other way about? Snapdragons, too, surely they were also called antirrhinums? If that were so, indeed the whole nomenclature of the plan would have to be altered, either to the popular or the official. That would be some job of work. Ludo's nose for the grindstone!

And although it would be impossible to connect up the mental processes involved, a further idea formed itself. What of that insignificant-looking uvularia? That seemed neither a well-known plant nor a suitable one. Why had it been put in the border at all? If new ideas be progress, he felt that he was getting along. He assigned to himself the afternoon for another desperate effort. Too priceless for words to take the wind out of Ludo's sails. To pretend the whole show was a washout and then, by accidental design, lead him unsuspecting to the scene of the dramatic solution!

He stayed behind as usual for his father. As they came out into the sunlight Burrows joined them. He had been seated at the back by the porch and ventured to compliment the vicar on the sermon. The latter shook his head as if to deprecate the efforts of humanity, and Wrentham cut in with, "What gave you the idea of that text, pater?"

"Why, Mrs. Walton's garden yesterday. Didn't you notice the lilies in the front of her cottage?"

His son confessed that he hadn't.

"It's a strange thing how we parsons are supposed to repeat ourselves, but I never remember having tried that text before. It shows how insular we can be and how bound up by the written word."

"Where are you off to, Burrows?" asked the Major. "I thought you were at Norwich."

The detective disregarded part of the question. "I was really coming along to see you. I had some news that wouldn't keep and seeing you in church—"

"It will keep until after lunch, I expect," laughed Wrentham. Burrows was beginning to fascinate him, much as that rabbit last night had been fascinated by the stoat. "Come along and make one. My birthday."

"Real or excuse?" smiled the detective.

"Oh, real enough! Pater, what about a bit of lunch for Burrows?"

"Do, do, please!" The vicar was insistent. "We've Christmas pudding, I believe," and he looked quizzically at his son.

"Lord knows what we haven't got! If my birthday or the pater's falls on a Sunday, Emma refuses to go to morning service."

So Burrows sent a boy with a note off to the inn and the three made for the vicarage. Emma's solemnisation of the occasion was marked by a noble duck, with its indispensable peas, and a pudding as brown as the coffee that followed it. Then came the health of the returned warrior and the sampling of the tin of tobacco.

"Have another spot of port?" said Wrentham when they were alone.

"Well, I will, Major, on this happy occasion, and once more, your jolly good health."

"Cheerio. Be rather funny, Burrows, if on this festive anniversary next year you were standing treat at Dartmoor or wherever you fellows hound me to."

The detective sipped meditatively. "Funnier things than that, Major. With all due respect to Mr. Wrentham, I once had the pleasure of getting a parson five years."

"The devil you did! Well, how's the case coming along?"

"Slowly. Too slowly for my liking."

"Then how about the old motto, *cherchez la femme*?" He tried to make his tone as flippant as possible, but the detective's start was too obvious to be missed. Wrentham deliberately kept his eyes away while casually filling his pipe; then he passed over the pouch.

The other decided to change the conversation. "The chap I wanted to see you about was your man Wallace."

"Wallace? What on earth has he got to do with it?"

"That's a pretty roundabout story. If you don't mind all the details I think you'll be interested. Roberts turned out to be a dead end. I saw Martin again and tried to shake him about seeing Roberts that night, but I couldn't upset his story, no matter how I tried. He maintained that it was Roberts he saw, and at about eleven o'clock near Lodge Cottage. So certain was he that it was Roberts he saw that he hailed him and said good night. I told you how I had got a bead on Roberts' movements and how he swore he was indoors for good that night at a quarter to ten. Well, I decided to work a bluff, or rather a double bluff. I tackled Roberts and told him the police knew he was lying. Further, I told him that if he didn't loosen up I should have no option but to bring Martin as a witness at the adjourned inquest, and I hinted at the probability of a coroner's warrant and so on. He fell for it right enough, and I never saw a man more scared out of his life."

This was distinctly exciting. Wrentham was sucking an empty pipe.

"He owned he had been out that night, and if I promised to say nothing about the matter he would tell me everything. Of course I couldn't do that. All I told him was that I would use my discretion and that was the best I could do for him. This was the story:

"It appears that Clark and he had knocked their heads together about netting a bit of layer on Saunders' farm—that bit that runs along by the woods and opens out at the back towards the cricket field. Your man Wallace appears to be an old hand at the game, and he supplied about eighty yards of silk netting to help out Clark's two nets. At any rate, they set off at about ten with the nets and Roberts' lurcher. If you remember, it was a pretty good night for the job, dark and windy."

Wrentham, who had had many a night's netting, agreed; with the proviso that he would have thought it a bit too damp.

"Apparently they thought the wind would blow everything dry, but they forgot that layer was sheltered by the south wood. To cut a long story short, they ran the dog over it, and the result was four rabbits where they'd expected at least thirty. So they packed up and separated at Church Stile. Roberts says he lost his lurcher bitch, who was chasing a rabbit on the meadows, or he'd have gone along home the back way by the church."

"You've tested his story?"

"Yes, and I'm afraid there's no leak in it anywhere. I checked up on Clark and Wallace. By the way, I should give your man the straight tip if I were you, Major. He seemed to be a decent sort of chap who has done his bit and was probably attracted more by the sport of the thing than the money they were likely to get out of it. I thought it would be better to have a word with you than Mr. Wrentham. I admit that poaching is no great crime when done by outsiders like Wallace, but it's fellows like Clark that make me riled. They're paid to protect against that sort of thing, and would probably run in any poor devil they ran across if he wasn't in their little swim. What do you think about it?"

"I think you're quite right and it's jolly decent of you to let Wallace off with a caution. I'll have a word with our ubiquitous gardener myself. I don't know that I don't envy him a bit, however."

"Envy him! Whatever for?"

"Well, wouldn't you like to chuck your hat into the ring occasionally? Sort of throw off your coat of ceremony—as my guv'nor wanted to the other afternoon—and have a real good time regardless? How about robbing Jerlingham's orchard some night?"

The detective shook his head; it might have been with regret. "Not much in my line, Major. If you don't mind calling it a bargain, however, I'll tell you what I will do. The next time you go looking for truth at the bottom of wells, take me with you, and the darker the better."

"*Touché!*" exclaimed Wrentham and the other could not help a modest smile. "All I am at liberty to tell you, Burrows, about that affair is this: Mr. Travers is coming down on Monday and we expect to do a good deal of inquiry into that particular business. And at the very earliest possible moment you shall know all there is to know. And I give you my word that it's all above board. Is that good enough?"

"Quite good enough for me, Major. But you ought to know at the same time that if it's nothing to do with the case I'm engaged on there's no compunction to tell me anything at all," and he rose to go.

"One more spot?" suggested his host.

"Not for me, Major. If I went looking for truth after a third it would be me who'd be found at the bottom of Rummage's well."

So much for that then, thought Wrentham. Rather funny about that silly ass Wallace! And what about tackling that infernal plan? Quarter to three; time for a good hour. Then he remembered that the vicar, away at the school and there for at least another hour, had the key in his pocket or else alone knew where it was. So he took a mashie-niblick and, screened from the gaze of scandalmongers by the outer trees of the orchard, tried back-spinners over the pear tree. And, for his sins, lost the only three balls he had.

CHAPTER XIX
BETWEEN CUP AND LIP

IT WAS WITH enormous excitement that he got out his beautiful file of papers and the books and propped the plan on the desk before him. The vicar had gone out to supper with Saunders, his warden, and he had the house more or less to himself. On the wool rug Tango was sleeping off the effect of the duck bones. The french window was slightly open and into the room came the heavy scent of the stocks, that fragrance which in itself has the subtle power to convey the perfume of immemorial gardens and give a haunting of beauty that neither time nor place can circumscribe. He recalled those April nights in Palestine when he would visit the wadi for the smell of the night-scented stocks, bravely holding their own in inhospitable sand and smothering the soil with small blossoms.

The problem was where to begin. The lilies seemed to be the strong point. If one had to consider the lilies, as a central feature or as the hub of a wheel, what radiated from them? He checked in various directions, with English and Latin names, but no sign of a clue could he obtain. Again there were fortuitous words but nothing that had a bearing on the problem.

How about trying which names were the commonest? Some seemed to be best known by their native names and some by the foreign. "Delphinium" was more common than "larkspur," or at least it appeared so to him. "Aquilegia" was not so well known as "columbine." However that would do as he came to it: better get straight on.

Well, then, what about having another go at the rows? There were few plants in the back row that seemed to have other than common names. The Michaelmas daisy was called aster, he had been right about that. Some names were very strange; holly-hock, for example, appeared to be known as *Althea rosea*. But all these could be tested at a glance. And the result was nothing. Very well, then, better try the second letters. Again a jumble. The third were equally hopeless.

By the time he had attacked the second and third rows he was exceedingly despondent. No amount of substitution would give the faintest suggestion of a message. The annoying thing about it all was, that if there were anything at all to Plumley's last message, there ought to be something in sight, very plain and obvious. Perhaps it was his density of skull that was at fault. So he filled his pipe, emptied his glass, and started all over again.

This time the assault was on the front row. He followed the same procedure, but as he had sufficient plants—over twenty-six, in fact—to try all the letters of the alphabet, he thought about attempting a cryptogram. It was beyond him. He neither knew where to start nor where to end. That project was still-born. He started at twenty-five plants back from the lilies and that gave no result. Second and third letters were equally inef-fective. The arrangements of English and Latin names merely served to complicate still further.

What about a plant recurring five times to make up the five vowels? No sooner had he got one than he did not know what use to make of it. Tango stirred uneasily and growled, then rose and trotted to the window. His master, save for a word of re-proof, made no comment, and the dog, after sniffing a bit and shaking himself, returned to his mat. Wrentham tossed the book on the desk and contemplated it moodily. Then he, too, rose and did a turn round the room. That stealing a march on Ludo sounded very well, but it was not going to materialise. He returned to his chair, rather tired and far from happy. He shut his eyes and tried to visualise the border. Three things came to him—the mass of lilies, the noble spikes of the delphinium, and the shabby blotches of the uvularia.

That was it, the uvularia. Hadn't Gordon said in his conversation that that was the plant Plumley had sprung on him unawares and had insisted on starting with? He consulted the book. There it was. Uvularia—slender leafy stems and pendent yellow flowers. Marked with a star to show that it was of dwarfish habit and suitable for rockeries.

Then another discovery, apparently of tremendous importance. He could not but observe that there was nothing else in the list that began with "u." He tried the index. No, nothing at all. Was that, then, the reason why Plumley had insisted on the use of that most unlikely plant, because it was the only one that began with that letter? If so, and he felt the extreme likelihood of the idea, he must have determined on the formation of some message that had to begin with that particular letter.

He started therefore with the uvularia and worked above it. It was ten minutes spent with no result. Could there be any connexion between the uvularia and the lilies? The front row he had already tried, so with a straight edge he tested the top of the triangle of uvularia and found a line of plants leading from it to the lily clump. That was something anyhow. Would it be better to put all the possible plants down or to take them as they came? He decided on the latter. There were few probabilities of variation and little chance of getting in a muddle. Then came the test. "U" for uvularia and "c" for catmint. Surely there wasn't any word in the language beginning with "uc"? He hunted round the shelves until he found a dictionary. He was right—there was no such word. Well, what did the book say about catmint? It showed varieties of nepeta. *Mussini* was that kind with lavender flowers and silvery, aromatic foliage. That was the kind they had in the Hall border. *Nepeta mussini* had it. Right-ho, then, "un."

The next was the doronicum, a yellow-flowering spring plant according to the book. There was an illustration too. He remembered it well; many of the village gardens had it. "Und"—that was all right. What was the next? Erigeron. "Unde." Then "r" must follow; rudbeckia. It was his own ghastly writing that was wrong. There it was in the book. *Newmanii* the best variety; autumn flowering, yellow with black centre. Of American origin and there called "Black-eyed Susans." Wasn't there a song some music-hall fellow used to sing,

Where the Black-eyed Susans grow?

Nepeta again, another variety of erigeron and then the white achillea. Hooray! He'd got it! "Undernea." "T" must come next. What had he down? Red-hot poker. What did the book say? *Tritoma* or *kniphojia*. Good Lord! Then "H" for the *Helenium Hoopesi*. "Underneath" was the first word.

Tango again growled and trotted to the window, but his master was too engrossed to heed him. What was next? He ran the straight edge over. Either sidalcea or lily would meet the case. Whatever happened it would be the first letter of a new word so there would be no harm in leaving it for a bit. He decided to try the next. Rocket. What did the book say about that? *Hesperis matronalis alba piena* (old double rocket)—noble spikes of large double white flowers. He put down the "h" with alternatives—"sr," "sh," "lr," and "lh." And the next? Thistle, no, globe thistle. *Echinops* appeared to be the classical name. "G" made no sense. That would give "sre," "she," "lre," and "lhe."

Then came flax—blue flowered, he remembered. *Linum perenne* the book called it. If "she" was correct the "l" would not be much good unless it was the first letter of a new word. However, to get on. Inula, that was easy. Then *Lobelia cardinalis*. That gave "lil." Extraordinary! The rest would surely be "ies." What was that long triangle? Poppies. Yes, but Iceland poppies, so Tait had said, and followed by another erigeron and the statice.

Hastily he put down the result: "UNDERNEATH SHE LILIES." Didn't seem to make sense. THE lilies, that must be it. Again he consulted the plan. What sort of lilies were that small group? The colour was orange, as far as he remembered. Tiger lilies, that was it. He felt like hollering "Hooray!" at the top of his voice. No wonder old Archimedes had yelled the equivalent. Then Plumley *had* made some kind of cryptogram after all. In some mad fit probably. A man who could get fun out of hiding notes in a book and playing with a toy engine no doubt found it devilish exciting planting out these word plants. He could imagine the quaint figure surveying the finished work and chuckling away to himself like anything. Did he forget all about it in his sane moments? However, why worry about the complexities of a madman's mind? He put the documents on the table and got up to stretch himself. Even Tango came in for a good rough and tumble. Rather extraordinary all this, for one who prided himself on that sure control of the emotions which is the heritage of his class.

Tango yet again went suspiciously to the window. His master pushed it full open and stepped out into the cool evening air. It was about ten-thirty. Surely the pater had come in. He returned to the room and so to the hall. Yes, the hat was there and it looked as if he had come in and gone straight up to bed. He had probably glanced in and had feared to disturb the earnest worker. He could afford to smile.

Well, to the serious business of the moment. He knew he had already determined to go at once to the Hall and test the discovery. He knew that unless he carried out the adventure to its only logical conclusion he would never sleep a wink. All the night he'd be thinking about it, and probably wouldn't bat an eyelid. In any case, with a job of work to do there was nothing like getting it over. He felt somewhat like a modern Luther; that were the very slates on the Hall roof legions of detectives, nothing should keep him away. The summary of his bodily fitness could best be expressed by the hoary phrase about pushing a church over.

What would be the best plan of campaign? Last night's joy-rags would be as good as any. Better add an electric torch also. And it wouldn't be unwise to take the Colt. There wouldn't be any need to loose it off, but it would give any too inquisitive an inquirer the devil of a wallop. A couple of deep pockets might be handy. The old shooting coat was the very thing. And then, in the middle of his private staff pow-wow of preparation, the lobby bell rang, viciously and loud.

It is necessary here that the geography of the small study should be understood. The east wing of the vicarage stood four-square, the french window facing the south lawn and the gravelled road through the drive gate. To the east was a shrubbery, and farther east still from this the right-hand fork of the drive, which was really the path to the kitchen and the stables, curving from north to west. At the back of the study was a tiny lobby, used principally by parish visitors, and those who came to consult the law. From this lobby one could proceed straight to the study or into the kitchen. Its outside door was set in a small porch, in the side of which was a pull bell.

There was only one thing to conclude: that the vicar was urgently wanted. Wrentham did, as a matter of fact, pause to wonder why the visitor, who must have seen the light from the study window, had not come direct to the obvious quarters of somebody not yet in bed. But there was, he knew, a strong disinclination on the part of the villagers to approach such a front door. Centuries of being kept well in place had removed for them any temptation to usurp the uppermost seats in feasts.

Tango, too, appeared to have heard steps, for he growled and went to the lobby door. Wrentham opened it and then stumbled over a chair in the dark. He swore and rubbed his shins. Then he felt his way gingerly until he came to the latch. He slid back the bolt and opened the door. There was nobody there! His first instinct was to step out from the porch to the brick path and look round. He called "Hallo!" softly, and then again, somewhat more loudly. There was no reply or sound of footsteps. Devilish queer that! Perhaps they'd gone to the kitchen door. He walked the few yards to the left, the dog padding at his heels, a steady yard behind. There was neither sign nor sound of a soul.

Perhaps they'd seen the light after all and gone round to the front. He left the lobby door ajar and returned to the study. He stepped out of the window on to the gravel and then to the grass and looked round. Not a sign anywhere. Again he called "Hallo!" but with no result. Very well! if they were as casual or silly as all that, let them ring again. He returned to the study and shut the window.

Well, what about waiting a minute or two to see if whoever it was came back, and then setting out for the Hall? He noticed a paper on the floor and stooped to pick it up. His plan. He put it on the desk and then with a start noticed that the papers had been scattered and tossed about as by a wind or a mischievous child. He looked over them hastily. There were odd accounts of his father's, portions of sermons, sundry jottings of ideas and a parish magazine or two. But the arresting thing was that his file of notes was gone! The plan and his final jottings which contained the clue alone were left!

To say that he was knocked all of a heap would be euphemism rather than hyperbole. He was so taken aback that for a second or two he couldn't even think at all. It seemed so incredible. Why, they were there only a minute before! The book was there but no papers. He jerked open the drawer. No, he had not replaced them. Good God! And in that file were the photos, copies of letters to Ludo, and enough matter to set the whole village by the ears. He had another hurried and desperate look. Oh, yes, they were gone right enough! He went quickly to the window and opened it. The dog followed him, wagging his stumpy tail. Some new game going on!

The thing was where to turn? Could it be Burrows who had taken them? Surely he would never have had the damn cheek to do such a barefaced thing, especially after that business of the shoes! Who else could have done it? But what was the use of thinking? Better do something.

He moved forward to the grass and stood listening intently. The night was so still and solemn that he appeared to be within the dim interior of some vast cathedral. And, as he recalled afterwards, the apple-like smell of the sweet-briar seemed to be everywhere, pervading the night.

Then, on his left, he heard, and Tango heard, what sounded like a rustling of the bushes. He did not stop to think, so furious was the surge of anger that rose within him. He made for the sound and he wouldn't have cared a hoot in hell if twenty prize-fighters had been waiting for him. He was almost at the gate, and was in act to stretch forth his hand for the leap. But he never reached it. His feet appeared to rise in the air, and a dull pain smote him. All that remained was the furious barking of a dog and then—nothing.

CHAPTER XX
THE TIRED CÆSAR

THERE IS A story of a Khalifa who, doubting the experiences of the Prophet and the miraculous passage of time, was command-ed to thrust his head into a pail of water. In that space between the submergence and the withdrawal, he married many times, saw his grandchildren, and lived a lifetime. So it was in a way with Wrentham and this the last few seconds before he awoke.

There was a humming as of millions of bees, a buzzing as of millions of immense flies, endless and nauseating. After centu-ries of that there came the sound of voices whispering, the voic-es of the drowned speaking from the profundity of a stupendous ocean. Then came a knocking, remote and dulled and dying ere it hardly began. There was a pressure on his head and binding his temples. He could feel the throb, throb as the blood pulsed its way. As he came nearer to consciousness there was a cool-ness. Something brushed his forehead and wrapped it as in a cool garment. The pain almost ceased; it was no longer madden-ing, but just a steady ache. His returning senses wrestled with the scent that seemed to envelope him and recognised it. He moved his head on the pillow and opened his eyes. He remained for a full minute, gazing inanely, like a baby from its perambula-tor. Slowly he came to full recognition, and the wonderment he showed might have appeared amusing had not the watcher been so concentrated on his task.

Wrentham stirred again and spoke. His voice, too, came from a far distance, if it was his voice at all. "Hallo, what's all this?" Ware came forward with something in a glass. "That's better, old chap. Just drink this." He slipped his left arm under Wrentham's head and held the glass to his lips. The patient gulped it down. Anything more like nectar he had never had, vile dope though it was. Ware propped a pillow under him, and he grinned cheerfully round. He called to mind the last things that he could remember: that rush for the gate, the leap into the air, and the barking of a dog. He went to get up in the bed, but the blood rushed to his head. He flopped down again helplessly and closed his eyes until the furious throbbing should cease.

When he opened them once more the vicar and Burrows were in the room. The former was terribly concerned. "How is he?" he asked Ware.

"Getting along splendidly, vicar. Be on his pins and as lively as a kitten in a couple of days."

The vicar caught his son's eye, and, unashamed, stooped over him. "My boy—" He remembered perchance the presence of the others, and withdrew within himself. "How are you feeling now, Geoffrey?"

"Like the morning after fifty nights," was the cheerful if feeble answer.

"I think I'll run along now, vicar," said Ware, turning to the patient and exhibiting a bottle. "Just take this, young feller, and you'll be feeling a different chap to-morrow." He turned to the vicar again and took his arm, and the two left the room, talking quietly. Burrows, left behind, drew up a chair and sat down by the bed. He too was greeted with a grimace, which he returned.

"Major, if I told you how happy I am at this moment to know you're all right you'd never believe me. There, don't trouble to talk," as the other made as if to speak. "You just lie quiet and I'll do the talking."

"Right-ho!" was the sleepy reply. "You tell me all about it. What time is it?"

"It's about six o'clock on Monday evening. Oh, no"—answering the unspoken question—"you've not been unconscious all the time. You've been more or less babbling away ever since you got that crack on the head, or at least until the doctor gave you a draught early this morning. Now don't trouble to move your head or exert yourself. Just move your lips and tell me what happened."

"I thought I heard somebody moving in the shrubbery and ran for the gate, that's all."

"Well, that dog of yours made enough noise to rouse the village. I was on the spot as soon as anyone, and found you crumpled up against the gate and the dog barking over your body like a mad thing. When I circled round him to get to your legs I found something—a line that had been stretched from the may tree to the far post. You'd evidently come a cropper over that and fallen pretty hard against the other post, where you were lying. I should think you went down as if you'd been poleaxed. I gathered up the line and stuck it in my pocket, and by that time your father and the housekeeper were on the move. Mr. Wrentham quieted the dog and between us we got you up to bed. Then I nipped off back and sent Rummage for the doctor. According to him you'd had a fearful blow, and were lucky not to have smashed your skull in. That reminds me. I didn't say anything to your father about that line. I thought there was no need to worry him unduly. He seems to think you just fell heavily. I thought I'd tell you that so that you should know what to say."

The other was hardly listening. Everything was coming back to him, and he recalled the anger that had seized him at the theft of his papers. If Burrows had taken them it was like his damn nerve sitting there and talking as if nothing had happened. It was not worthy of him was that thought; most likely it was not himself who spoke but the querulous thing with the enormous aching head. He did not mean to ask it, but the question came out: "I ought to tell you, Burrows, that last night I was running for the gate because somebody had just stolen from the study a collection of very private papers of mine. Do you know anything about them?"

The detective went a violent red, although the questioner was not regarding him. He felt the insult was deserved, and yet he did not expect it from where it came. He answered calmly, however. "Major Wrentham, I give you my word that until you just spoke of them I had no idea you had any private papers. As for the rest, you should have known me better."

Some devil of spite must have possessed the invalid, because his next remark was more unpardonable: "That's all very well, Burrows. It was no harder to get into the vicarage than into Lodge Cottage."

Again the detective flushed. He looked as if about to make a furious retort, but the sight of the other stopped him. "I won't say what I intended to, Major, because I know you don't realise what you are saying. I repeat, I don't know anything about your papers, and I can't say more than that."

Both were silent for many minutes. Wrentham lay with closed eyes, deadly tired, and making an effort not to think of anything. The detective was watching and wondering—wondering how on earth the other had known of his breaking into that house, wondering what those lost papers had been and who had stretched that damnable line. His thoughts ran over all the ground he had already covered so many times, and dwelt upon the infinite possibilities of this new event; this reconstruction, as it were, of the earlier crime. In his heart was no resentment for the hints the other had thrown out against him. His was a trade that had to have a thick skin. He thought much of the man who lay there with eyes closed and face unwontedly pale. The summing up of character was his business in life, and he did not think he had made a mistake with Major Wrentham—a *sahib* to the finger-tips, as Wilfred had described him.

He was right. Wrentham's nature was one that could not long harbour or express thoughts that were so foreign to his real self. He made his apology—feebly because he felt feeble, and haltingly because of the shame of the attack. "I'm sorry, Burrows. I shouldn't have said that—"

The detective smiled and patted his hand, as one would humour a sick child. "I knew that, Major. I knew you didn't mean it. If I had got a crack on the head like yours I should have said anything." He got up to go, for he thought he could hear footsteps on the stairs. "You lie quiet now. I'll drop in again later."

But the other had another question to ask. "You said I had been babbling. What had I been talking about?"

"The biggest lot of rot I ever listened to," was the reply. "You know the old jokes about coming round after gas at the dentist's? That's the sort of thing you were talking—all kinds of twaddle mixed up. There was a bough of a tree falling on a lady, and you kept shouting to her to get out of the way. Then you kept asking for a message and said you were going digging. And in the middle of all that you kept shouting for Ludo—Mr. Travers, I supposed you meant—and then you'd moan with the pain in your head until it was enough to make one's blood run cold. If it hadn't—"

He stopped speaking. The vicar and Ludo were entering the room. He greeted the latter, and had a confidential word or two with the former, and went out. The two whispered together for a minute and then went over to the bed. The invalid was asleep. There had probably been something in the draught which Ware had given him and it had taken effect. So, but for one short waking spell, he remained all night. When he awoke the sun was high. He felt free of that sickening pain of the night before and as hungry as a wolf. Emma was in the room. She waddled over to his medicine bottle and poured out a dose. "How are you, Mr. Geoffrey?"

"Fit as a flea, Emma," was the reply. He looked up at her, and to his consternation thought she was going to cry, her usual method of recognising the happiest events. He stopped that ere it began. "Come on now. Produce that dope! Filthy muck! What about some breakfast, Emma?"

"Well, Mr. Geoffrey, the doctor said you was to have eggs if you was hungry."

"Right-ho! Poach 'em, and get a pail of coffee."

Emma's message on descent must have been reassuring. The vicar and Ludo carried up the breakfast between them. Afterwards he had a cigarette and announced his intention of getting up. Only by the earnest solicitations of his father was he persuaded to remain in bed, at least until the doctor should call.

The head still felt tremendously sore. Several stitches had been put in it. But except for that occasional pain he felt very much himself again. Ludo forbore to make either the obvious remark about thickness of skull or the reminder that his words of caution had come true. By the time the doctor had gone, with the assurance that the invalid might get up for an hour or two after tea, provided he got back to bed again at once as soon as he felt any swimming in the head, he was actually feeling in quite good spirits. To be propped up well in bed with a pipe was, after all, almost as good as getting up. He gave Ludo an account of the happenings of the Sunday. "And now, cough up all your news."

"I'm afraid there isn't any," apologised the other, "at least to compete with yours. I should like to see that plan, however." He fished the key out of the trousers pocket and went off and found the cardboard drawing. He followed the other's explanations, given often with an unspoken request for confirmation or approval. Ludo was most enthusiastic. It was simply splendid. But when was it to be tried out, to see whether the final, and after all the only real, test proved it true?

"I don't think there's any enormous hurry about that," was Wrentham's opinion. "As you observe, the plan and the notes with the solution were not taken, and I'm absolutely certain that nobody could do anything without them. Suppose that whoever has got all the rest makes up his mind to go upon the same lines as we have indicated for his benefit: unless he is an expert or has free access to the border, it will take him at least half a day to make a plan. Then he will want another to solve it, even if he is extraordinarily lucky. My idea was for you to go to-morrow night."

The arrival of Burrows stopped the discussing of plans. The detective looked very tired and worn. He was very apologetic, about not having shaved. "Call it a sore chin if you like gentleman, or what you will, but there it is."

"Before I do anything else," said Wrentham, "I want to thank you, Burrows, for all you did for me the other night. It's thanks to you, and you only, that I'm feeling as fit as I am now."

The detective was plainly embarrassed. He mumbled something, including a remark about the doctor. He seemed to be gratified, none the less.

Wrentham sized up the situation. "You may say what you like before Captain Travers," he said. "He knows as much as myself about all this business. Tell us now, what is your opinion about that attack on me? I don't see how we can call it anything else, do you?"

"I own up," replied the detective frankly, "that I haven't an idea. But"—and he included them both in his intense look—"if you two gentlemen would tell me all that is at the back of your minds I should be better able to find out."

Wrentham looked at Ludo. What he saw was non-committal. He decided for himself. "Give us a day or two, Burrows. I tell you honestly the business we are mixed up in, even if we solve it, will not, in my opinion, go an inch towards answering the question of who killed Moulines. For all that, I'm sure we should be doing right to lay our cards on the table. I can't go farther than that." He glanced at Ludo, who was looking out of the window and nodding agreement.

"Very well, gentleman." The detective was patently resigned. "I'll do as you say. I ought to tell you, by the way, that I've given the strictest instructions that not a word of your accident is to be let out. Do you think your housekeeper and the maid can be trusted?"

"I'd trust anything in the world to Emma, if it concerned our interests," was the verdict. "I've no doubt, too, she'll see the maid says nothing, not even to Wallace. But won't people notice the doctor's visit?"

"That's easy. Visit to the vicar about the adjourned inquest. Also I've already told your housekeeper she's to be slightly unwell."

"The devil you have!" exclaimed Wrentham. "You're a fast mover! Oh, there's one thing I've been wondering about. How's the inquiry about Tait?"

"I'm glad you asked me that, Major, because two very interesting things arose out of it. First, we found no less than fourteen gamekeepers' caps within a radius of four miles from Hainton. Also during the same inquiry we had an extraordinary piece of good luck, nothing less than discovering the whereabouts of Tait's last job. We found that he was discharged from his last place in Hampshire for disposing of garden produce without permission, and, of course, pocketing the proceeds. I should like to know exactly how he got the late Mr. Plumley to take him on."

"Theft is surely by no means akin to murder," remarked Ludo.

"That's true, sir, to a certain extent. At the same time, suppose Tait met the dead man, who knew his past history and was bound to tell about it. There'd be no improbability about the suggestion that Tait would feel like putting him away, rather than have everything come out."

Wrentham agreed. In one way he was sorry, and in another glad. Burrows' revelations meant that there would be a chance for Gordon to get back. He was inspired to utter a truth and at the same time put the detective off the scent. "What you have just told me about Tait is very closely connected with those inquiries I was talking about," he said. "A man of your discernment will probably put two and two together."

And while Burrows was trying to see what it actually did mean another interruption—this time lunch—broke off the conversation.

CHAPTER XXI
ADVENTURE BY PROXY

SHERLOCK HOLMES on a certain famous occasion staggered his henchman Watson by following the latter's train of thought and doubling along ahead, as it were, to meet him again at the end of it. I forget the exact sequence, but a picture of General Gordon was in it.

It might be interesting to follow the consecutive recollections that, in their course through Wrentham's mind, led to the location and the method of the killing of André Moulines. Not that he took any credit for the discovery, but rather recognised himself for a fool who had blundered into a path a wiser man had had no chance of treading.

As he lay resting quietly after lunch—over-much pipe was inclined to make his head swim—he thought of outside and the sun. Followed the walk to the heath, the country-side generally, the ride home from Marnham, getting a bicycle, and so to his first bicycle ride. Here we must be reminiscent and detailed. He and Ludo had borrowed an antiquated machine from Wallace and departed with it to the top of one of the few local inclines— Padley Hill. The learning was simple. One merely got on the machine at the top of the hill and was given a push. Both sides of the road were ditchless and with wide grass borders; there was consequently no harm in taking a toss.

After an excellent trial or two, Geoffrey was emboldened to pedal to a greater speed. Far beyond the foot of the hill the bicycle crashed into a deep roadside cutting, and over the handle-bars he shot, like a stone from a catapult. In the fraction of a second before he fell he could see a heap of broken stones, lying ready for the road. So straight for them did he appear to be going that he could feel the impact. But he fell beyond on the long grass, and, when his horrified companion found him was much as usual, except for a bit of a shaking up and a certain whiteness about the gills.

So from that fall and the imminent stones to the fall of the other night. A crack against the post had been bad enough, and the surface had been perfectly flat. Suppose he had struck two feet to the left against the brick-piered flint wall? The thought sent a shiver down his spine: his skull would have been smashed in like an eggshell—something like the injuries Ware had described in the case of Moulines. Was it possible for the murdered man's injuries to have been caused like that? Where was there a likely wall of the same kind. Of course—the long wall sheltering the kitchen garden at the Hall and running along the back path until it rejoined the house at the main drive.

Then it might not have been murder after all. Why shouldn't Moulines have crashed into that wall or a similar one? No, that couldn't be right or the machine would have been smashed up. Moreover, if the affair had been an accident, why had the unknown removed bicycle and body? Yet the death must have occurred at the Hall. No, even that wasn't certain. The only certainty was that the dead man must have come to the Hall and the bicycle had been put where it was by him, and him only. The bicycle was his. Burrows had told him that the registration had been proved. Well, if there hadn't been an accident, why shouldn't Moulines have been lured into running and tripped up just as he had been? If so, he must have been enticed by somebody climbing the wall. There was no other reason for anybody to run straight into brick walls, and that one must be eight feet if it was an inch.

Right or wrong, it appealed to him, so much so that when Ludo came up a minute or two later the whole of the arguments were expounded to him. Remarkably sound, too, the listener thought it. Wrentham was feeling in good fettle. "I don't mind telling you, Ludo," he said, "that my little grey matter is in very good form at the present moment."

"I'm not at all surprised at that," was the reply. "It's probably due to the fact that for the last few days you have not been able to indulge in your usual gross over-eating."

"Ludo, in your senility you are getting vulgar."

"Not at all. Even if I am I glory in it. The functions of the body are men's own and abiding topics. There'd be precious little discussed in smoking-rooms without them."

Wrentham took refuge in his usual "Perhaps you're right," adding, "I've got a scheme of which I was about to tell you if you hadn't put it out of my head with your very intimate remarks. Would you mind finding Wallace and sending him for Burrows? Tell him it's desperately urgent. I'll explain to you all about it when you get back."

The scheme was this: Wrentham, in the presence of Ludo, was to tell the detective his new theory about the death of Moulines. It was more than probable that, unless he had already worked at and discarded some such theory himself, in view of the imminence of the inquest, he would go at once to the Hall and test the idea. Ludo was to be happening to go in the same direction and was to offer to accompany him. An opportunity was bound to arise for the latter to slip round and visit the border. The lilies would have to be looked at and the geography of the immediate locality, especially from the point of view of night-work, would have to be memorised. The grand attempt on the lilies was to be made at night, and Ludo was to be prepared for all contingencies likely to arise in connexion with the proposed excavations.

"I withdraw my remarks on your grey matter," admitted Ludo. "If everything works out according to schedule, we ought to be having a Brock's benefit at about midnight. One thing struck me, however: if Burrows finds anything suspicious at the Hall, won't he be more than ever certain to be prowling about there to-night?"

"My opinion is the other way round. If he finds anything I'll lay ten to one that he'll hare off to Norwich like a streak of lightning to confer with Delane; if not Norwich, to the nearest telephone, and that's eight miles away. After that he'll have his evidence to prepare. No, I don't think there will be any sleuths round the moated grange to-night."

Luck was certainly with them this time. It could not by any stretch of the imagination be said that the detective was outwardly enthusiastic, and whatever his private thoughts he kept them to himself. He and Ludo set off, however, just before tea, while Wrentham dressed himself under the watchful eye of his father and came down to an easy chair in the drawing-room. Emma had prepared a meal more suitable for a dozen, and it felt very jolly to be out of that infernal bedroom again, if only for a change of wall-paper.

Ware dropped in during the meal and expressed himself astounded at the condition of the patient. "What you fellers don't understand," said Wrentham, "is that there are people whose lives are so virtuous or well ordered that little things like this have no more effect on them than an attack of measles. Hearts of oak, my dear chap! Hearts of oak!"

"Skulls of oak!." interrupted Ludo, entering the room. They all laughed, none more heartily than the claimant for virtue.

Ludo's account was very satisfactory. He had left the detective searching the wall as if his life depended on it. It had been easy to slip away to the border where the clump of lilies, now past their best, had stood up clamouring for dislodgment. He had discovered the best method of approach—over the cricket field and then round the park in front of the house would also be the easiest. When he had returned the detective was still at the wall, back towards him, so he had made a graceful and unobtrusive exit.

"There's just one other thing now," suggested the owner of the grey matter: "you must go to Rummage at about seven and ask for his car. If he's in I shall be very surprised. However, if he is in, you'll have to take the car and go to Thetford or some place or other. If he's out, you're bound to be told where he is. That will give us a line on the whereabouts of Burrows. I'm afraid you're becoming orderly man for the day, Ludo!"

"My dear old chap," was the reply, "I wouldn't add to your conceit by telling you so, but I'm so dashed glad to see you sitting in that chair that I wouldn't mind being in orders to-night as orderly corporal. I think I deserve a stripe."

The luck still held. When the orderly returned from his visit to the inn it was with the information that Rummage and his guest had taken the Norwich road. That didn't convey much, and yet, if the detective had wished to telephone, he would surely have gone to Thetford, and not the twelve miles to Longham. Ludo had done his best, but the famous suavity had produced no other news except that Mrs. Rummage didn't know when they would be back. Her husband had told her so.

"The chances are certainly Norwich," was Wrentham's opinion. "Now I've another scheme to submit. Up in the workroom is an iron rod—an old curtain rod, I think it is. I propose we go up there and you cut it off to the length of a long walking-stick, twist round the top to form a handle, and sharpen the other end. If you stick that well down its three feet into the ground you should be able to locate any box or solid container. That ought to save a lot of time in the long run by giving you an indication as to where to dig. By the way, it will make a pretty hefty weapon if you should want one. One jolt in the guts with that and—" The rest was panto mimic.

"A very sound idea! And another struck me while you were talking. When I was looking at the lilies it was certain that if I had to uproot them altogether I should never be able to replace them in the dark without leaving as many traces of my visit as if I were a flock of sheep. With your gadget I ought to be able to dig between plants and tunnel under them from the side, leaving the bulbs absolutely untouched. And that reminds me: how far below the surface do the bulbs go?"

"We'll soon find that out," said Wrentham, consulting the book. "Here we are. About three times the depth of the bulb. Say six inches before you strike the top of them and nine or ten right through. Allow a further six for roots, and there you are."

It was a trying wait that Wrentham had while his fellow-conspirator was away. Imagine Cæsar abed with the mumps while the Nervii were attacking his camp, or Columbus with the gout and unable to come up on deck for the first sight of land. Or, again, so might stout Cortes have felt had he tramped the poisonous undergrowth of Darien only at the last to hear at second hand the report of that great vision of the Pacific. There may be something in the misfortunes of our friends which, as the Frenchman recorded, is not wholly displeasing to us. There is often, too, in some very indefinite way, something about their abilities which is hardly as satisfying as our own, saving, of course, all mention of those geniuses who, in their particular line, leave us aghast. Had he felt fit, the waiting would have been intolerable. Shortly before ten he went up to bed, as his father suggested. Ludo was to lock up when he came in, and his report would be made in the bedroom. By half-past he was a bit worried. Devilish awkward if Burrows had turned up after all and run Ludo in! At eleven he was resigned, and at half-past sound asleep.

That was how Ludo found him. It took a good stirring to get him awake. He woke very drowsily. "Good Lord, Ludo! What's the time?"

"Round about midnight." He spoke so tersely that the other guessed something was the matter. He was fully awake now. "How did you get on?"

"Nothing doing."

"Nothing doing? What do you mean? Cough it up, Ludo."

"I'll tell you just what happened. I got round to the front of the Hall and the border easily enough, and deposited my spade and gadget at the back. I ought to tell you that in the afternoon I'd stuck a sheet of paper in a clump immediately behind the lilies, so I knew exactly where to start from. Well, as I said, I left the tools there and had a peep round the Hall end of the border to see if the coast was perfectly clear, and if I didn't see something moving from the direction of the rose garden I must have been blind." As if to refute that statement, he removed his glasses and polished them vigorously.

"I kept low down, between the junction of the border and the stone path, and waited. Whoever it was came straight for me. Thinking I wasn't far enough out of sight I went to move back, just as the feller was almost on top of me. All I did was to fall tail over tip against something. I didn't make such an awful row, but it was quite enough to scare him, because I heard him take to his heels as hard as he could hare. The noise sounded rather as if he were wearing rubber shoes."

"Was it Burrows?"

"No, I'm sure it wasn't. I couldn't give my reasons for saying so, but I'm sure it wasn't he. However, I knew you'd be getting jolly anxious about me, so I only waited a few minutes and ventured out again. Then I scouted all round the Hall. I wasn't specially keen on getting a bat over the head, so I didn't hurry over it. As far as I could judge he'd gone. I didn't detect anybody or hear any movement, and I flatter myself I did the job very thoroughly. Then I got back and made a start with the gadget.

"I thought it best to come in from the back and keep crouched down, as then I should be absolutely invisible. It was black as your hat inside there, but it was child's play to find the lilies, because, even if I hadn't marked the spot, the scent was so heavy. I guess I was more excited than you would have been, Rouster"—under the influence of the boyish escapade he slipped into the old name—"but my heart was going like a kettledrum when I started pushing the rod down. There wasn't a thing there!" Ludo took off his glasses with one hand and gesticulated with the other. "I stuck that rod down in every direction and couldn't hit a thing. Oh, yes, once I thought I had something, but it must have been a stone because I could get all round it. What do you think I did next?" Ludo was desperately anxious to justify himself, to show that the lamentable failure was no fault of his.

"Don't know. Don't see what you could possibly have done."

"That's what I thought at first. Then I dug down a couple of feet and tried the rod again. I did the same all round these lilies. I actually thrust the rod through from side to side under the bulbs. That meant five feet down for a diameter of at least three feet. If there's anything under there I'll buy you the best hat in London."

Wrentham was certainly surprised. There had seemed no possibility of drawing blank. It was beyond him entirely. "I reckon you did better than I should have done, Ludo. All the same, it's most extraordinary."

"That's what I thought, so after I'd tidied up everywhere and made things look as much like normal as possible, I got the idea that perhaps I'd been trying the wrong lilies and that one of the two side groups might be meant. Well, I did try those two groups of tiger lilies. This time I had to work quickly because I had to come in from the front and consequently was in full view. According to the rod there was nothing there. I got my things together, ready to come back, and was just nipping round a bed at the angle of the house when I ran into a man. Really ran into him, I mean. I hit my head a devil of a wallop, and over we both rolled. By the time I'd got up he simply bolted. It was the same man I'd seen before, I'd swear to that. The really annoying thing was that I couldn't find my glasses for quite a bit, and as soon as I did get them I came straight up here."

"Which way did the man go?"

"The first time round by the rose garden, the second, down the drive."

"What I'm really getting at is this: he knew his way about?"

"Oh, rather! He ran like a jack rabbit and without the slightest hesitation."

"Tait for a fiver," said Wrentham. What a night Ludo had been through. Poor old chap! He looked knocked to the wide. "I think you've been simply splendid, Ludo. There's no doubt the fault lies in our preliminary inspection and not in anything you've done. Don't you think so?"

"I certainly think there is something wrong that we ought to find out. What's more, we'll have another go to-morrow night if you're fit and game."

But the morrow was to prove the most amazing day of all, and to bring with it a certain sign that matters were approaching a climax.

CHAPTER XXII
LITTLE GRAINS OF GRAVEL

THE VICAR evidently expected that the adjourned inquest would bring a party for lunch. Jensil had been written to, and both Delane and Burrows would probably come along. As in the house of the Franklin of old, it was apparently going to snow meat and drink. In such a small village as Hainton it was rare that the opportunity arose for hospitality, and the war had made a big gap in social continuity. Emma never made any difficulty: company in the house always meant company in the kitchen.

Wrentham decided not to go to the inquest. Ludo was of course required, and the vicar wished to be present. He took his duties very seriously, and already his son's accident had kept him on the Monday from the Bench, where he was chairman. As Wrentham confided to Ludo when they left, he would go over the ground once more and see if anything had been omitted. A connecting link must have been left out somewhere, but he was not too hopeful of finding it.

The inexplicable failure of the previous night had been a considerable shock to his complacency. When Ludo had set off to the Hall on his expedition it had seemed to him a case of going, seeing, and conquering. Surely Plumley had not been playing some mad prank, an April fool trick! That would have been a mordant jest on his son, but surely not the action of a man who knew himself in the presence of death. The fault must lie in the way the clue had been interpreted.

Underneath the lilies—so much was certain. If Ludo had been accurate in his investigations, and there seemed no reason for doubt about that, there was nothing under these lilies, unless it was at a greater depth than five feet. Hardly likely that. Plumley would never have excavated a hole of that depth; why, the top of his bald head would hardly have been visible. (You will perceive that the rule of *de mortuis* had gone by the board. A wallop on the head is apt to leave you little courtesy for the pates of others.) Then there must be some more lilies at the Hall, and, if so, a prominent show group.

Why not ask Wallace? Not, perhaps, the best authority on flowers, for they had never gone in for them much at the vicarage. Still, out of the mouths of babes and sucklings. . . . He found the gardener planting out cabbage plants on ground cleared from early potatoes. "Morning, Tom! We got any lilies in the garden?"

"Lilies? Yes, sir. There's always been a bed against the cold house."

"That's funny. I don't remember them." Just shows, he thought, how a man can often not see the wood for the trees, and doesn't know he has a thing till he wants it. "What sort are they?"

"Madonna lilies, sir. This way"; and in the corner where the cold house met the wall he pointed out an untidy mixture of stalks and dark green dwarf leaves.

"Surely those are not lilies," said Wrentham in astonishment.

"They are, sir, and if you'd seen them a fortnight or three weeks ago you'd have thought how well they were looking." He pulled away some of the disfiguring stalks. "They've been here as long as I can remember, sir, and I must have dug scores of bulbs out during my time. Leave'm alone and they're like weeds, unless they get the disease."

"What are these young shoots?"

"Lilies that have done flowering some time, sir. The Madonna lily never loses all its leaves. As soon as it stops flowering it starts again. If you want to move lilies, sir, now's the best time."

"You're a regular encyclopaedia, Tom," said Wrentham. "Now I've a poser for you. Suppose you saw some actually in bloom now. How would you account for that?"

"That's cushy, sir. They must have been planted late."

"But I thought you said they were a kind of evergreen."

"So they are, sir. Whenever you plant them there's green on them, but that don't make no difference."

"Right-ho, Tom. I'll give you in best. When we make our border we'll have a good clump of those chaps in it." Wallace was wondering why the Major was suddenly taking an interest in things. Wrentham was wondering whether the book, or Wallace, was right.

The book confirmed the gardener. It was all there: Madonna lily (*Lilium candidum*)—best moved in July after flowering—increases rapidly—best left undisturbed for some years—not fastidious as to soil—subject to disease—sand for roots and dust with sulphur.

The lilies at the Hall had been planted late, and that would account for their flowering. But there remained one final test: what of the lilies his father had seen and on which he had composed his sermon? As soon as he went out he would have a chat with Mrs. Walton. Young Masters, too—the very chap. He would probably be able to say exactly what orders Plumley gave when planting them at the Hall. He would know also exactly what Plumley had been doing in that interval between the dismissal of Gordon and the arrival of Tait. But wouldn't he be likely to talk? Well, suppose he did? The time had gone now for too much wariness. The one who got there earliest would get the worm. It certainly looked as if he would have to pay another visit to the Hall. The first lot of lilies he tackled he would have them up by the roots and excavate down as deep as coal.

These were the medley of thoughts that passed through his mind as he waited for the return of the others. There were also thoughts less pastoral—a revival of furious anger against the one who had come near to ending his life and the beginning of a deep feeling of suspicion against the man Tait.

But the wait was a long one. Emma came out and asked him if he wouldn't have something, and made remarks on the impossibility of keeping things hot when you never knew when people were coming in to their meals. When the party of five did arrive it was nearly two o'clock and he was as hungry as the proverbial hunter.

Jensil's booming voice and cheery bulk seemed to fill all the house. He was as good as a tonic for the vicar, and with Delane made the centre of one trio and found time to cut in on the third. Burrows looked a bit out of his depth. The work of the last ten days had doubtless proved trying, and late nights seldom agree after forty. While the others were engrossed in some discussion after lunch Wrentham signalled to Ludo and gave Burrows the tip to go out. He led the way to a shady spot under the elm where deck chairs invited. "Now, you people, tell me what happened. How did the inquest go, Burrows?"

"Better than I thought this time yesterday, Major, and thanks to you. The jury brought in the usual 'Death at the hands of some person or persons unknown,' so that tells you we haven't found what we're looking for. Still, I'm hoping."

"That's good," said Wrentham, passing over his tobacco pouch. "What did you actually find yesterday?"

"Well, I went to the wall as you suggested. I'll own up that when I started I wasn't any too optimistic."

"You didn't look any too boisterous," interrupted Wrentham, "but I put that down to the unfortunate fact of your having to accompany Captain Travers." Ludo waved an airy hand.

"As I was saying, I went to the wall and examined it inch by inch. That didn't give me much information. Somewhat in the way of one section of the wall was a load of gravel, for the paths, I presumed, heaped up almost to the coping. I wanted to be sure when it was put there, so I asked Masters about it on the quiet—perfectly casually, as I didn't want it to be repeated to Tait. Well, Masters said the gravel had been there a fortnight but they hadn't had time to use it. I went off back, and was just going to start on the wall again when about ten yards along it I noticed a smaller heap of gravel, about a couple of pails full, I thought at the time. It looked to me at first like the scrapings of the cart, but I soon realised it couldn't be that, as the cart would have been scraped with the shovel wherever it was kicked up. Curiosity got the better of me, and I had a good look at that heap. I cleaned some of it away, and underneath it I found—"

"Blood!" exclaimed both.

"You're right. That's where the murder had been committed, if murder you call it. I should say Moulines was struck by something, maybe a blow on the head or body, and fell backwards, smashing his skull on the flints. The person who struck him probably tried to see if he was dead and came in contact with the blood. The bleeding would soon stop, but in order to conceal the traces he got handfuls or hatfuls of gravel and covered the spot. He possibly therefore knew of the existence of the gravel beforehand."

"Surely that looks more and more like Tait?" suggested Wrentham.

"Maybe, maybe not. I had thought all along that your theory of the dead man being enticed into running, just as you were, Major, must be wrong, because the wound was at the back of the head. It would hardly have been there unless the action of striking a taut line had caused him to turn over in the air. Another thing that arises, therefore, is that the killing of Moulines and the attack on yourself were not necessarily by the same person. One other thing I ought to have told you: in spite of the quantity of rain which had lashed that wall I found on one of the flints some hairs and traces of blood."

"I think we ought to congratulate you on a very successful piece of work," contributed Ludo. "And what are you going to do now? I suppose you will go on with your inquiries. No fear of Scotland Yard butting in?"

"They can't come in unless the county asks them," replied the detective hopefully, "and we're not likely to do that yet, whatever we may have to do in the ultimate future. Yes, I suppose we shall go on with our inquiries, though probably from different angles and cast the net wider. We know the time Moulines crossed the railway at the gatehouse, but we haven't found a soul who saw him after that until he was found by Clark."

"A strange business," said Ludo, "but I suppose your job consists of little else."

"By Jove, that reminds me!" exclaimed the detective. "I shall have to be moving again. Maxwell came to me before the inquest with an extraordinary story, and I promised to see him about it afterwards. Mr. Wrentham asking me to lunch quite put it out of my mind." He rose to go. "Tait came to him this morning with an extraordinary story. Somebody had been at the Hall during the night and pulled up dozens of roses by the roots. They hadn't only pulled them up, but some of them had been dug up deeply and, according to Maxwell, earth was thrown about all over the place. But there you are: you never know what a tale was like originally after it has been through Maxwell's ears, and this one sounds to me like the doings of a lunatic or somebody's silly mischief."

"Is that all that was touched?"

"Well, practically. Tait had a good look round to see if any other mischief had been done. All he could find was traces of footsteps on the border and signs of earth being disturbed, but nothing actually upset. However, there's the tale for what it's worth. Will you make my excuses to Mr. Wrentham, Major, if I'm not back in time? I'll just nip up and see Tait for a minute. I ought to be back in under half an hour."

The faces of the two had betrayed merely polite interest in a ridiculous episode. "Seems rather too absurd to be true," said Wrentham. Ludo, not so sure of himself, fell back on the usual polishing of his glasses.

"If you're interested, I'll tell you what I found out when I come back," said Burrows as he got his hat from the hall.

"Please do," replied Ludo. "I expect we shall be in all the afternoon."

When he had gone, Wrentham regarded his now blushing assistant with an eye of mock reproof. "Now what about it, young feller? Pretty nice sensation you've created in this peaceful corner of England."

Ludo was on his defence. "Honestly, I didn't leave any traces. Unless, of course, the freshly turned earth was a bit noticeable. You heard what he said about the roses?"

"Did I not! It seems to spoil the Tait theory pretty thoroughly."

"How's that?"

"Have a heart, Ludo. Tait is a gardener. Can you imagine any gardener deliberately destroying his own garden? If you had something that was your bread and butter, and which you had made yourself, would you feel like destroying it for anything?"

"Certainly I might, if there was something better to tempt me. Tait might have imagined he was throwing dust in our eyes."

"Well, I don't agree with you. Still, whoever did it was the swine who had those papers of mine. I'll tell you what we'll do, Ludo. We'll get Burrows to help and go up to-night and lie in wait for the blighter."

"I don't think we could quite do that. It would mean telling Burrows more than we are quite prepared for yet. And if we went up alone we should have the risk of dodging Burrows and anybody else—probably one or two of the under-gardeners—who are bound to be on the look-out. Let's think it over for a bit."

"Right-ho! You apply your brains to it if you like. I'm going to speak to the others and then collar the paper if some hulking brute connected with the police hasn't already got his talons on it."

Ludo went off pensively to his seat under the elm and started the mental wrestling-match. His colleague passed into the dining-room, where a great pow-wow was going on. Jensil was illustrating something with the spoons; the other two, with chairs drawn up, were listening to his exposition. They certainly did not notice the appropriating of the unopened paper. Like a sparrow with a crumb Wrentham bore his spoil to the tree.

"Steady with the grey matter," he flippantly exhorted the other, and opened the paper at the sports page. This took a whole pipe to finish. Then came a very business-like search of the financial columns, where nothing of import. Next, the pictures on the back page, chiefly girls showing teeth and legs in the gentlest of sad sea waves. Then, "Hallo! What's this? 'The House at Hindhead, the Property of the late Henry Plumley, and the Scene of Yesterday's Inexplicable Outrage.'" He had another look. Henry Plumley's house. Yes. But what outrage? He turned over the sheets until they rustled—so much so that even the patient Ludo swivelled an inquiring eye. He scanned every sheet—ah, there it was! "Strange Occurrence at a Hindhead House." A whole column of it.

He read it slowly, every word of it. At the finish he pushed back his chair with perplexity. Phew! What on earth next! The fat was in the fire now, and somebody else seemed to know there was milk in the coker-nut.

He passed the paper over to Ludo. "Have a dekko at that, old scout," indicating the exact spot with his finger. Ludo indulged in a tantalising polish of his glasses. He too got furiously interested. "Well, that about tears it," was his eloquent comment.

Which was probably justified, for this is what they read.

CHAPTER XXIII
BEAUTY IN DISTRESS

STRANGE OCCURRENCE AT HINDHEAD HOUSE
CARETAKER'S AMAZING DISCOVERY
IS OUR SOLUTION CORRECT?

AN AMAZING OCCURRENCE took place during the night of Monday last at "The Larches," formerly the residence of the late Henry Plumley. "The Larches" is of quite recent date and stands well back from the main road, the approach being by a long carriage drive. Of moderate size and containing only some dozen rooms, the house was a great favourite with its late owner, who was accustomed fairly frequently to spend his week-ends on the local golf course. On account of events arising out of the late owner's death the furniture had been removed on Saturday last, and Mr. and Mrs. Keymer, the caretakers, had retired to a small cottage near Greyshott. The house was therefore deserted although securely fastened. It was nevertheless the intention of Mr. Keymer to pay a daily visit of inspection to see that all was in order. He had actually gone round the building on the Sunday and Monday and had found both house and grounds in perfect order.

Our readers may not know that the late Henry Plumley took an enormous interest in gardens. He practically remade the very extensive gardens at "The Larches," and his special pride was the immense rose garden. This was in front of the house, facing south, and contained some hundreds of bushes tastefully arranged in beds. Although they had been unattended for some days when our correspondent saw them yesterday, such as remained were a mass of bloom. In the very front of the house, between it and the roses, were various beds of annuals. The whole must have afforded a feast of colour to the eye.

Yesterday morning, however, when Mr. Keymer made his visit of inspection, an amazing sight met his gaze. The flowers in the beds had been pulled up and scattered everywhere, and in the centre of each bed a deep hole was dug. Further, the rose beds had been ruined; not a single one had been left intact. Roses had been torn up by the roots and had been scattered about, and again each bed had been dug in. Some beds actually contained two or three excavations. Furthermore, a fine specimen fir tree on the west lawn had been sawn off within a foot of its base and had crashed against the house. The fact that the nearest residence is two hundred yards away will explain the failure of anyone to remark on the unusual noise.

Two things were at once apparent. The perpetrators of this amazing outrage must have been at work through most of the Monday night. Further, the object was not the theft of the roses. Mr. Parker, formerly head gardener at "The Larches," interviewed by our correspondent, informed him that when the numbers of the bushes were checked they were found to be correct, and that if a thief had stolen them it would have been almost impossible to replant them at this particular time of year.

It is needless to say that the police were at once informed of this extraordinary outrage, and were on the spot immediately. If the purpose of the actors in this absurd drama (for the police incline to the belief that more than one man was concerned) had as their object mere wanton damage they are likely to pay very heavily for the performance. The police have already secured what are believed to be valuable clues, and hope to be in a position to make a statement shortly.

There is a theory of our own, however, which we offer without any apologies to our readers. It will be remembered that the late Henry Plumley died in the act of making a speech on unemployment at the People's Hall, Aldgate. In that speech, purely as illustration and in a metaphorical sense, he alluded to buried treasure. Was there a person or persons that night among his audience sufficiently naive as to take these remarks seriously? It almost seems so. In our opinion there can be no other explanation of this peculiar outrage. If ours is the explanation we believe it to be, the police will doubtless take steps to guard the other properties of the late Henry Plumley against a continuation of such senseless and wanton destruction. A special article on the latest developments of the case will appear in to-morrow's issue of this paper.

Wrentham had been regarding the other's face with interest during the reading. "I don't agree with you about this being a disaster," was his opinion. "For one thing, I should imagine there's nothing gone."

"Oh, there's nothing gone," admitted Ludo. "If there had been, they wouldn't have dug up every bed, unless they had the good or bad luck to find what they were looking for in the very last job they tackled."

"I never did believe in the roses being of any use to us. You remember what I told you about those at the Hall. Only a few put in, and those to replace losses or disappointments. There couldn't have been any clue or message with them. What's our policy now? To let Burrows in on the whole thing?"

"Strange to say, I'd been thinking about that in quite another connexion. I should say 'No.' I really think, Geoffrey, that our policy should be to hand out to Burrows no more than is absolutely necessary; and that amount at present appears to me to be *nil*. I propose we simply hand the paper over to him and ask him if he has seen the news. He has already given us an opening in reporting the discovery at the Hall."

"I think you're right, as usual. Still, we've got to hang on here all the afternoon in case he comes back. I think you ought to add this, however, when talking to Burrows"—and he confided his idea to the other, who, after raising several objections, agreed to it in a modified form.

"No more brain-work for me," was Wrentham's final word, "or for you, young feller. You brought down a collection of iron-mongery and we've also the balls you doubtless brought too. Come and try your hand with a mashie. The one nearest the flag. Threepence a time."

Ludo had not made any statement as to his having taken up golf pretty seriously during the previous few months. That was how most of his leisure had been spent. This unrevealed fact probably accounted for the position when Burrows made his appearance, Wrentham being four and threepence down, to his vast astonishment. Indeed, he was in the act of regarding, with mingled consternation and astonishment, his opponent lofting a ball to within a few feet of the pin when the detective came up.

"Thank God for this!" he exclaimed. "I was praying for Blucher or night. This home-made Cinquevalli has damn near ruined me."

Ludo snapped his eyes and looked exceedingly apologetic. "I thought you wanted me to play."

"Hark at him, Burrows! Four and threepence I owe to this masquerading Shylock." He grimaced with mock despair as they went back to the tree. "What happened at the Hall?"

"Pretty much what Maxwell told me. The place is in a fearful mess."

"In other words, a horticultural shambles," suggested Ludo.

"That just about describes it," laughed Burrows. "There were enough footprints for an army if they hadn't been made by the same person. At least all those round the rose beds. Those on the border were quite distinct, but my own opinion is that they were nothing to do with the business at all."

Wrentham passed over the paper. "Have a look at that."

Halfway through the detective looked up and saw the intent watching of the others. "Rather queer this," he remarked. Each was thinking of what would be his impressions when he came to the paper's treasure theory. His remark, however, was too shrewd for at least one listener. "More people looking for truth, Major!"

The Major for once found no apt answer, but Ludo came to the rescue. "I wanted to ask you personally what ought to be done about the Hall in the light of this, Burrows. Don't you think there ought to be some sort of guard kept?"

"I think we can soon fix up that," was the detective's reply. "A relief for Maxwell ought to meet the case. They can do duty turn and turn about for a night or two. I shouldn't think there will be any repetition, however, especially when this Hindhead affair gets out. The job was probably done by the same crank. I may know more when I have heard from the Hindhead police."

"You'd look a bit silly if they did roll up again," said Wrentham. "Mr. Travers was thinking of taking a look round himself during the night. It might be just as well if you gave your man his name and description in case he puts in an appearance."

"That's just as Captain Travers likes." The detective didn't seem any too keen. "Where's Delane, by the way? Gone yet?"

"No, I think they're still holding the fort," said Wrentham, leading the way in. The fort was indeed being held. The voice of Jensil reached to the porch. You could hardly see across the room for smoke. The vicar looked very guilty when they came in, perhaps at having had no afternoon nap. Their entry served as the necessary signal for breaking up the party. Jensil declared he had no idea it was so late. Delane also bustled round as if he were now in a hurry. He announced that he had to get back to Norwich, and Burrows was going with him. "I'll see to that little matter for you, Captain Travers," was the detective's parting remark to Ludo as they saw them off from the porch.

"Rather like the tennis parties of the old days before the war, pater. This has done you a lot of good." Turning to Ludo, "We shall have to get him about a bit more. The Carews were asking the other night when we were all going over." The loss of his nap seemed to have done the vicar no harm, but rather to have renewed his youth. He announced his intention of paying a visit or two. He had promised to look in on old Wharton for one thing.

"I'll tell you what we'll do, young feller," said Wrentham. "We'll have an early cup of tea and a game or two of billiards. What about trying out that set of snooker balls you brought us?"

Ludo agreed on one condition: "The first who says a thing about Plumley or any of his works pays a bob."

"With you every time," agreed the other. "It's a filthy occupation for a summer afternoon, but I don't feel like walking. By the way, you'll excuse my mentioning the fact, but I suppose you haven't spent your life on a billiard-table since you were here last?"

But new matter for a May morning was at hand. In the middle of the umpteenth game, with Ludo's start of four and three-pence reduced to fivepence, Helen appeared with a note. "No answer, sir." Wrentham didn't trouble to read it until the game was over. When he did open it he could hardly believe his eyes.

DEAR MAJOR WRENTHAM,

A matter of extreme urgency has arisen on which I must speak to you. Realising the danger there is of scandal in villages, I will not ask you to come to my house. If, however, you will meet me about a hundred yards down the small lane that turns off the forking of the heath road at about ten p.m. I shall be more than grateful.

Yours very truly,

SYLVIA FORREST

"If that isn't the limit!" He passed the note to Ludo.

"I won't make any of the ridiculous comments to which this note lays you open," he said chuckling. "All the same, it's devilish funny."

"Can't see the joke myself," said the other, running his hands through his hair. "Hold hard a minute, though," and he rang the bell.

"Who brought this note, Helen?"

"One of the village boys, sir. I don't know his name. He just said there wasn't any answer."

"Right! Thank you, Helen."

He read the note again, then put it in the empty grate and set a match to it. "What would you do about it if you were I?"

"I should certainly go," was Ludo's opinion.

"Yes, but how? Alone, or with you?"

Ludo hastily withdrew from any possible complicity. "I don't think it would be very wise for me to go. Why should I? What cause for danger is there?"

"Lord knows! The whole thing is so startling that I don't know what to make of it. There's one thing I am jolly bucked about. When I connected her with the Plumley business I wasn't far wrong. It's a certainty that that's what she wants to see me about. Look here, Ludo. Open out a bit. What am I to do about it?"

Ludo was plainly flustered and remained non-committal.

"There's one other thing, however," continued Wrentham. "The idea may be to get me out of the way for another search of the study. I'll lock the drawer in any case, Ludo, and you'll be on guard."

Ludo appeared to have made up his mind. "If I were you I should most decidedly go. As you say, if the idea is to get you out of the way, I'll certainly hold the fort at this end. Slip on your trench coat and put the Colt in your pocket. You don't know if any of her pals may be round. One other thing I'd do. Will Tango come to heel?"

"Oh, rather! He'll keep within a foot of me if necessary."

"All right, then. Take him on a lead with you and keep him to hand. If there should be anybody moving about he'll give you warning. Probably you'll look a bit of a fool—perhaps I should say bigger fool—carting round a dog with you if she happens to be absolutely alone, but you'd look a bigger one still if you ended up with another crack on the skull."

"Yes, but why should anybody want to go cracking my skull? There's nothing now they can get hold of."

"It does seem a thankless task, I admit," was Ludo's final summary. "Still, there you are. That's what I should do."

And that is what Wrentham did. He donned his discoloured waterproof and slipped the Colt into the big pocket. An old hat of Ludo's added to the disguise. Indeed, as he told his aide-de-camp, who had received strict orders to keep the light going and to sit up for him, he wanted nothing but a tin mug in the front of his coat and a "Blind" placard to be made for life. The vicar had gone to bed early and the coast was clear. The night was fairly light, with a young moon, and of the three who parted at the drive gate Tango was the most excited. It was the first night operation he had ever been present at.

CHAPTER XXIV
SYLVIA FORREST'S STORY

HE KEPT CLOSE to the left-hand side of the road with Tango trotting along at his heels. Near Puddle Pond a trap passed them, but he assured himself he was not recognised or even seen, for he flattened himself against a tree and the shadows cast by moving lights are treacherous. He was, however, feeling most unhappy about the whole business. Beauty in distress was one thing, but clandestine appointments were quite another. If by any unlucky chance he should be recognised the news would be all over the village in a few hours, and over half the county in a week. For all he knew, the whole scheme might be simply one to discredit him in people's eyes.

From the pond, however, to the end of the main road no soul was seen. Where the trees ended the so-called lane was but a track in the grass. Tango whimpered excitedly as a rabbit ran from under their very heels, but a curt order from his master soon quieted him. He stood perfectly still for a minute or two, but could hear no sound save the many voices of the night. The two moved on along the track with its remnant of hedge, straggly and broken.

About a hundred yards down, as he judged, they came to a great oak, standing back from the drift, its branches reaching over to the broken hedge. A likely spot, he thought, and with one's back against the tree easy to keep off any surprise attack. As he came under the denser shadow, walking warily, with his left hand thrust out before his face as a guard against stray boughs, he caught the faintest scent of a perfume and heard a voice which he recognised.

"Is that you, Major Wrentham?"

"Yes, Miss Forrest." His voice sounded very strange in his efforts to speak low. Tango growled again and was quieted. Beyond the tree the line of the horizon could be plainly discerned up the slope. It would be impossible for anybody to approach that way.

"Major Wrentham, you must have thought me mad to write to you as I did." He did not know what to say, and did as many a better man has done—kept quiet. "I am in such trouble. I didn't know which way to turn."

He could not see her clearly; just an outline, a pale thing which might have been her face, and the smell of that delightful perfume. She seemed to be crying, dabbing her eyes with a handkerchief. He had no more idea than Tango what he should do, and yet he found himself patting her arm. "Don't worry, Miss Forrest; tell me all about it."

"But it seems so incredible. You will never believe me."

He was feeling more sure of himself now that he had taken the header. "The world is full of incredible things. Please tell me."

"Do you mind if I start at the beginning. It's a dreadfully long story."

"Please do. Just tell me everything there is to tell."

They were speaking in unnatural whispers, but when she began her story she raised her voice ever so slightly. The other drew his back against the tree, then stooped and pressed the dog down to his feet. He could by now see faintly the line of hedge that marked the track. If a rabbit had moved he thought he could have seen the flash of it.

"People in the village have already remarked on the strange thing that I should be connected with the Masons. What they do not know, Major Wrentham, is the story of her brother, my father. He ran away from home when he was quite a boy, as I have often heard him relate, and went into service with a doctor as a sort of page-boy. When this doctor found him remarkably quick and trustworthy he began to take a great interest in him, and as his wife was dead and he had no children of his own he actually sent Daddy to a school, where he did simply splendidly in his examination and even gained a valuable scholarship. The doctor helped with his fees, and he did wonderfully in his medical examinations and actually ended up as assistant to his benefactor. When the doctor died Daddy succeeded to the practice and quite a lot of money besides. Of course I don't remember anything about that, but I have often heard Daddy talk about it. He was not the least bit ashamed of his origin. He died only about five years ago, and then mother sold the practice and we took a smaller house much more in keeping with our means.

"I always wanted to be a singer. People had often complimented me on my voice, and I was constantly asked to sing at private concerts. Then, at one of these—a charity concert in Mayfair—I met Mr. Plumley: Henry Plumley. I can't explain how it was, but he seemed to take to me from the first. He called round to see us several times, and finally suggested that he should pay my fees—and very expensive they were—so that my voice might have the proper training. Of course I hardly liked the idea of that, and yet I was very much flattered. My mother urged me to accept the offer, and Mr. Plumley said I need only regard it as a kind of investment for him, and when I was getting the big money I was sure to get some day I could repay him.

"Well, I accepted his offer, and three years and I don't dare to think how much money were spent over my training. In the meanwhile I ought to tell you that Mr. Plumley had persuaded mother to let him reinvest our capital, and we were in consequence much better off. When my training abroad was finally over and I went to see him he had a great surprise for me. He said he had intended from the first that I should marry his son. All he needed in his life was a good woman to pull him together.

"You can imagine that was a great shock to me. I asked for time to think it over, because I knew his reputation even if I did not know George Plumley himself." She hesitated and again dabbed at her eyes.

"Then two things happened. First Mother died and then there was a dreadful scandal about George Plumley's marriage. When I next saw Mr. Plumley after it was all over he was just as kind as ever to me, although anybody could see he was desperately broken up. I told him I intended selling the furniture, giving up the house, and then going into rooms, and then he asked me if I would go to Bellingham House as housekeeper. I couldn't very well do that, and again I had to put him off with excuses. Then I had pneumonia and my voice went. I could still sing, but my voice wasn't a bit what it had been. The doctors said that with time—a year or two—it would be as strong as ever.

"I went to see Mr. Plumley, but he was not at home. I went again two or three times, with the same result, and then I began to be a bit suspicious. I began also to realise that it wasn't that he could not, but that he would not, see me. On two occasions when I was sure he was there the door of Bellingham House was shut in my face. I wrote to him and got no answers at all. I was very worried about it all, because it was so inexplicable. I was not worrying about not being able to follow my profession, because I had plenty of money to live on. I could easily have afforded a service flat if I had cared for that kind of thing. Finally I saw an announcement that Mr. Plumley was to speak at the People's Hall, Aldgate, and I made up my mind to go there and see him after the meeting was over. Oh, wasn't it dreadful!" and her voice broke.

Wrentham waited for her to recover. "I was at that meeting," he said. He did not mean to say it: it just slipped out of its own accord. She gave a gasp of surprise.

She went on. "Yes, and I couldn't understand why he was pointing at me and staring at me so fixedly when he was talking about that hidden treasure. Major Wrentham, I am as sure as that I am standing here that he had some message for me. When I saw the solicitors the next day I was sure of it. All my money had gone. Beyond a few pounds for immediate needs I had nothing in the world."

She waited, as if for some comment from him, but he gave no sign.

"I didn't know what to do. I had already got my aunt to let me have Lodge Cottage when she went away, and it was the first thing I thought about. At first I intended to come here and live quietly for a bit. Then when I thought it all over I knew Mr. Plumley intended that I was to have that money to make up for what he had taken from me. And I couldn't do anything. The message had said that I should see the money in front of me in grass and trees and flowers, and so I went to the Hall and sat there and tried to see. I tried so hard, but I could see nothing— nothing at all. Oh, Major Wrentham! won't you help me?"

"How can I help you? You mean to find this supposed money?"

"Major Wrentham, you were at that meeting. You know as well as I do that that message was real, whatever the papers may say."

"The papers?"

"Yes. Didn't you read how people had been trying to get the money from Hindhead? Oh! I am sure, I feel it inside me somewhere, that you know all about it."

"Miss Forrest, I have no more idea than you of the whereabouts of this supposed money."

She was crying again, very softly. It was unbearable. Again he did not mean to speak but he did. "If the money is yours, Miss Forrest, it is yours, but I'm afraid a court of law would hardly take the same view."

"What has the law got to do with it?" This with all the illogicality of woman's reasoning. "If Mr. Plumley gave it to me and I am likely to starve for want of it, why shouldn't I take it? Major Wrentham, you must see that. Won't you help me?"

"If you will be explicit and tell me how, I will do anything I can." At the moment he would have promised anything. "But why did you hit on me?"

"Because I thought you were trying to get the money yourself!"

Blunt that! and certainly a bit of a facer. His reply was very lame, and gave away more than he intended. "I don't admit that, Miss Forrest, but suppose for the moment that I was. If you knew the circumstances you might consider that I had as good a right to it as anybody. Also"—he added this as an afterthought—"I didn't then know of the existence of your claim."

"Then you will help me, Major Wrentham?"

He did not know what to say, feeling the ground being cut away from under his feet. He temporised. "The position is very difficult. Mr. Plumley gave you what was not his own. Suppose anything were found it is not ours, and the penalty for taking it would be very severe. The most I could do would be—if, of course, anything ever was found—to take you to where it was and then let your own conscience be your judge."

"Oh! will you do that?" In her excitement and relief she grasped his arm. "Oh, Major Wrentham! How can I thank you?"

He thought she was going to start crying again, and cut in quickly, "Don't thank me, Miss Forrest, until after the event. After all, I may be of precious little use to you."

"Oh, you're so splendid! I'm sure we shall succeed. What are we going to do, and when are we going to begin?"

"That's one thing I'm afraid I can't tell you, Miss Forrest. You mustn't expect too much from me. What I will promise you is that if I think we are on the point of discovering anything I will let you know. And what I have already promised about your having your share shall be true."

"You say' we.' Whom do you mean?"

He recovered from the slip. "I mean you and me. Now can you tell me anything you have discovered?"

There was regret and excitement both in her voice. "I'm absolutely useless. I haven't discovered a thing. All I have done is to sit like a broody hen on her eggs and watch where I thought something might be. All I can say is that nothing was removed while I was there."

He couldn't help smiling at the *naivete* of it. "I don't think they'd try to remove anything by daylight. Still, it's a capital start. Have you heard about last night's attempt?"

There was a catch in her voice, and again she grasped his arm. "What attempt?"

He told her, adding the assurance that, in his opinion, nothing had been found.

"Oh, Major Wrentham, we must do something quickly!"

"Miss Forrest, whatever is done will have to be done quickly. I think I can promise you that." A silence fell between them, and Tango stirred restlessly. Wrentham suddenly recalled his preparations for attack, and how ridiculous they now seemed.

"What are you going to do with yourself, Major Wrentham, now the war is over?"

"I'm afraid I'm a man out of a job. Still, something's bound to roll up." Again the silence. Tango got up and strained at his leash. "If there is nothing else we can do at present, I think you ought to be going," he suggested.

"No, I want you to go first. I shall come on later."

"I say"—he stammered somewhat—"it was jolly plucky of you coming out here all alone."

"I didn't feel at all plucky. I felt as nervous as a kitten. Shall I expect to hear from you then?"

"Yes," he assured her. "I will find means of getting you a note somehow if there is anything certain doing. Will you be in, by the way, the next few days?"

"Yes, I shall be indoors all the time. If I am not, my maid is to be trusted implicitly." She held out her hand. "Good night, Major Wrentham. Have you forgiven me for bringing you out on this foolish errand?"

The fragrance around her may have had something to do with his answer. "Miss Forrest, I can't say how glad I am that you did send for me. You're sure you'd rather go back alone?"

She nodded her head and he turned away and was gone ere she could have been aware of it.

He was so intent on regaining cover and busy with the thoughts aroused by that strange meeting that when Tango leaped at the flash of a rabbit the lead went, and Tango too. Wrentham dared not whistle or call. He could hear the panting of the dog. Damn the animal! Chasing rabbits with the lead on, too. Might get himself tied up in some hedge, and then there'd be the devil to pay. Well, no use hanging about. He started off again, and from time to time sent back a glance to see if he could discern the other following. There was neither sign nor sound. Half-way along the main road Tango caught him up and came crawling on his belly for the expected cursing. His master took the lead without a word, and again they jogged off. But the next time he mustered courage to try a leap he was jerked back on his hind legs with a shock that nearly throttled him.

"Funny things, men!" Tango might have thought. "Devilish funny things, women!" his master was thinking. Sylvia Forrest was thinking how hungry she was. Ludo was yawning: "They must be having an all-night sitting." The vicar, who for once had an attack of insomnia, was wondering what was keeping those boys up so late. The next night he was to wonder still more.

CHAPTER XXV
EVENTS OF JULY 31ST:
RECONNAISSANCE

WHEN WRENTHAM AWOKE it was with the recognition of having suffered a sea change. It took him some seconds to realise fully the events of the previous night, and now, in the cool light of morning, they wore for him a very different aspect from what they had seemed beneath last night's stars. He could understand now why Ludo had been so unappreciative of his story. He must have got devilish fed up with waiting all that time, and, not having had the stimulus of being an actor in the dialogue, could not but regard things in a pessimistic way. By Jove! that conversation made a huge difference. Had he done wrong to let out so much? Had he been unwise to commit himself to help her without first consulting Ludo? And was that what the old ass had been so grumpy about? Well, what was done couldn't be undone. Better go and rouse Ludo and see what he was thinking after a good night's sleep. There was Emma coming.

He slipped on his dressing-gown and met her at the top of the stairs with "Bright and early this morning, Emma!" He relieved her of the tray. Ludo was sound asleep, and took some rousing. "Here you are, young feller. Swallow this down and nurse will give you a chocolate." Ludo groped for his glasses and tried the mixture as prescribed. Over a cigarette they discussed the situation.

"After I turned in last night, or rather this morning," said Ludo, "I went over all that interview of yours in my mind. I got out a list of things I wanted to ask you about. Frankly, I think the whole business begins to be remarkably fishy."

"Of course you're taking into account the fact that you've never had a thing to do with a woman in your life—your misanthropic tendencies, so to speak. You're sure you're not prejudiced?"

"Just a minute." Ludo found up a piece of paper and started to scribble. "Let me jot down what I was thinking last night while it's reasonably fresh in my mind and before your infernal chatter drives it out. That's it. Now then; answer me these questions. In the first place, did she during the whole of the conversation tell you anything which could be checked up on, to see if it was true?"

"Of course, heaps and heaps!"

"Right-ho, then; tell me something."

Wrentham thought for a goodish bit. "Well, if you put it quite like that, I don't think I can."

"All right. Now for concrete instances. What was the name of the doctor who acted as benefactor to her father?"

"She didn't say."

"Quite so. And we can't look him up, unless it be in the Æsculapian directories of heaven. Where did he live, or, if you prefer, where did they live until her father's death?"

"Lord knows!"

"Exactly! and therefore we cannot check. What was the name of her school?" (No answer.) "Where did she study music?" (No answer.) "Coming to dates, did she mention when she got from Henry Plumley permission to go anywhere on the Hainton estate? And did all the dates she gave you fit in?"

"Here! Have a heart, Ludo! I come in at about midnight and get off to bed at about one in the morning, and you expect me to have ready a complete analysis of everything she told me. I don't remember anything of what you've been asking me. All I do know is that to me her story rang absolutely true."

"To you it might. To me it sounds extraordinarily queer. However, you've given your word, and now I suppose we shall have this woman hanging on to our skirts. Next time I say my prayers I shall add, 'Please God, don't make me fascinating!'"

Wrentham at that left his companion master of the stricken field and went off to his tub. However, by the time breakfast was over he was feeling fairly resilient again and sufficiently confident to propound yet another scheme, fire new from the mint. This time it was to interview Masters and try to get from him all the information which seemed necessary to fill in the gaps. "I asked Wallace," he announced, "what time the Hall gardeners knocked off for dinner. He said about half-past twelve. If we start from here at about twenty past we ought to meet him as he goes to his cottage."

Ludo was still feeling somewhat disgruntled. "It's by no means certain. The probability is that now these people have nobody to keep an eye on them except Rendell they make their meals as long as they like and take them when they jolly well please."

Wrentham agreed gracefully. "Will you come along and chance it?"

Ludo thought he might. The other, exasperated, threw a cushion at him, and after sundry wrestlings and contortions managed to get something like normality out of him. The installation of a flower-pot in the tennis court and the informal opening of a complete short hole from the corner of the paddock further served to clear the atmosphere. When they did set out ultimately round by the village it was in quite good spirits.

As they approached Mrs. Walton's cottage Wrentham remembered the question he intended asking her. She happened to be at the gate talking to the baker. To mark time he did up a perfectly fastened shoe-lace, and as they arrived before the small gate the baker was swinging again on to his bicycle. "Good morning, Mrs. Walton. I wanted to ask you something about those gorgeous lilies of yours. Madonna lilies, are they not?"

"Yes, sir. I think that's what they call them."

"Well, now. How is it that ours at the vicarage have finished flowering long ago and yours are still out? Did you move them this year?"

"Yes, sir. That's just what I did do. Or, rather, my boy, who works in Peter's nurseries at Norwich, he sent me a lot of new bulbs this spring, and when he was home for a short holiday he put them and the old ones into this bed in the front garden. A rare lot of people have been admiring them."

"I don't wonder at that. Would you mind if Captain Travers had a look at them?"—and he motioned Ludo to the gate.

"Why did you ask about those lilies?" he asked as they went on.

Wrentham told him. "Those lilies at the Hall ought to have been dead days ago, but they were still flourishing when I saw them last. I just wondered whether Plumley had new bulbs or transferred the old, or what happened. Also, if we do catch Masters there'll be some ground to work on."

"But won't Tait be with him?"

"Oh, no! Tait shares half the double cottage where Roberts lives."

They arrived at the stile and were lucky enough to see Masters coming towards them, halfway across the church path. "He's your pigeon," said Ludo, "so I'll go on."

"No, you don't! You keep with me for moral support. It will also save my repeating it all over for you again afterwards." The gardener came abreast.

"Morning, Masters. You're the very chap who can help us out if you're not in too much of a hurry."

"How's that, sir?"

"Well, Captain Travers and I have been having an argument about lilies. We just had a word with Mrs. Walton about hers. It's like this: ours at the vicarage are all dead, and those of Mrs. Walton's and yours at the Hall are still out. Now, did you replant them last spring?"

"No, sir. We didn't replant them. Mr. Plumley said he was going to put in some new bulbs."

"Said he was going to? Didn't he plant them?"

"Well, sir, he did and he didn't. He showed them to us in the afternoon, and fine big bulbs they were, sir. Never saw such bulbs in my life. Mr. Plumley he measured up the border and stuck a stake in to mark the place where he was going to put them. When we come along next morning to carry on with the border he already had them in."

"He'd done them himself?"

"That's right, sir. He must have done them the night before. I was sort of foreman, because we only had Barton as kind of rough digger, and he pointed them out to me, and I remember he said they weren't on no account to be moved. He said, sir, them bulbs had cost a lot of money and they'd take several years to grow into anything like. One thing he had done, sir: he'd smothered them with flowers of sulphur because all the ground was covered with it."

"Why had he done that?" asked Ludo.

"So they shouldn't get the disease, sir. Sulphur allust keeps it off. Well, as I was saying, sir, he give strict orders that we weren't to touch them lilies on any account whatever happened to them. He said he'd made up his mind to have the best border in Norfolk, and them lilies was to be the centre of it."

"Did Mr. Plumley do any more planting by himself?"

"No, sir. Not as far as I know. We got the whole border replanted by the Tuesday, and Mr. Plumley he said we'd have the border better than it had ever been before."

"I don't think he was far wrong about that, Masters," said Wrentham. "At any rate, you've settled our bet, and it's only right you should share in the proceeds." He handed over half a crown. "Drink my health!"

"Thank'ee, sir. Thank'ee." The young gardener was plainly taken aback at this unexpected windfall. He touched his forelock with one hand while grasping the *pourboire* with the other.

"Oh, just one other thing, Masters. Are there any other lilies at the Hall except those in the border?"

Masters rubbed his chin and appeared to be making a mental Cook's tour. "No, sir. There aren't any other lilies at the Hall. That I'm sarten of."

"Good! Are you doing anything, by the way, about guarding the gardens after that business of the other night?"

The gardener looked very surprised at the extent of Wrentham's knowledge. "No, sir, not that I know on. Martin, he have orders to go out during the night, that's all." And the parties moved on.

"We'd better go on to the church and round by the meadows for appearance' sake," suggested Wrentham. "Now, Ludo, what's your opinion about those lilies?"

Ludo was most perplexed. "I'm damned if I know. One thing I am sure about, and that is, that there wasn't a square inch under them that I didn't explore. That is," he added hastily, "the central lilies. I own I didn't do the side groups so thoroughly."

"Never mind about those. I've got a brain wave, and it's so absurd that I won't tell you anything about it until I've had time to think it over. Anyhow, I've an idea that to-night we shall have stirring times. Tell you what I'll do, Ludo. Bet you a new hat that the whole thing will be settled by this time to-morrow, that is, if it isn't settled before."

"I'm not taking you on. My middle name always was Cassandra. Were you not afraid, by the way, that Masters would repeat what we asked him to Tait?"

"I don't care a hoot in hell if he does. I expect he'll find some difficulty in putting it all together again. But what's it matter? There's a pretty big kitty in the pool, and we've just jolly well got to take a risk. If you ask me, it will be all a flick of a feather which way things go."

They went through the churchyard and by the side path to the Hall drive. Each gave a surreptitious glance as they passed the cottage, but no sign of life was there save the scarce seen grey of the chimney smoke. No mention was made of the unseen occupant, yet each was glad in some indefinable way when the cottage lay behind them.

"One thing I'm looking forward to," said Ludo, "and that's the latest in the paper about the 'Hindhead Outrage,' as they called it."

"Rather late in the day for us, I expect. There'd be a bit of a sensation, Ludo, if we two started spilling the beans into the receptive ears of editors—what?"

The paper, however, was very lukewarm after the previous day's hot air.

THE AFFAIR AT HINDHEAD

LATEST INFORMATION

With regard to the mysterious affair we reported in our columns yesterday there is little to add. The police have the matter well in hand, and are still inclining to their own theory that the question is one of damage and destruction for destruction's sake. A further theory that has now arisen is that some sufferer by the collapse of City Corporations has had his revenge by inflicting as much damage as possible on the estates of the late unfortunate head of that concern. If this is so, the act must have been that of a madman, since, as a creditor, he would have been destroying his own property.

The extraordinary interest aroused by our own theory brought forward yesterday in these columns is shown by the large numbers of letters which have already reached us, a selection from which is printed elsewhere in this issue. Our readers may rest assured that we are by no means disposed to let the matter rest where it is, and any further developments will at once be reported.

The pictures were the usual thing—any sort of padding which could anyhow be said to bear on the case. They were: a photo of the felled larch, Mr. and Mrs. Keymer and their cottage, a general view of the Hindhead golf course, and, finally, a ghoulish resuscitated picture of Henry Plumley himself.

They had a look at the letters. "Lord, what tripe!" was Wrentham's comment.

"Why not?" inquired Ludo. "If you keep a tripe shop I should imagine you have to keep it in stock."

The comment was not wholly unmerited. It consisted of unburdening of souls by "Judex," "Countryside," "Lover of Gardens," "Anti-Socialist," and all the dozen or so of mute, inglorious scribes who doubtless blushed to find themselves in print. Wrentham turned in relief to the sports page, and Ludo wandered off to the billiard-room to try his hand at a few red losers—the foundation, somebody had assured him, of a good game.

But he was not to be allowed to continue in peace. Just as he thought he could do three out of four from any position on the table, the sight of his partner in detection coming into the room and, carrying what looked like an enormous onion in his hand, warned him that the day was likely to continue fine and warm. There had been a few clouds; the paper had produced wind and the rest of the weather forecast he would not have cared to predict.

CHAPTER XXVI
EVENTS OF JULY 31ST:
PREPARATION AND BARRAGE

LUDO WAS HAULED out to the study, and the other bore the apparent onion with him. He placed it on the desk with its paper wrapping, dirt and all, hitched up his trousers, and stoked up his pipe. Ludo, mystified and a bit worried, contributed to the proceedings by polishing his glasses. "Well, young feller, I fancy we've arrived at the last sitting of this society. If that unmentionable swine hadn't pinched the records I'd read the minutes of the last meeting."

"Meetings!" exclaimed Ludo. "Good Lord! What else has there been but meetings?"

"Well, what do you want better? Perfectly friendly and keeps us out of mischief. However"—and he gave his trousers a further hitch to indicate that the business of the day ought to be proceeded with—"this session is going to be thrilling enough for anybody outside a graveyard. Can you remember that famous list of yours?"

"I think so. One of the few things left to me is a tenacious memory. I can't guarantee the order, however."

"It doesn't matter a cuss about the order. I'll sing out what I can remember of the things you had to get, and you add any I leave out. Now then. Pine needles, cones, suitcases, tennis balls, cement, damp-coursing, wire. Anything else?"

"Yes, information about glass."

"Right-ho! That completes it then. I don't think the last matters. Sort of inverted fox and grapes. I mean it doesn't matter because I can't find any use for it or make it fit in. Now then, this is what I want to ask you"—and he produced the onion. He shook it vigorously until the last speck of dirt was left on the paper; then held it in the palm of his hand so that the other might see it plainly. "Remembering that list, what does this remind you of?"

Ludo regarded it much as a thrush might contemplate a new sort of worm. "Well, it looks like a very ragged onion and might be stretched to resemble a tennis-ball."

"Good!" Wrentham threw the onion up to the ceiling and caught it again. "Only it isn't an onion. It's a lily bulb. I stuck the fork into the clump while Wallace was at his dinner, and took the biggest bulb I could find. I cut the young growth off the top and here it is."

Ludo was paying more attention now. "What do you deduce from it then?"

"This. You are perfectly sure when you thrust down the rod the other night you didn't go near the bulbs?"

"Of course I didn't. We agreed that the bulbs must be a certain distance below the surface, and I allowed for the roots and kept a good foot below. I wanted to be perfectly certain I shouldn't injure them."

"Good! And when you thrust the rod through parallel you still kept well below?"

"Not exactly well below. All I worried about was not disturbing the bulbs in such a way as to make them wither and so calling attention to the fact that they had been disturbed. What's the idea, Geoffrey? You're not implying that the money is under those lilies after all?"

"Well, not exactly under them. Among them if you like." Ludo's face showed incredulity. "And there's no blame attached to you. You did precisely what I should have done under the circumstances, only probably more thoroughly. Also, it's by no means certain that even this theory is correct."

"I think I'm tumbling to your idea, even by process of exhaustion: if something is under the lilies and it is not where I tried, it must be either higher or lower."

"Exactly. 'Under the lilies' needn't mean of necessity 'under the bulbs.' The flowers constitute the lilies as much as anything else. My scheme is that the money is inside tennis balls and among the bulbs. To keep them from rotting Plumley might have done one or two things. He might have covered them with the bitumen felt or have given them a coating—'rendering', I believe the correct term is—of the waterproof cement. What did you say the name was?"

"Pudlo."

"Pudlo, that's it. He might have coated them half an inch thick all round with that. Can't you imagine the old boy at it? He probably found it most amusing and exciting, and there wouldn't be such an enormous difference between a ball and a bulb."

"Well, there'll be no harm in trying it. What about going up after tea and having a daylight raid?"

"Too much chance about that tip-and-run sort of business. The risk would be too great; besides, I don't think there's any need to worry about anyone else having been mad enough to think of anything of the kind. Further, I've got a great idea about getting Burrows away. I'll get you to ask him along at about ten-fifteen. I shall go up there alone at about ten, which ought to give me heaps of time."

"Why shouldn't you ask him along? It will sound better coming from you. If he gets here before you get back I can always make excuses. And that reminds me. What are we going to talk about when he gets here?"

"If the plan goes wrong, we might do worse than take him into our confidence. If it goes right, I don't know. Sufficient unto the visit is the talk thereat. Disposing of Martin is more to the point. He always strikes me as too thick-skulled to be much of a nuisance. I think I shall just chance my arm with him. Now what—"

"Mr. Burrows, sir!" announced Helen. Wrentham swept the bulb, paper, and soil into a drawer. "Show him in, Helen."

"Afternoon, Burrows. What's blown you along?"

"Good afternoon, gentlemen. I really came to get some information from Captain Travers. I didn't care about approaching Rendell, and I thought, sir, you'd be better able to tell me what I want to know. What was done with the surplus vegetables at the Hall? Had anybody any authority to sell them?"

"Certainly not. Twice a week hampers of vegetables, fruit, and flowers were sent up to Bellingham House. If there were any surplus we knew nothing about it. I think we used to assume there was no surplus. I believe there were occasional donations to the hospital. Why do you ask?"

The detective was on quite good terms with himself. "I don't know that I ought to give information as I'm out to get it. I rather think, however"—looking archly at the pair of them—"that in the process of prowling about the Hall I've managed to unearth what's been intriguing you two gentlemen."

Wrentham dared not look at Ludo. He felt a rosy glow suffusing his own face. The detective went on.

"I believe I told you, Major, that Tait was dismissed from Sir Thomas Warrell's place in Hampshire on account of graft. You seem to have suspected it, and I can assure you that that's what has been going on at the Hall. Rummage hasn't an inch of garden, and he apparently has been getting all his vegetables from there. I dropped across his man West last night with a hamper, and got a good deal out of him. I imagine the hotel at Longham has been getting its supplies pretty regularly from the same source. Furthermore, I strongly suspect Rendell is in it; at least he was present to-day when another hamper was put into the butcher's cart that comes from Longham. The trouble is that I don't know who is to bring an action unless I report to the Official Receiver and see what he suggests."

Wrentham breathed again. He was by no means displeased with the news. "Well, we're very grateful to you, Burrows. Isn't that so, Ludo?" Ludo nodded. "However, I do think Gordon should be most strongly recommended to those in authority and Tait given the option of clearing out or standing the racket. You have brought this business home to him, I suppose?"

"Not exactly. He knows that I know, and that's all there is to it at present. After all, the stealing of vegetables is hardly a matter for which you can hold a man, and if he does a bolt it will be because he's scared of something far more serious. I'm disposed to wait. Rendell I may speak to. You know anything about him, Captain Travers?"

"I have run across him once or twice in purely a business way," Ludo acknowledged. "Never was particularly taken with him. These horsey men in non-hunting country strike me as specially anomalous."

"Well, if he makes his living, or loses one, at that sort of game, there's no wonder he isn't above a little graft. Still, there we are. Lot of queer fish about."

"How's the case going, Burrows?" inquired Wrentham. "You seem fairly cheerful."

The detective immediately sobered down, like a man who suddenly discovers himself whistling a comic song in a cathedral. "Not too bad. Not too good. Ask me more to-morrow."

"Really! You honestly think you see the end of it?"

"I won't go so far as that, gentlemen, but I think I know the probable whereabouts of the man who killed Moulines. A little luck and I might have my hands on him in less than twelve hours. That's all you'll get out of me. If you know a man who wears a seven boot, smokes John Cotton No. 1 and Russian cigarettes, then you probably know him as well as I."

"I don't know that *I* haven't done all these in my time," confessed Ludo, "but not simultaneously."

Wrentham cut in. "You seem to have remembered, Burrows, my telling you that Captain Travers and myself were engaged in a particular piece of work. It appears that we also are getting very near the end. Could you possibly drop in to-night at about ten-fifteen to see if we have any final news for you? I don't guarantee any, but it might be worth while."

"Suit me very well, Major. I confess I haven't quite fitted in that well business yet, and I'll own I should really like to know just what it all means. I shan't be able to stop more than a few minutes, however. I've got pretty big fish to fry. I don't mind owning I'm going along now for an hour or two's nap. Can't keep on burning the candle at both ends."

"See you later then," said Wrentham as the detective rose to go.

"Yes, Major. I'll be along there or thereabouts."

"Now I wonder what he's got hold of," said Wrentham. "Devilish funny his thinking we were after Tait for pinching the baronial potatoes—what? You got any ideas, Ludo?"

"Precious few. It isn't I and it isn't you or Uncle Peter, and the rest I'm not certain about. Rummage, of course; he can't run to John Cotton and Russian cigarettes unless he steals them. What are your exact plans for to-night?"

"Me? Oh, I shall probably arm to the teeth and put on breeches and a woolly so as to be free either to run or scrap. I thought of taking Wallace's small trapping spade also, for turning up the bulbs. It's pretty light and won't be much more trouble than a stick. Devilish good weapon, too, if I should happen to want one. How does that fit in with your ideas?"

"I think it's all right. I know you're more of a scrapper than I, but I wish I were going up instead. I feel in my bones that something's going to happen, and I'd rather it happened to me. Let's get the damn thing off our minds or I shall be getting morbid. How about a cup of tea and a stroll on the heath?"

"Suit me down to the ground." He fumbled over the next words, and in trying to be casual succeeded only in becoming incoherent. "This is a rotten sort of holiday for you, Ludo. If things don't turn up right to-night we'll chuck the whole concern. See the Carews, get some golf and tennis. Cars aren't frightfully dear. Might get about a bit."

"Don't worry about me," Ludo assured him. "I'm enjoying every bit of it, but I wish it were all over. If that business of Moulines and your own cracked skull hadn't come into it I should have been more pleased still. But there you are. The moral for us in this little adventure seems to be, 'Gawd help them wot wants to help themselves.'"

It was rather a bit absurd. Still, men who had slept through hell's own barrages had been known to be scared at a Zeppelin attack when on leave. The two were rather like children who on the eve of Christmas can scarcely sleep or eat for thinking of what the morrow will bring. They had about six miles at a killing pace, considering the late experiences of one of the pedestrians, and I don't suppose there were half a dozen sentences exchanged all the way. The great thing about getting these miles from home is that you have got to get back, and there is no hailing a taxi or catching a train. After dinner a billiard enthusiast or two dropped in and were initiated into the mysteries of snooker. Great excitement and amusement, as may be imagined. The vicar was specially rueful when his best efforts met with what seemed quite unmerited disaster.

Wrentham left Ludo holding the fort. An idea had come to him, and to him an impulse was as good as action. His word had been passed and he meant to stand by it. Had it been morning he would never have harboured the idea. Darkness, we are told, is beloved of doers of evil, and the night with its thousand eyes beholds more foolishness than the day which is all-seeing. He scribbled his note and stuck it in an envelope.

DEAR MISS FORREST

At ten o'clock to-night I am making a final attempt at the Hall. If this does not succeed I must ask you to free me from the promise I made you, unless you have further definite knowledge upon which I can act. If you know Martin, the caretaker, and could get him out of the way for a quarter of an hour at the psychological moment it might help.

G. W.

Now, how to get the note there? He strolled down the drive and then slowly along to Jerlingham's farm. He was fortunate in meeting a boy. He didn't know him. All these village boys seemed to have sprung up during the war. "Where are you going, boy?"

"Home, sir."

"Look here. You want to earn sixpence?"

"Yes, sir." No hesitation about that.

"Right-ho, then!" The coin was produced. "You know Lodge Cottage? Yes? Well, take this note to Miss Forrest from the vicar. Stick it in your pocket, and don't lose it. And see how quickly you can get there."

The lad cut away over the low meadows, and Wrentham went back. The billiard players were still in the thick of it, but at about a quarter of an hour before he was due to set off he got hold of Ludo. "I say, Ludo. This is absolutely topping. I didn't think of the billiards when we were making our arrangements. You go on with the night-club stunt and keep them at it. When Burrows comes give Helen the tip to show him right in. He's not likely to miss me then, and it will give you a good chance to keep him here."

"Suppose he says he can't stop?"

"He can't do that at once. All these policeman are frightfully keen on the game. Lure him into giving an exhibition. If he positively insists on going, tell him you don't know where I am—and I can promise you that you won't have any idea at that particular moment—and will he drop in again later or in the morning."

So off to get the spade and to dress for the part. It was too late for the breeches, so he retained the grey flannel trousers and pulled a woolly well down over the tops. This and a shooting coat completed the equipment. Into the pocket went torch and Colt. He felt perfectly cool now. He even chuckled aloud at the thought of how he had saved Ludo's conscience. He certainly wouldn't know where he was going to be at any particular moment from now on.

As a matter of fact, at the precise moment when Ludo was making that identical statement in answer to Burrows' question, it was extraordinarily true. Not only was Ludo completely ignorant of the whereabouts of his fellow-conspirator, but Wrentham had not the faintest idea of them himself.

CHAPTER XXVII
EVENTS OF JULY 31ST: MAIN ATTACK

HE DECIDED TO FIND a wholly new line of approach. By the church path was too risky; there might be latecomers from the Woods Cottages or the Hall. By the drive was unthinkable, and through the orchard had not proved too successful on a previous occasion. Back of the far cottages was impossible; if there were paths he did not know them. He had decided therefore on cutting the main road between Church Stile and the village, hugging the eastern end of the cricket field and then approaching the Hall by a detour from the south-east. The only risk was the possibility of stumbling across a pair of entrenched lovers. However, he accomplished his task more successfully than he could have anticipated. By keeping close to the fringe of the main park woods he was able to arrive absolutely unperceived within twenty yards of the hedge which separated the grassland from the front lawn of the Hall.

The night was an ideal one—the very night that Clark and his friends should have chosen for their onslaught on Saunders' layer. It could not be called dark, and yet the little light there remained was singularly illusive. There was a heavy dew and the wind blew gently and scarce perceptibly, and yet very present. Away at the junction the distant trains could be plainly heard.

Secure in the shadow of the trees, he surveyed as far as he could. Now he had come to rest he noticed the green afterglow that backed the horizon. By this time his eyes were more used to the darkness. He could discern nothing, however, but the dark indication of the hedge and in the middle distance a blackness that must be the Hall. His luminous watch had gone out of action, but, squatting behind the bole of a huge elm, and with his coat to conceal the flash of the torch, he consulted the one he had borrowed from Ludo. Five minutes to ten. No harm in trying the next step. This was easy, for the shadows of the wood reached almost to the hedge, and in a second or two he was at the first objective. In one place the hedge had been tramped through or else had decayed with time, for roughly placed rails repaired what else had been a gap. He knelt behind this and peered over. What he saw made him lower his head quickly and peep instead through the gap in the battens.

Ten yards away was a figure—a policeman in uniform. It was not Maxwell, that was certain. No mistaking Maxwell with his lanky frame once you had seen him. This man was burlier—a Hercules of a fellow; unless it was that the unnatural light made a monster of him. Perfectly still he was standing; so much so that he might have been mistaken for the trunk of an ancient tree or the thicket of climbing roses round a pole.

He could not have been standing so still unless keyed up by some straining of the senses. He moved to the right a little and stopped again. Evidently he was listening for some sound that was evading him. In a minute or two he moved again, but now in a regular beat; from the eastern corner of the house to the west edge of the border. It was a sort of patrol at ease. The watcher at the hedge could make out the tune of the popular song that came through his teeth in a suppressed whistle. Once he stopped, pulled out a watch and consulted it by the light of a match. "A damn fine sentry that!" smiled Wrentham to himself.

But things were not so amusing when this patrolling continued. The time was going on. Had the walker been certain of the extent of his beat or its continuity it would not have been so bad. Nearly every stage, however, he would stop and listen. Too risky that, thought Wrentham, for a dash across the border. The idea came to him to throw a stone towards the house, where it would rattle against the stone path or the wall of the house. It was discarded as likely to betray its point of origin by the whistling of the stone through the air. When a good five minutes had gone he was desperate. There was little chance of getting through the hedge farther down, and if he did he was bound to make a row. Besides, there might be another policeman farther along. If the damn fellow didn't soon stop there'd be nothing for it but to go back and round the kitchen garden.

Then he caught sight of a dark patch in the intermediate distance, half-way to the border. It was, though he did not know it, a large gypsophila, three feet high and nearly as much through; and round it in the small circular bed were pale pink snapdragons. There was his chance. He felt the rail at the bottom: it was loose. He drew it gently to one side until there was plenty of room for his body. Then as the policeman was in reverse and almost to the far end of his beat, he slipped the fifteen yards to the dark shelter and there he crouched. He dared not peep to see, but waited until the sound of his feet marked the return of the patroller. He was not conscious of the destruction he was causing among those pink blossoms. All he knew was that the feet were coming nearer and nearer. As they drew level he moved around his shelter, then listened again for the return. He rose to his feet and went swiftly the final stage, doubling round the west end of the border and behind a clump of hollyhocks. They were taller than himself. He stood at his full height and pulled aside the flowering stalks. The constable was in the act of beginning a return towards the border. From his unvarying pace and the distant sibilance it seemed he had neither seen nor heard. At that very second Wrentham remembered something—his trapping spade! He had left it the other side of the hedge!

He was at first rather bewildered at the unexpectedness of the catastrophe, and then vastly furious with himself. It would mean that the spade had to be recovered somehow. Wallace's name was bound to be stamped on the handle, and it would be easy to bring home to the owner any damage which he might be forced to commit. The job had to be done in any case, annoying though it was. Like hunting the world for eggs to make an omelet and then, in the act of cracking, to let all fall to the floor. Still, those who spoiled their omelets must content themselves with bread. He knelt down and tested the soil. Apparently it had been recently hoed, for it felt far from hard. He would have to use his fingers. So, synchronising his movements with the walk of the constable, he crept along to the centre of the border. There was no smell of lilies this time; yet the air was heavy with the smell of flowers in which the unpleasantness of the phlox predominated.

He knew the spot, however. With the other a good forty yards away at almost the limit of his beat he made a tentative step inside to check his position. He was quite right. Just in front of him was the lily clump, and now he could catch the smell of the few blooms that yet remained. He stepped out again, with head behind his tall barrier. What he did not see was a figure moving behind him in the shadow of the rhododendron hedge, and not ten feet away. It was a curious triangle, with the policeman alone unconcerned. As he walked, Wrentham reconnoitred, and as he followed every step of the unconscious patroller so the other watched like a terrier every movement of his own.

Then with a suddenness that was thrilling in its terror a shriek rang out. Horrible and discordant it sounded, as of one in deadly pain or under the influence of some swift and awful fear. Hardly human it was, and Wrentham felt his heart stop like the ship of the Ancient Mariner, and then make a sudden and fearful leap. It was repeated—long drawn out and diminishing to an unearthly and stifled scream. It was like the cry of a madwoman, the strangled shriek of the demented crying for help. The thought rushed to his mind, "Sylvia Forrest! My God, someone's killing her!" She must have come down to help him and been surprised in the trespass. Who was it? Tait or Rendell, or who? He could not see the policeman, nor could he be heard. Over to the left he fancied he could still hear that ghastly clamouring for help. What was he to do? He would make his attempt first now the coast was clear. No, he couldn't do that. He would reproach himself as long as he lived.

He slipped quickly round the border nearest the house and ran along the stone path, so plain was it to the eye even in the dark. As he left the border the figure left the shelter of the rhododendrons and came to the border at the spot where he had emerged. It stepped round the hollyhocks and was lost to sight. Wrentham himself stopped suddenly at the corner of the house and peered round. He heard voices. He drew back into the creeper and remained motionless. Round the angle of the house two figures appeared, Martin and the policeman. They were talking excitedly.

"I should reckon I did hear it. My wife she say to me, 'What's that, Fred? Go and have a look.'"

"Where do you think it come from?" asked the policeman.

"Well, that sort of fared to me to come from down in the holler, by them trees," and Martin pointed out the shadowy blur of oak and elms that guarded the lawn on the north.

"That's just what I thowt. Now—" The sentence was never completed. At that word the cry rose again. This time it began as a shriek and ended in a moan—a long-drawn "Oh!" of agony. It was as if a human were caught in a trap where steel jaws were biting to the bone. Wrentham felt his blood run cold. The other two darted off towards the sound, the policeman first and Martin following.

Their going made up Wrentham's mind for him. Whoever it was that needed help the policeman and Martin would be sufficient. He must not risk being seen, and the chance was too good to be missed. He ran for the gap, leaned over and recovered his spade, and then nipped again round the end of the border like a stoat. Whew! that was quick work!

No time to be lost, however. He returned to the centre of the border and slipped quickly inside. He avoided a tall group of something whose name he had forgotten and got on his knees before the lilies. He felt curiously self-possessed, although his heart was still hammering away from the effects of the sprint. He felt his hand shaking as he shortened his grip of the spade. He thrust it well under the scarcely discerned tangle of blackness and tried to lever it up. The plants were in the way. This method of dislodging the bulbs was evidently ineffective. He tore furiously at the stalks and leaves. With his grasping, some of the bulbs came away in his hand and the white of them was plainly visible.

He scooped away with his hands and, working his fingers well into the soil, tore away like a badger. He felt something hard. What was that? Only a big bulb. What was this? A stone? He got his fingers well under it and pulled it out. Round and heavy and certainly no bulb. He had been right. It was a ball of some kind!

He stuck it between his knees, and, tearing away like a madman in the small pit he was making, found amid the bulbs another ball. So on, until he had gathered six. And explore how he might, there was nothing else. He left his small heaps of discovery and, getting to his feet, thrust the spade in the ruin where the lilies had been. There was no striking of steel on stone. The cache was rifled clean. Behind him from a dark mass on his left a figure rose and a hand was raised as to strike, but then, unearthly as before, but this time far round to the right, there rang out a scream, or rather scream on scream of a woman's voice. She was in deadly danger. This time the call could be distinguished: "Help! Help!" rising to a maddening crescendo. The south-east wind bore it clear.

At the same time voices were heard, and Martin and the policeman, panting with their run, came pounding along. The screaming died again to a long moan. The two stopped before the border. Wrentham crouched with his head almost in the soil and held his breath.

"Damned if I can make it out. Do you reckon there's somebody carrying the woman about? Where is it, Martin?"

Martin's teeth were chattering, although the perspiration was running into his eyes. "I don't know. Sort of sounds as if it might be in the wood yonder."

"You show me the way and we'll have another try. If anybody's playing a trick on us, Martin, I'll twist their blasted necks if I get hold of 'em." And the two made for the gap by which Wrentham had entered. There was the sound of a fall and a muttering as the policeman took a toss over the other side of the rails. Then came the sound of running feet.

At the same time Wrentham's ears caught the suggestion of a rustling near him. He stopped as if shot, and strained to listen. The wind blew a gust. That would be it. The rustling of the flowers as they swayed. He felt for the pile of balls and stuffed one in each pocket of his trousers. He started to fill the pocket of his shooting coat, and to do that he had to remove the Colt. He kept this in his hand and put two of the balls in each pocket. Then he rose to his full height.

As he did so the blow fell. Had he not been in the act of stretching, whereby his head moved slightly, he would have been felled like an ox. As it was he crashed back against a scarce yielding clump, and, staggered as he was, caught sight of his assailant. He felt the lunge he gave to be useless. It was the knowledge that he was at last face to face with the man who had nearly killed him that struck, and not he, numbed as he was by the blow. He felt a crashing to his face and then fell groping helplessly. The last thing he remembered was a knee in his ribs and a hand taking his revolver. Then came a thud, and as far as he was concerned that was the last of it.

The assailant grasped him by the collar and dragged him behind the border. Then he got to his knees and hitched the body over his shoulder. He rose with some difficulty, and, using the spade as a support, staggered away. When he reached the rhododendrons he did a curious thing. He raised his voice in a long "Coo-ee." The sound rang and echoed among the trees and undergrowth. Then he moved more quickly to the right, shuffling almost to a trot. With no hesitation he went past the roses, through the already opened door of the quadrangle, and so to the kitchen garden. There the shadows swallowed him up.

Back by the border the policeman and Martin lumbered up, harassed and perplexed. In the kitchen Mrs. Martin and her sister stood frightened in their nightgowns, and jumped with nervous apprehension as the grandfather struck the half-hour. The figure of a woman appeared at the back of the kitchen garden and slipped into the orchard. At the vicarage Burrows was inquiring, "Haven't you any idea where the Major is?" and Ludo was replying, "I haven't a notion," and then less truly, "But he'll be in any minute now."

Elsewhere the Recording Angel dipped his pen and settled comfortably as to write. A doubt appeared to strike him. He frowned, hesitated a minute as though weighing the case in the everlasting balance, and then regretfully replaced his pen. Ludo had received the benefit of the doubt.

CHAPTER XXVIII
RETIREMENT IN FAIR ORDER

WRENTHAM STIRRED many times during that long period, but his final awakening was a kind of stupor, dull and heavy. His head was aching as if to burst, and his throat was like a Sahara limekiln. Arms were lifeless and legs were cramped. He wanted to be sick—very sick. He realised why: a gag of some sort was in his mouth, and round his chin was something that hampered his jaws. He bit viciously on the cloth or whatever it was, and at the same time knew that his arms were tied behind him at the wrists. His fingers were numbed and dead. His legs were tied too. He raised his head a bare inch and could see the rope lashed round ankles and knees.

Full consciousness returned, though with no diminution of the ache that was all over him. He appeared to be lying in the manger of a stable—a lofty, airy building—and over his head was an iron hayrack, with mouldy remnants protruding through the bars. Above his knees was the crossbar of the manger, and to this his legs were fastened at the knee. He moved his head back and regarded the pillow. Hay, but last year's or even older. He turned as well as he could until his back received a certain support. Inside his prison was a light as of late twilight, but outside the noise of birds told that it was still day.

He lay there for some minutes, his eyes growing accustomed to the unusual light. A squeak came from the end of the manger, and perched away at the side he could see a mouse, its long tail pendulous, nibbling away carelessly. It was joined by another. Regarding them he thought of himself. It was not hunger he had but thirst, as if he could drink for hours. Then he lay quietly, trying to collect his thoughts, but his brain was too bemused and bewildered. A hurtling of thoughts began to run through it like those that go feverish through the mind of one who cannot sleep. The theme of the previous night's *dénouement* occurred over and over again. There emerged the recognition that it had been all his own fault. If he hadn't been so infernally self-suffi-cient he wouldn't be lying there.

He roused himself to an effort to get free, but whoever had tied him had done so with dexterity and a reticent simplicity. He could not pull up his legs because of the fastening of his knees. He could not bring his hands into play because they were fas-tened above to an iron ring. Tightly they were not tied. It had been the cramp of the arbitrary position that had hurt him. He could not even drum with his heels on the manger bottom, since it was filled with hay. If only he could get rid of that thing out of his mouth he might do a holler. He bit again and again at the wet mass, but the effort only made him feel violently sick. He settled down with his head on its pillow and fell to kicking out with his feet. The effort was too much for him, and he felt trembling and very faint. His head began to swim. The room seemed to be getting darker and darker.

He must have gone off into some sort of sleep, for when he again opened his eyes it was dark. When he knew where he was and had remembered the earlier awakening he became conscious that his limbs ached and his body was wholly compact of bruises. Something felt cold about his neck. It was the wrapping that had come loose. In his feverish tossings he must have rubbed it violently against the wooden side. He levered himself over to the manger's edge and spat out the abominable thing. He breathed deep in the cool air and filled his lungs to bursting. He spat again and cleaned his mouth and once more let fall his head.

Already he felt better. He could even feel angry, more with himself than with the assailant. So the blighter had won the second trick. If only there might be a third round! What had happened to the girl? Was she, like himself, tied up by now in some obscure outhouse? It was not Tait who had struck him, he was certain of that. The man of last night had been clean-shaved. But of course Tait might have shaved. But the whole attitude of the man had seemed curiously unlike Tait. What a night! All for nothing, too. He knew his pockets were empty. He tried a confirmatory roll against the side of the manger. Nothing there. Yes, there was! but not in his coat pocket. It was the pockets of his trousers that still held the balls he had put there. Lord, what a relief! The sweater must have concealed those pockets, and the chap who tied him up must have been pressed for time. The feeling that after all something had survived, that adventure had for once been justified of its children was a fine tonic. He was feeling a new man.

After that he moved his aching body into some kind of ease. The feeling of thirst was still there, and a vast hunger with it. Thereafter he must have dozed off at odd intervals, for when he was fully awake the stable was again light. The coldness of the air announced that the hour must be early. He tried to shout, and although the effort brought the blood to his head he persisted. It was of no use. Better lie there and wait for some sign of movement outside. What stable was it? He did not recall ever having been in it before. It was too well built to belong to a farm. Then it must be at the Hall. If so, all that was needed was a little patience and there was bound to be someone about. As if in answer to his questioning, a sound reached his ears—the 'Ma-a-a' of a goat. That was it. He was in the old stable at the far end of the orchard. Then it would be a pure slice of luck if anybody came that way. It would probably turn on the question as to whether the goat was a milker. If not, he was likely to be there for hours.

So the time went by. There were distant sounds of life. From time to time he shouted with all the strength of his lungs. It seemed as if the voice did not escape the closely sealed room, for it bellowed and echoed round him and seemed as unreal as could be. Once he heard the sound of whistling, and once the braying of a donkey. He judged it must be about breakfast-time. In spite of that sore lump that seemed to take up the whole of his head he could do with some himself. And wouldn't a cigarette be topping!

A swishing noise—the sound of running feet. They came close. There was no need to cry out, for the unknown could be heard panting with haste. There was a fumbling outside and the rattle of a key against a padlock. A bar fell and the door was dragged open. A policeman! Maxwell!

All out of breath as he was with running, he came forward. He appeared like one who sees what he expects and, at the same time, what he ought not to be seeing. He was, as it were, incoherently apologetic. "You all right, sir? I couldn't believe it, sir."

Wrentham indicated the bonds. "Get your knife out, man! Don't stand there!"

In a minute he was free. The policeman helped him out of his bed, but when his feet touched the ground his body joined them. It was impossible to stand. They fell to rubbing his legs and arms. The pain of the returning blood was almost worse. When he felt more normal he dispatched the constable for a pail of water. "Don't say anything to anybody why you want it, Maxwell."

"That'll be all right, sir. They'll all be in at breakfast."

He still could not manage his feet very well, but he knelt before the pail and drank deep. He rinsed his mouth and gargled; then, stripped to the waist, washed with the icy cold water. There was a lump behind his ear which felt so tender that it was pain to approach within inches of it. His jaw was bruised and sore. His chin was feeling rough, and his hair was all over the place. Still, he could get to the vicarage if necessary without meeting a soul. He dried on his own and Maxwell's enormous handkerchief, and scraped his hair into something more presentable. He wondered just what the policeman was thinking of it all, and then realised with a start that he did not know himself what had brought him there at that hour and why he had come at the double.

"How did you find out all about this, Maxwell?"

"Had a letter, sir," was the reply, and the policeman dived into an inner pocket. "A registered letter. I happened to be standing outside the post office when the postman came in, and he give me the letter. It had this key in it, sir."

Wrentham took the letter and read it:

To the Hainton Village Constable.

Upon receipt of this letter you are asked to go as quickly as you can to the old stable at the end of the orchard at Hainton Hall. The key herewith will undo the padlock. Inside you will find a gentleman sleeping off the effects of a dirty night.

Perfectly ordinary paper of good class. No date, no name, no address. He gave the letter back. "Is that the envelope you have there, Maxwell?"

It was, but it afforded little in way of a clue. Posted at Leicester Square the previous morning. Not much good that. He decided, however, that the policeman should be given some sort of explanation.

"I expect you're wondering what all this is about, Maxwell. The fact is, I was actually very near the Hall last night—what is to-day, by the way?—Saturday? Well, on Thursday night I heard some terrible screaming from somewhere. I was trying to make out where it came from when some feller gave me this swipe over the jaw and another over the skull, and the next thing I did was to wake up in this stable."

The constable looked by no means incredulous. Had he been asked he might have given the other stranger information about the happenings connected with that night.

"You got a cigarette on you, Maxwell?"

He had. Wrentham fumbled in his pocket and then remembered that he had no money on him. "Now, Maxwell, can you keep an absolutely still tongue in your head? Not a word to a soul about this—not a single soul, mind you, not even to Sergeant Burrows. If you can you're on a ten pun'note."

Maxwell touched his helmet. "That's all right, sir. I won't say a word to anybody."

"Right-ho! To-day's Saturday. Come to me after breakfast on Monday and collect your money. Only, mark you, if a single word has leaked out I shall hold you responsible and you won't get a cent. There's nothing for you to worry about in any case. I've been attacked, but if I don't choose to lay any information against anybody that's my funeral."

It was clear that any spilling of the beans would not come from the constable's side. Ten pounds is an excellent mental soporific. "If you're seen, you must make your own excuses, Maxwell," said the Major. He peeped out of the door, and then, his gait steady but by no means rapid, came out of the orchard by the large gate and, crossing the rough grass, emerged at the drive. He turned away to the left for the low meadows, and then noticed a peculiar thing: where Sylvia Forrest's house had stood was nothing but a heap of black. Even the chimney breast had fallen. Lodge Cottage was burnt to the ground!

He came out at the road where lay an uncracked heap of stones. A thought struck him. Nobody was in sight. He took one of the balls out of his pocket and threw it as hard as he could at the stone heap. Nothing happened. He put the ball on the heap and, seizing the largest of the flints, brought it down full on top. The ball smashed. He examined it and what he saw pleased him. He returned it to his pocket and moved on.

The excitement caused by his appearance was enormous. Ludo saw him half-way up the drive and fluttered round him like a hen with a lone chicken. His father was no less concerned.

The story that he had been suddenly called away did not for once convince the vicar, who looked hurt at his son's reticence. After all, a stubbly chin, a black eye, and a face like putty take more explaining away than a casual visit. However, he conciliated his father by the promise of full unfolding later. There was a letter for him from godfather Hallett. That could wait. He crammed it into his pocket. For the moment breakfast was the thing, and coffee—hot, and gallons of it.

After breakfast, while changing his clothes, he gave Ludo all his news. At the conclusion he fished out the broken ball, with a "Take a look at that." Ludo held it reflectively. It certainly did look a strange object. Thanks to the chipping that had come off, it was easy to determine the structure. A tennis-ball had been neatly cut so as to remove a circle of rubber no bigger than a shilling. When the ball had been filled, the hole had been covered by strips of bitumen felt, running crossways. Above all was a layer of cement put on about half an inch thick all round. Two small white spots on each side marked the final fillings of the holes where it was being held by some instrument while the rendering was being applied.

With a pair of scissors they tried to remove the contents without enlarging the hole. It couldn't be done; the ball had to be ripped open. Inside were twenty-five banknotes, each for a hundred pounds. The other doubtless held the same, but it was decided not to mutilate it. A new cache was made for the lot, in a tin of nails placed unobtrusively away on a shelf in the workshop. Nobody ever came there, unless it was Wallace when invited for the annual spring-cleaning.

"What's to be done with them?" asked Ludo.

"Ask me something hard! Why not wait and see what happens? By the way, what exactly did happen at your end on Thursday night?"

"Burrows came round, a bit late too. I should think it was a good twenty past ten when he got here. Of course that wasn't bad from my point of view, as I said you'd gone out, thinking probably that he wasn't coming. He left, or rather was leaving at about a quarter-past eleven. Uncle Peter had gone up, and three of us had been playing snooker afterwards. When we came to the door we noticed a fire over by the Hall. I was a bit anxious about what you were doing. You see I thought if you had got on well you would have been back in half an hour. However, the fire got bigger and we decided to walk over that way. As soon as we got to the meadows we found it was Lodge Cottage blazing away like a little Hades. Half the village was there, trying to get water from the well. As you can guess the speed that meant, you can imagine there wasn't much doing in the fire brigade line.

"I nipped off back after a minute or two and waited for you to turn up. When midnight came and you hadn't put in an appearance I didn't know what to do. However, I waited till one and then hopped it for bed, leaving a couple of messages, one in the study and the other in your bedroom. When I got upstairs I couldn't sleep, so I came down again and finally set off to the Hall to look for you. The fire was still burning at the Lodge, but I went round the orchard and had a good hunt through the gardens. As you know, I found nothing except your spade, and that was in the middle of the drive, as if you'd dropped it in a hurry.

"When I got back at about four I found you hadn't been in, so I really did go to bed. I was the first one up in the morning, but there was nothing doing. I decided to tell Uncle Peter that you had been called away suddenly and would probably be back during the course of the morning. Then I went off again to look for you. I don't mind owing up that I was scared absolutely stiff. I had a peep at the border and saw the mess you'd made there, but nobody else had noticed it, because the men had been up all night at the fire.

"There were two sensations in the village: Tait was missing, or, at least, he was not at his work, and his wife didn't know where he was. Also the women from Lodge Cottage couldn't be found. Burrows was up to his eyelashes in cinders when I saw him last, hunting for bones, and Ware paid one visit in the afternoon and had a pow-wow. All through the day I was getting more and more scared. At last I didn't give a damn for anybody. I took Tango and hunted over the woods round the Hall and Robert's cottage and anywhere that your body might have been put. I was up at the Hall too, and again last night and had a fearful time evading your policeman friend, who came on duty about midnight. Burrows hasn't been here at all, by the way. I expect he's got a new job in hand in view of the fire and the disappearances. When I saw your long legs coming down the drive this morning I believe I nearly fainted."

"Well, all's well that ends well," was Wrentham's somewhat obvious comment. "But I wish I knew where that woman was." It was on the tip of his tongue to tell about the note he had sent that night, but something restrained him.

"Yes. It would be pretty horrible if they had both been caught upstairs in that place. When I first saw it the flames were simply pouring out of the upstairs windows."

The other said nothing. He felt in the pockets of the discarded clothes to be sure that nothing had been left in them, and came on the letter. "Good Lord, Ludo! I'd forgotten all about this." He slit it open and read it.

ST. GILES' CHAMBERS
NORWICH

Private.

DEAR GEOFFREY,

I am in a position now to give you the news I promised you. The whole of the Hainton estate is in the market, for sale by private treaty. We are acting for Sir Herbert Sprent, your old Colonel, who has spoken of you very well. Sir Herbert has always been desirous of having the Hainton shoot, and a meeting has been arranged with him and Mr. Hare and the others concerned at our London offices on Tuesday next.

I may say that I am almost certain that the Hainton estate will pass into Sir Herbert's hands, and in that connexion I ventured to recall your name to him, for which he was very grateful. He would welcome your services as agent for the estate, feeling confident, as I do, that he could have nobody with interests more bound up in the village than a Wrentham. The salary would not be excessive—probably in the neighbourhood of six hundred pounds. Immediately after Tuesday next Sir Herbert will write you and will suggest an appointment, probably here.

There is a matter I have to add, and it is a matter to which neither of us need again refer. I am not a young man or a rich one. The little that I have, however, will be yours. The worries you have had over the unfortunate business of Henry Plumley's affairs must have been many. But you will recall my last words to you when I saw you in London: *Forsan et olim hæc meminisse juvabit.*

My good wishes, and to your father.

Your afft. godfather

WORTLEY HALLETT

Ludo was hilariously delighted. The other was soberly incredulous. He was pulling at his pipe and staring out of the window when Ludo left him.

CHAPTER XXIX
ENEMY INFORMATION

THE MIDDAY POST brought another letter. He scanned the writing; absolutely unknown. Postmark—Victoria. Date—the previous afternoon. Frowning slightly, he slit open the envelope. "My dear Wrentham . . ." There seemed to be pages of it, and he turned for explanation to the final signature. "Good Lord!"

Ludo had disappeared somewhere half an hour previously, but he slipped into the vacant study to digest at leisure what gave every promise of being an amazing epistle. Here and there the writing was almost illegible, so much did it sprawl and leave the lines. It did not need a Lecocq to fathom that it had been written in a train, although that gentleman might have worked out the route followed by the carriage wherein it was composed.

MY DEAR WRENTHAM,

A mere hour or two has elapsed since I was with you, and now I fear I am going to surprise you considerably. This letter is being written during the journey from Thetford to London. You may know the interminable time taken by this so-called "mail." It was a long tramp that we had from Hainton to catch it, and my wife, who was very exhausted, is asleep on the opposite side of the carriage. All I can do to pass the long hours is to write to you. First a brief word of apology. As you will realise, I have to write straight on; I may therefore seem illogical or even incoherent. And as I have to write at length or be bored to extinction I shall certainly be long-winded. You will pardon all this.

I start as nearly as I can at the beginning, to preserve a certain chronological order. Again an interpolation is necessary. As I was furnished with your own private musings, as well as your correspondence with your partner—the Ludovic Travers for whose "Economics of a Spendthrift." I have the intensest admiration—I am able to write from your point of view as well as my own. I am regarded as a blatant person; for my over-intrusion of the *culte de moi* I therefore crave your forbearance.

My adventurous or hectic past is doubtless known to you. To go over it would be tedious; to defend it impertinent. For me the culmination was a so-called forged cheque. I do say frankly that it was Moulines who let me in for that. In him I thought I had a friend: an error of judgment on my part which proved expensive to both of us. For all I knew I was likely to be arrested at any moment, and the only thing to do was to clear out, temporarily at least, abroad? That would have been to confess guilt. Where to, then? That was a problem but not an insoluble one, as you shall see.

Some months before, during a house-party at Hainton, two of the maids were suddenly taken ill, and Mrs. Mason, at that time living in retirement at Lodge Cottage, was good enough to lend a hand. Unfortunately for her the butler reported to me, in the absence of my father, certain suspicions. On her way home one night we stopped her and recovered a set of Georgian spoons. I do not know why I did not prosecute, but something warned me to hold my hand. I told Morris to say nothing, and impressed upon Mrs. Mason that she had had a lucky escape. It was thus that when later a city of refuge was desperately needed one came to hand. I interviewed Mrs. Mason. I told her certain complexities had arisen and that I did not see how a prosecution could be avoided, unless perhaps she were to leave her cottage and depart for some place unknown. She was to announce an invitation from a fictitious sister, with whom she proposed to spend her last years, and announce further the arrival of a niece to take over the cottage. Hence Sylvia Forrest.

It was a rôle that I had played before. If you know my degenerate past, as I think you do, you may remember the affair of the lady seen emerging at an unseemly hour from the rooms of the Master of Cranmer and my subsequent and hurried departure from Oxford. My wife was to accompany me as my maid. Here we might live as in a sanctuary until the affair blew over and it was safe to emerge.

It was, however, a remarkable thing that no sooner was this sanctuary prepared than information reached me that there was no danger of any warrant. Thereupon I recognised at once that my only hope was to see my father at the earliest possible moment and explain things to him. I had no money: practically all the proceeds of that cheque had gone to Moulines for moneys advanced to me from time to time. I seemed to have a very fair case. My father—I give him that credit—had generally treated me pretty decently. What I was not yet wholly aware of, however, was either the peculiar condition of his mind at this time or the ascendancy that Moulines must have had over him. That Moulines had double-crossed me I was of course aware. As to what extent he was prepared to maintain his position I was far from well informed.

I made my attempt then, but the information given me was that my father was not in. On the whole, I was not surprised. But when it turned out that there was an organised and elaborate scheme for shutting me out I was not only desperate but furious. If I called to see my father the door was slammed in my face. I once waited for several hours and caught him just as he was entering the car at Bellingham House. The chauffeur pushed me out of the way as if I had been a tout and my father got in quite unconcerned, waving me away like dirt. There must have been some pretty hefty greasing of palms to have accomplished that. And what made me more furious was the fact that Moulines was hedged in just as thoroughly. I could not take it out on him.

My wife and I talked it over and came to what may seem to you an absurd decision. If I was to see my father, it would have to be out of the influence of Moulines. It was his custom to run, for a day or two at least, down to Hainton, and that seemed to be the best place to see him. Sylvia Forrest actually came into being and we took up our residence at Lodge Cottage. I neither ask nor expect you to understand the twist in my nature, the *diablerie* that inspired this feminine masquerade. You will admit, however, that as myself I should have been speedily recognised, and my father would have been aware of my whereabouts. There would have been complications also with regard to Mrs. Mason and the non-arrival of the expected niece.

We were perfectly quiet, reasonably happy, and thoroughly economical down at the Cottage. Every day we expected my father to turn up. From time to time I went to town to try to find out just what was going on. During one of these visits I actually missed my father, who spent two days at Hainton. Then I learnt of that meeting—that final meeting at Aldgate which you yourself attended. I made up my mind to be there and to see my father, by hook or by crook, at its conclusion. What happened there you know as well as I. But it was to me that my father spoke; it was upon me that his pointed finger rested. It was to me that he tried to convey the secret of the salvage from his financial wreck. When I knew he was dead the bottom seemed to have dropped out of most things. The following morning told me the worst. So back I came to Hainton to keep an eye on my buried inheritance; to lie low, as it were, and see what would turn up. I expected Moulines for one thing, and by keeping an eye on him to get some idea of what those last words of my father really meant.

Again I must ask your forbearance in the matter of Moulines. If only on the principle that it is as well to leave the best wine to the last, we will say no more at present about that unsavoury person. He will make a later reappearance, but he must wait a little longer if that moment is to be really dramatic. Moreover, there now enters a much more interesting character—yourself.

I confess you were beyond me that first morning. To give some excuse for my watch at the Hall I posed as an artist. Of the theory I knew a good deal, but had I attempted to put brush to paper the most ignorant village lout would have known me for an imposter. There I was sitting when you came by, and I confess I gave you no further thought. But your next visit set me thinking. What a gallant and reasonably brainless officer should be doing prowling about other people's gardens did, I confess, intrigue me. Then came the upsetting of my easel and your view of my sketch. A friend of mine had done that from a photo and certain descriptions which I sent him. He was an expert at his job, and I had therefore no fear of your scrutiny. Still, I was uneasy.

But not about my disguise. When one is as fair as I am and of the Jacob type, it does not even matter much about shaving. My voice was ever "low and sweet," which is, we are told, "an excellent thing in woman." Then, too,

I had worn that disguise so much that I was case-hard-
ened. The fur helped to make me invulnerable. Even
when you and your father paid later a not unexpected visit to the Cottage I needed only a slightly darkened room
to become in a few seconds an interesting invalid.

Well, as I was saying, you began to intrigue me. I decided to look you up. There you were at night, scribbling
away for all you were worth, and if I knew anything of
your army its tendencies were not usually to produce
very earnest workers. I decided thereupon that it would
be really interesting to see what you actually *were* writing. It was child's play. How it succeeded and how your
notes came into my possession you know only too well.
But I will state most earnestly that I had no desire to injure you. That tripwire was laid so as to delay possible
pursuit. I expected to dash into your room and dash out
again with you at my heels. Still, there we are; spilt milk
and all the other proverbs won't help it.

On the value of your notes I will not enlarge. They
told me what you were after. They gave me the chance
to go down to Hindhead and try out your theories, and
above all of those theories that my wife and I were able
to evolve. With the roses we had no luck whatever. With
the larch tree, or whatever conifer it was, we were much
more successful. Three large cones were attached by
copper wire to a fairly low bough. The cones appeared
to have been soaked in some kind of tarry water-proof-
ing, but their colour camouflaged perfectly the wire. The
base of each cone had been hollowed out, a small wad of
banknotes inserted, and the hole then plugged carefully
with some damp-proof bitumen stuff. What the amount
was that each contained I am not prepared to say. All I
will admit is that it was not so bad. One night a week on
similar terms and I'd soon buy a bank. Some excitement
seemed to be created in the Press. By the way, the letter
which was published from "Lover of Gardens" was sent

in by myself. In the light of this read it again, my dear Wrentham; it will amuse you.

But there was more to collect, and I saw no reason why you should profit by that singular inheritance of mine. But just what you were up to and how much you really knew I had no means of finding out. Hence the pathetic appeal to you by Sylvia Forrest. What a night that was! Stars and the honeysuckle and the way of a man with a maid! You were really quite decent and, which was far better, most informative. And when you sent me that message to put Martin off the scent, Lord! did you ever hear of such a bit of luck? My wife deputised for me. Rather good, wasn't she? Those groans, for instance— amazingly natural. They almost frightened me.

I was sorry to knock you out, but it had to be done. The time was overdue and we had arranged to meet in the old stable. I couldn't leave you on the ground; your groans would certainly have been heard by that flat-footed pair who were prowling round. You were a bit of a load, but the contents of your pockets were a very sound reward. To tell you the truth, I expected more, but where I am going it will last quite a long time. We had to tie you up for the same reason. For all I knew you might have recognised me, and then the fat would have been in the fire. I hope you will not get loose too soon. This afternoon I shall send a letter advising the village constable of your whereabouts. This letter I am writing will be posted at a more convenient season.

So at last we arrive at Moulines. But there, you have doubtless guessed by this time what happened. That Saturday night I ran into him full tilt. We were both of us scouting so carefully that we were on each other before we were aware. I wish to God I had strangled the swine myself rather than what actually happened. Mark you, I will not swear that he raised his hands to strike me or that he merely raised them against what he thought a provocative or threatening attitude of mine. But, at the time, I thought he was going to strike and I struck first. I shall not forget the sound of his skull as it thudded against the wall. Nor shall I forget the rest of that night: obscuring the blood, the damnable load he was to carry off, and the concealment of the motor-cycle. I did not mean to put him in the pond. It was sheer exhaustion made me drop him there, and the machine had to follow. Worse than all was the fear that I had left some trace behind. But, what do you think I found in his pockets? Five notes of a hundred pounds!

You see the connexion? It is, I am sure, simply this. By some means or other Moulines got hold of the cloak-room tickets for those suit-cases, and getting them out on trial, found much more than he had calculated on. The rest of the boodle he must have had elsewhere, for that was all I could find on him. You may ask, "Why the suit-cases?" Well, what else was there? At the time I own I merely relieved Moulines of those notes to defray current expenses, but when I got hold of that curious list I began to see daylight. At this minute I am certain, and this is why. With one exception, and I hope to refer to that later, everything is accounted for. The cones and wire (collected by G.P.); the balls, cement, and damp-proofing (collected by G. P. via M. W.). Now, whereas Moulines knew nothing of that list, any fool who finds a cloak-room ticket can go and collect the proceeds. Moreover, hundred pound notes are most uncommon things, and I don't see from what other quarter Moulines could have secured them.

As soon as you were tied up nice and cosy we returned to the Cottage, dodging a sleuth *en route*. It is true that the problem of the glass remained unsolved, but there was no time for that. We realised that we had done re-markably well from our various contributions, so we bolted. That the Cottage should have got burnt down was fortuitous. We were both getting the least bit scared, however—my wife in particular. Not only was there the pale ghost of your robust self lying up there, but there was that visit paid by somebody or other—I expect by yourself—during one of my absences. We had the substance, and the shadow was not worth it. So here we are, at this moment, in the suburbs of London, for the houses seem to be getting more thick every minute.

I think everything is explained, and there remains therefore one thing only to do—to say a further farewell to you as speedily and gracefully as possible. And here we revert to the glass. Two digressions and I am done. That wonderful night when you and I stood beneath the sheltering oak (ah, me!), I recall the words you then used: "Miss Forrest, I am" (or was it, 'You see before you'?) "a man without a job." Again, it is said that a certain blood and iron general, viewing London for the first time, exclaimed with the yelp of his tribe, "What a city to loot!" You see the connexion? That glass, opaque glass, hiding somewhere thousands of pounds. What a job! and what loot! I shall be out of your way; there will be no competition. New climes are about to claim me, since I have an idea that safety lies in innovation. Be no longer, my dear Wrentham, one of the unemployed, who appear in market-places and cannot even afford phylacteries. Be a man with a job.

Success to you and your bat-eyed friend. But for the Lord's sake do not let him wear those glasses in the moonlight. They shine like the very devil!

We are running into Liverpool Street. I send my thanks and every good wish, and in this my wife joins me, and

I beg to remain
Yours gratefully
GEORGE PLUMLEY

P.S.—May I remind you that my father possessed what was probably the finest collection of Waterford and Bristol glass in the country?

Wrentham's face during this reading was a screen whereon were registered divers emotions. At times he turned red, at others he scowled like a thundercloud, once he laughed aloud, and on more than one occasion he swore. And after the reading he remained long in thought, the letter lying idly to hand. Then, as by a sudden resolve, he got up. He fetched the tennis balls from the workroom and put them and the letter into his pocket. Where the devil was Ludo? Must have been an hour since he hopped off.

With hands shoved deep into his pockets, and wearing a most unwonted scowl, he went down to the hall. No sign of the wanderer. But a look through the open door was more reassuring. He was coming down the drive and Burrows with him. As they got nearer it was noticeable that they were conversing but little. It was more like a rehearsal for a procession of mutes. Wrentham lit a cigarette and waited.

CHAPTER XXX
CEASE FIRE

"AFTERNOON, BURROWS. What's all the gaiety about, Ludo?"

Ludo twisted his features into the semblance of a smile but said nothing. The detective, with the air of a man with a grievance, found his tongue and spoke for both.

"It's like this, Major, as I was telling Captain Travers here—as far as I can see I'm for what they call the high jump."

"What's been happening?"

The detective gave a gesture of disgust and despair. "Happening? Oh, nothing at all, sir. I only had in my hands the chap who killed Moulines and let him go; that's all."

A slight red suffused Wrentham's face. "The man who killed Moulines! Who was he then?"

The detective was by no means loath to unburden his soul. "I don't know how you got to know it, Major, but I made an entrance one night into that place they call Lodge Cottage. I can't very well admit it officially because I had no apparent reason, and I certainly hadn't got a warrant. There you are; I got in and I found among other things a pipe, some cigarettes, a pair of socks, and the print of the boots that made those marks at Puddle Pond."

Nobody made a remark to fill in the detective's dramatic pause and he went on. "He must have been a friend or relative of that Forrest woman; I knew that at once. She probably hid him up there for a bit. And then I had to go and be too clever."

"How was that?" asked Wrentham, again feeling perfectly sure, and on the whole rather relieved, that Burrows was on the wrong track.

"Well, in two ways. First, I wanted to get him myself, on the job, so to speak, and had a couple of men, one marking the Hall and the other the Cottage, with instructions to hold anybody they didn't know or who fitted the description I gave them. What I should have done was to arrest the Forrest woman as an accessory and hear what she had to say. Then, again, I must send along a footprint to Hindhead to see if there was any connexion with that affair there. And then while I was waiting for this and waiting for that the damn cottage gets burnt down, and if you ask me that's the last I'll ever see of either the man or the woman."

"Any bones in the ashes?" asked Ludo.

"Devil a bone, except those of a cat. Well, there's only one thing to do now, gentlemen: that's to own up we're beaten and call in Scotland Yard."

It was hard work for Wrentham to feel other than pleased at the turn events had taken. Certainly he was sorry for Burrows, but after all there must always be a certain pleasure in being a cutter of knots. He patted the detective on the back. "Cheer up, Burrows! Things aren't so bad as all that. Look here now," and he led the way over to the tree, "will you do something for me?"

"Anything I can, Major." It was plain that Burrows regarded himself as in the deuce of a hole.

"Well, it's just this." He pulled out the letter. "Here's a letter I want Captain Travers to read now. As soon as he has finished it I want you to read it and I'll bet you a fiver most of your troubles will be finished with."

Burrows was too incredulous to reply. Ludo, too, took the letter without comment and settled to his reading. Wrentham stoked up his pipe, passed the pouch to the detective, and then glared away beyond the trees. He felt within a small sense of triumph, but after Ludo's reading he knew he would once more become a bubble, and if not burst at least decidedly flabby. Still, there you were. Better get it over and done with. What was it his old housemaster was always repeating? "It's only the fools who never make mistakes." Well, he had been a fool; not for the first time and certainly not for the last.

His pipe was nearly burnt out when a grunt from Ludo announced that the reading was finished. Wrentham glanced round quickly. Ludo was looking decidedly sheepish, to say the least of it. The other took the letter and handed it to the detective. He also drew up the small rustic table and placed on it the tennis balls.

"Now, Burrows, have a go at that. You probably won't understand the whole lot, but have a good go at it." He glanced at Ludo. "Captain Travers and I have one or two things to talk over. You'll be here all right when we get back?"

Burrows was emphatic. "I certainly will, Major, even if it isn't till to-morrow."

Wrentham laughed. "Right-ho, then, Burrows. We'll be back in a few minutes in any case and spill all the beans there are to spill. I think you'll find that letter interesting enough." He took Ludo's arm and they moved off through the garden and round to the orchard.

At first neither seemed very anxious to speak, but it was Wrentham who made the first move. "Burrows was saying he'd been a bit of an ass, Ludo. I reckon I've been the whole thirteen kinds, and then some."

Ludo's reply was ready in a flash. "Good Lord, Rouster! I think you've been perfectly marvellous."

"Oh, I don't know. Look at the whole of that Forrest affair."

"Well? What of it? I was just as big a fool as you; so was Burrows; so was everybody; so was George Plumley himself if you come to that."

"How do you make that out?" Under Ludo's exoneration Wrentham was beginning to feel himself again. "It seems to me he's the only one who has come damn well out of it all."

"Oh, I don't know. I think his missis is the only one who really comes out of it well. A jolly plucky little soul that. George Plumley seems to me to have been just the least bit too clever. I mean if he hadn't wanted to write to you and score at your expense he'd have kept his mouth shut altogether. If the police really want him, you can be certain they'll jolly well have him, however 'new' the clime he refers to. Besides that, in heaps of ways he hasn't been as clever as he thought."

"Well, the picture may not look too intelligent, but you'll admit it has an excellent gold frame."

"Just a minute." Ludo polished his glasses. "What I said was that he wasn't half as clever as he thought. Take the tennis balls. Didn't he imagine he walked off in that instance with the whole of what he calls the boodle? Was it clever to leave two of them in your pockets?"

"That may be so. Still you'll admit, Ludo, that getting away with two-thirds after someone else has done all the work is pretty good going."

"Granted. Again, however, there is the matter of the glass. He evidently imagines this is quite beyond us and therefore brings gifts—informatory gifts I mean. After all, if you look at it fairly and squarely, George Plumley did nothing that required brains. The balls broke well for him, and it isn't so frightfully difficult, if you have the taste for that sort of thing, to pose as a twopenny odalisque."

"I think, perhaps you're right, Ludo. By the way, I've got a jolly good theory about that glass business. Of course you know the old riddle, 'What is it that purrs, has fur and lays eggs?' The answer's, 'A Cat.' Then you say, 'A cat doesn't lay eggs,' and then the other bloke says, 'Oh, that was put in to make it harder.' Now then, Ludo, don't you think that's exactly what Plumley

222 | CHRISTOPHER BUSH

did? What was the use of making a lot of trails and having no red herring? Don't you think the glass was put in to make the whole bag of tricks more difficult?"

Ludo smiled, in what was for him a peculiar way. "I'm afraid I'm a bit too prejudiced to answer."

"Prejudiced! Oh, I see. You mean you read the book of words sent by that glass firm about making glass opaque, and so you know all about it. What did that prescription actually say Ludo?"

"I'm afraid I've forgotten all about it that I understood, and that wasn't much," confessed Ludo. "As you know, I'm not a very scientific sort of chap. I do know there was, first of all, something about the use of hydrofluoric acid in etching glass. You see that firm actually made its own opaque glass. They would never have to take transparent glass and mess about with it. Oh, yes; I remember too there was something about the action of minute fungi and the cumulative effects of sea-sand. But what I will say, and most emphatically, is this: Plumley could by himself have never made any use of the information contained in the memorandum. I really think that is why my mind discarded the whole thing."

"In other words, we're worse off than we were before. What about that postscript of George Plumley's, Ludo? Anything to it?"

"You mean about the collection of glass." Again the spectacles were removed and rubbed. "I wonder if you'd mind my spreading myself a bit Geoffrey?"

Wrentham looked at him, blinking away there in the sun, and an overwhelming desire came to him to laugh uproariously. Good old Ludo! What the devil was he up to now?

"I just want to put one or two things to you. I'll confess that I knew all about the Plumley glass, and that this isn't the first time I've gone into the whole thing. If you were a collector you'd hardly have the heart to spoil a bowl or candlesticks or a goblet by making them opaque. If you were such a vandal, what purpose would have been served? It would only be inside the glass itself that you could even then hide anything. Isn't that so?"

Wrentham nodded.

"Now then, take the man in the street, and for the purposes of this argument Plumley is included since he must have soon recognised that he would have to adopt ordinary and not highly technical methods. Very well. Take the man in the street and say to him, 'Glass.' What does he understand?"

"Beer!" replied Wrentham, without the least hesitation, but the remark was ignored.

"Does he think of museum pieces? Certainly not, but the glass he looks through—window glass, in other words. Now then; suppose you have a window which is badly overlooked by a neighbour, for example, and you want to make that glass opaque. How do you do it? You would either paint it inside or else put on one of those transfer things you can buy anywhere and stick on for yourself." Wrentham made as if to speak but the other went straight on. "Assuming all that, doesn't it remain very plain that anything hidden by those means would have to be put between the paint and the glass or between the transfer and the glass? And that is to say it wouldn't be hidden at all, since it would be visible through the glass from outside."

"In other words, Ludo, you've proved conclusively that we're up a bigger gum-tree than ever."

"Not necessarily. Let's take a hypothetical case. Suppose there were a perfect double window, looking out, as it were, two ways. Again, suppose you painted or transferred both windows from the inside space: that window would then be opaque as far as concerned the space inside or between the panes."

"I don't quite follow."

"All right. I'll still be hypothetical but much more explicit. Suppose I am accustomed to solve acrostics. Often there are lights which escape all my efforts, and yet as often, when I wake up in the morning I find the answer all ready for me, prepared by the magic of my subconscious mind. As a matter of fact, that has happened to me and to hundreds of other people, hundreds of times. Haven't you worried occasionally overnight about the name of a person or place, and then thought of the answer next morning when you had forgotten all about it? Well now, I ask you to imagine that during lunch something of the same sort happened to me. For example, we will say my brain was suddenly presented with the facts which I have just given you. Further, the same subconscious self actually showed me a window which really did have a transfer on it, a window which I saw but did not notice—mark well that tremendous difference—yesterday when I was looking for you up at the Hall. Imagine that so illuminating was that revelation that on the spur of the moment I went up to the Hall and found that window where I expected; that it was a circular one of about eighteen inches diameter, let, shall we say, into the north-west corner of the dining-room, and facing, or if you prefer it acting as a background for, that new artistic top to the old well. Imagine, further, that the design of the transfer of this window was a group of lilies. What would you have thought?"

Wrentham grinned. "I should have thought it was just about time the alarm went off."

Ludo's face remained impassive. "I know it's all very far-fetched. Still, let's go on with the hypothesis. I should think to myself, 'Underneath the lilies.' I measure the thickness of the wall to the glass. I go indoors to Martin and ask him to accompany me to the dining-room. There I find not the back of the transfer but a new one, facing inside! I measure again. I open an ordinary window and check. Things become rather obvious. There are two circles of glass, two transfers, and a space between! Nobody has ever spotted this because the light is so dimly religious. 'Martin,' I say, 'when did Mr. Plumley have this window altered?' 'Last April,' says he. 'Very well then,' I say; 'look out for yourself.' And with the poker I smash the outside pane. There, at the bottom, lying in the space between the two circles of glass I find this," and Ludo put his hand into his pocket, and after some fumbling, produced with a somewhat naive sort of grin—a bundle of notes!

"You mean to say—" stammered the other. But Ludo was rather embarrassed with his triumph. He was already moving over to Tango, who was leaping at his chain like a mad thing and begging frantically to be loosed. Delirious with his freedom, he circled the orchard twice and then came back, jumping up at the pair of them.

"Let's go and see Burrows," suggested Ludo, and the three of them moved out of the orchard, round by the shrubbery and so to the front lawn. Burrows was still sitting under the tree, making, as far as could be seen, a careful examination of the tennis balls.

All at once Wrentham clutched Ludo's arm. "Just watch Tango a minute!" For this is what was happening, spread out as a comedy before them. Emma was obviously looking for somebody, and there on the lawn she stood, perfectly still, gazing intently towards the paddock. Her Tango espied. He crawled to within ten yards on his belly and then made a desperate dive. He ripped at the skirt until Emma's wild shriek told him she was no dummy, but very much alive. Tango fled, ears well back, as if the devil were after him. Ludo laughed uproariously.

"By Jove!" exclaimed Wrentham; "there goes one more bloke who'll remember the Plumley inheritance!"

THE END